Embers of Liberty

Embers of Liberty

Trever Bierschbach

Copyright © 2018 Trever Bierschbach
All rights reserved.
ISBN-13: 9781726636186

For my mother, without whom this dream would not be possible

Chapter 1

I imagine if you asked people, before everything changed, what would America look like in a couple of decades, this wouldn't be it. It didn't take nearly that long. Some people believe the beginning of the end of America was in the early part of the century. America elected an extremely progressive president. No one remembers, or no one cares, whether he was a republican or democrat. It doesn't really matter anyway. Others said it started long before, before the Great Wars, or during the Great Depression, as many theories as there are people to think them up. All I can say now is it doesn't matter anymore. What's done is done, and all we can do is live with our mistakes.

-Excerpt from the journal of John Evermann

John took his jacket from the locker marked with his number, pulling it on over his sore shoulders. He grabbed his steel lunchbox from the bottom of the locker and turned to leave the break room.

The floor manager stood in his office doorway, catching John's attention as he walked by. "Your line is down twelve percent with Hernandez out again."

"I'll come in early tomorrow and catch up," John said, his normally soft voice rough from hours on the dry factory floor.

Several of the workers in the room gave John a disgruntled look.

"It will be outside your contract time, John," the floor manager said. "We can't give you extra time off later."

"I know, Terrance," John patted the dark-skinned man on the shoulder as he passed.

The drab walls of the break room and hall were broken every so often by a colorful poster espousing the merits of hard work and doing one's part for the community. In stark contrast, most of John's coworkers stood, exhausted, waiting in line down the hall for their turn at the time clock. Work was something that many did, not something they wanted to do, or cared about. John could remember a time, when he was younger, when his father and grandfather used words like work ethic, and pride had meaning. Now it was all about getting through the day with nothing to look forward to except the same tedious tomorrow. He picked up a broken chair that had been leaning against his locker before leaving the break room.

One of the last men in line stepped out and followed John toward the front doors, stopping him where no one could overhear.

"What are you doing, John?" He asked in a hoarse whisper. "You know our contract with the feds means no extra rations for extra work."

"Work has to get done, Carl. It's not about the pay."

Carl scratched at the short stubble atop his head and looked back at the line of workers. He waited while one of their coworkers passed on the way out the doors, then he turned his eyes on John again.

"It makes everyone look bad. If we still had unions they wouldn't stand for it," Carl said.

John shrugged and look back down the line of people, standing complacent as cattle outside a slaughterhouse.

"No one should feel bad, we're all the same now right?"

There was a hint of sarcasm in his voice, and they both knew without looking at the wall that John was standing in front of a poster depicting three androgynous, faceless people in gray coveralls, standing on the edge of a cliff or building. Each held a different tool but they were otherwise identical. Against the red background, printed in gold letters, were the words *Free, Fair, and Equal.*

"Just be careful, John," Carl said before returning to the line. "Don't draw more attention than normal."

John exited the mill and looked up at the lettering over the main doors of the *National Department of Agriculture Stewart Mill*. The sky over the sign was leaden and the air was colder than the day before. He sighed and started the long walk home, hoping the coming winter would be milder than the last. John's family did not own a car, not that anyone else *owned* a car either. The government denied John's application for a car because it was determined he lived close enough to his workplace to ride public transportation. When he appealed, stating that Stewart, Illinois was too small of a town to have public transportation, his application was denied citing a new ruling that five miles was close enough to walk.

John scratched an itch on his shoulder blade as he passed Stewart's hardware store, his fingers passing over the white stenciled numbers on the back of his grayish-blue jacket. His digits were always there as a reminder that he was just a number in the system, not John, but a series of numerals to pass through the databanks and bureaucracy faster. He waved at Mike Connors, the old man who used to own the hardware store. Mike was sweeping the steps under a sign reading *National Hardware Supply, Stewart Unit*. Mike stopped sweeping and nodded in greeting, watching John pass by.

John saw people he had known since childhood, walking around town with no apparent purpose. When work was done for the day, many people had no idea what to do with themselves. Most forms of entertainment had been eliminated or changed to meet new regulations. People used to go out, meet friends, and date, but few saw the point anymore. People still had to get out of the house. Meeting in groups was against the law, as was loitering on government property so most just wandered around town until they got bored and went home.

Just a few store fronts down from the hardware supply was a furniture repair shop where Stewart's only contracted furniture carpenter worked. John put his hand on the glass door that still bore the faded letters naming it Jerome's Woodworks under a newer sign stating *Furniture Repair, Stewart.* He pushed the door open and walked through a shop that was piled high with rows of broken chairs, tables, cabinets and other pieces of furniture. No one else in town was authorized to do their own repairs; it wouldn't be fair to take the work away from another citizen.

"Jermone, I have a chair here that needs fixed," John called out. He didn't hear any power tools running in the back to drown him out.

"That you, John?" Jerome's mellow voice called out from the back.

The man entered the room, wiping wood shavings off his jeans with a large rag. Jerome was a giant of a man, at least a head taller than John. Ebony skin rippled with muscles across his bare arms, and sawdust clung to the sweat of the workday. His wide face broke into a smile when he saw John.

Jerome took the chair from John as if he was handling a wounded animal. "What happened to this guy?"

"Thomas was leaning back in it again and it tipped," John explained.

"Your boy all right?"

"Bumped his head, but nothing serious."

"Well, I'll get the chair in line." Jermone gestured to the furniture that surrounded them. "Not sure when it will be done."

"No luck getting some help around here?" John asked.

"Stewart's too small to support a second carpenter," Jerome said in a tone as if he was quoting a letter from the *National Labor Board*.

John just shook his head and offered his hand to the big carpenter. Jerome took it in his strong grip.

"Say hi to Amanda for me," Jerome said.

John nodded and headed out of the store, giving another quick wave as the door closed behind him.

John turned the corner and started up the Harper Street hill. He passed by a rundown brick building with a faded placard above the door that read Jerry's Pub. He remembered the day Jerry had to close his beloved bar. Nearly the whole town showed up to say goodbye to the old place that had been a Stewart institution since the end of the first Prohibition. Now the building sat like a forgotten friend, empty windows staring out onto a town that had long since given up hope of ever entering those welcoming doors again.

Beyond the abandoned pub stood a long line of houses that ran up the street in front of John. They were classic American, small town type houses, some of which had been around since the turn of the last century. Most had small fenced-in yards with little concrete porches. A few toys lay in the grass among fallen leaves recently dropped from the surrounding trees, but not many. He remembered when the sound of dogs barking could be heard in the neighborhood, but as far as he knew there weren't any pets, anywhere. Owning pets had been ruled inhumane, and most of the animals had been put down. The useful ones were turned into work animals for the government, but the rest couldn't just be released. Some owners could not turn their pets over and released them out in the country. The farmers were still dealing with the packs of feral dogs that attacked national livestock.

John smiled when he saw some kids playing tag near the top of the hill. Children were the exception to the law that prevented adults from gathering in large groups. Believed to be no threat they were permitted to gather and play between the end of school and curfew. They all had little grayish-blue jackets over their school uniforms. He almost didn't notice the numbers anymore. The children ran about, squealing and laughing while he watched. Their game was silhouetted against the gray October sky, and for a time John forgot everything except what it had been like to be a child and have no care except to enjoy the moment. When one of the kids looked in his direction, he waved and two of them came running over, shouting goodbyes to their friends. After a quick hug, the trio continued to walk up Harper Street.

"More kids than usual out," John commented.

"The bus broke down again. Everyone had to walk," the boy said. The district had one bus so kids at the end of the route wouldn't be home before dinner.

"Well, walking never hurt you two," John said. "At least they'll get home in time to have dinner with their folks."

John and his wife wanted their kids home for dinner every night, so rather than ride the bus and be one of the last ones off, they walked to the top of Harper Street and met their dad on the way home.

The little girl took John's hand; he smiled down at her. "How was school Susan?" He asked.

Susan kicked a small stone, sending it skittering and bouncing down the road. "Fine, daddy."

"Just fine?" John asked.

Susan nodded her head, causing her brown curls to bounce a bit. She squeezed his hand and giggled, then ran off after the stone to give it another kick. John watched her and chuckled at her antics. She was tall for eight, and smart. He was a sucker for those big blue eyes, and Susan knew it too. John would move heaven and earth for those eyes. The boy was walking quietly next to him, hands in his pockets and his face turned down in thought.

John patted his shoulder. "Thomas?"

"Huh?" Thomas looked up, snapped out of his thoughts.

"What's on your mind son?"

"I was thinking about class today. Do other kids have to learn history when they get home?"

John watched Susan skip down the road for a moment before answering.

"I don't know Thomas. It's important for you though, to learn the truth, because things won't always be this way." John waved his hand, indicating the world around them. "When things get put back the way they should be, the world will need people who know how it got this way in the first place."

"We were reading about that Chinese guy, Mao, who lived a long time ago. The book at school said that he was a great leader, and helped the world, but didn't you tell us he killed lots of people?"

John nodded grimly, taking a moment to stifle the rising anger that he felt, not toward his son, but toward the school.

"Yes, Thomas. He killed lots of people to get what he wanted. That's why we study this at home. So we remember."

"It just makes me sad," Thomas said quietly.

"Me too son," John put his hand on the boy's shoulder.

The trio rounded a corner, turning onto their street and saw federal agents parked outside a home a few doors down from their own. Two black cars were in front of the small house, and two officers were standing by them, watching the street. John and his kids could hear shouting coming through the open front door of the small, white house. A crash sounded form somewhere inside and a moment later two more officers exited, pushing a small Asian man out in front of them. His hands appeared to be cuffed behind his back.

"Mister Li, you are charged with overdrawing rations and hoarding food," one of the officers said loudly.

John had stopped walking at the sound of the crash and all three were close enough to the house to hear everything. Seeing his neighbor's face pulled at his heart, especially since John had considered finding a way to draw more rations himself. With the shortage, everyone seemed to have just enough to get by. He hadn't realized it, but his fists were balled tightly, and he took a step toward the officers.

"I'm sorry," Mister Li was saying. "We need the food, our son is sick."

"Everyone needs the food Mister Li," the arresting officer said in the professional monotone that all federal officers seemed to use.

Mister Li looked up and saw John and the kids looking on. The defeated look in the man's eyes brought John forward another step. He didn't know what he would, or could do, but he felt like something had to be done.

"Move along citizen, this is none of your business," the voice of one of the other officers snapped John out of his thoughts.

For a moment the approaching officer became the target of John's simmering rage. He could feel every muscle in his body tense as if preparing to lash out, but it all came crashing down with a tug on his pants and his daughter's voice.

"Daddy, I'm scared," Susan was pulling at his pocket to get his attention. Those blue eyes that always touched his heart were on the verge of tears.

"Can we go home?" Her voice shook a little.

John tamped down his anger and picked her up, all thoughts of doing something that would put him in jail forgotten.

"Let's go see what Mommy has for dinner."

Chapter 2

If you knew your history, then the formation of the Federal Police Force scared you to death. I know it did me. The President had promised to give us a kind of national security force, stronger than the army, but we all thought it would be to combat terrorism. Some warned that this force could be used against the citizens, but most did not listen. Conspiracy theorist became a phrase often used against people who usually weren't considered such. I think the first indication that federal officers were not just in place to stop terrorists is when they confiscated every firearm in the country. The Feds claimed dissenters were domestic terrorists if they owned firearms and used that excuse to take their guns. Then they went a step further and took the rest, claiming that without terrorists next door no one else needed guns either. A lot of people died in that first day.

-Excerpt from the journal of John Evermann

John and the kids arrived home after the long walk and crossed the sparse front yard to the door. John's neighbor Steve was sitting on his own porch, watching the flashing lights down the street. He glanced at John briefly and nodded, John gave a smile and a thumbs up, and then ushered the kids into the house. He knew Steve would understand the signal and be on the phone soon to arrange a meeting, that night, at John's house.

John and Steve had grown up together, and been friends as long as they could remember. Steve's mixed heritage had made him the target of bullies and John was always there to back him up. Steve had introduced John to the woman John would marry, Steve's cousin on his mother's side, which tied the friends together as family.

"Hey Amanda, we're home," John called as he pulled his jacket off and hung it on the hook next to the door. He took the kids' jackets and hung them up as well. His house keys clinked when he dropped them into the ceramic dish on the little hall table.

"Back here," John's wife Amanda called from the back of the small house.

The kids ran back, giving the requisite hugs and kisses, before sitting down at the kitchen table to do their homework. John entered the kitchen and smiled at the scene that greeted him. The kids were opening books and shuffling papers. Thomas had hesitated when he saw the old milk crate in place of his chair, and had turned an almost offended look on his father. John just gave him a stern nod that indicated any argument would be pointless and Thomas sat down.

Amanda was at the counter, finishing dinner. She was dressed simply, in jeans and a t-shirt, and her long, dark hair was damp from steam. Dinner smelled great as usual. Amanda had a knack for turning their rations into something enjoyable. He stepped into the room and watched her from the doorway.

"Smells great hun," John said.

"Thanks. What's going on up the street?" The flashing red and blue lights were reflected faintly inside the house.

"Someone turned the Li's in for getting extra rations. They are taking Mister Li in," John explained. His voice carried the outrage he felt inside.

Amanda knew her husband well enough to know what he was feeling. She wiped her hands on a towel that was lying on the counter and went to him. Wrapping her arms around his neck she gave him a quick kiss. The gesture broke his dark mood instantly.

"You know there's nothing you could have done but get yourself arrested too," Amanda said quietly.

"I know I just hate feeling powerless to help."

"You are far from powerless, John. We just have to remember we can't help everyone."

John nodded and let her go, knowing she was right. It wouldn't help anyone if he were arrested, especially the Li's.

"How was work?" Amanda asked after John released her.

"Oh, fine. Jerry didn't show up again today, so I'll be going in early tomorrow to catch up," John said, washing his hands before helping with dinner.

"Of course you are dear," Amanda said. She was moving a pan off the hot burner and set it down a little harder than intended.

"You know if I don't people will notice. They're used to seeing me cover," John said.

"I know, I'm just tired of barely getting by and you working extra for nothing," Amanda said in a strained voice.

"I'm sorry dear," John broke the uncomfortable silence that followed Amanda's outburst and put his arms around her again.

"It's not your fault," Amanda said quietly.

John looked at the kids, who had been staring, and nodded toward their books. They both whipped around and got back to work.

"You don't think Jerry's been caught do you?" Amanda went on after taking a moment to relax in her husband's embrace.

"I don't know Amanda, let's just hope he made it west like he planned," John said firmly. His wife nodded and turned back to put dinner on the table while he helped.

The kids moved their books aside while John set down steaming plates of meat and potatoes, with a slice of bread on the side. John sat down in his chair and Amanda handed over a napkin. He sat staring at his food momentarily, the hard-earned fruits of his labors, no more and no less than was determined to be his family's need.

"Eat before it gets cold," Amanda chided.

John smiled and started to eat. As usual Amanda turned otherwise ordinary rations into something good. The meal went on with the clinking of silverware on plates.

"What about your day, dear?" John asked.

"The kids were good as usual," Amanda said. She worked at a daycare facility for children who were too young for school.

"Good," John said.

"Rations were delayed again. No early pickup this week either," Amanda said after a few minutes of silent eating.

"We'll get by," there was more confidence in John's voice than he felt.

They finished dinner, cleared the table, and the kids helped Amanda with the dishes.

John settled in his chair in the living room and picked up the National Newspaper, hoping he would find something new, but knowing he wouldn't. It was always the same with the one newspaper in the country. Articles about how much the government is doing for the people, new community welfare programs for every problem that could be cooked up by some faceless politician. In the past people might have wondered how the government was going to pay for it all, but once the President signed the executive order that claimed all wealth, the United States Government became the richest in the world.

John tossed the paper on the coffee table in disgust. He looked at the one television they had been allocated, but did not turn it on. It would just be the same. All the programming was government filtered news, or mediocre sitcoms that extolled the virtues of their society. The network didn't even televise news about the war with the Republic of Texas because America wasn't winning. John thought back to the day that shocked everyone. An executive order was signed that abolished the states, bringing them all under the umbrella of the American government. Four states refused and seceded. Arizona, New Mexico, Oklahoma, and Texas decided to declare their independence and formed the Independent Republic of Texas. They created a very limited central government and kept their state governments pretty much the same. Most of the soldiers that lived and served in those states stayed, and many more flocked there, citizens and soldiers alike. By the time the American government responded Texas had a large force of armed men and women ready to defend their rights. The war was brief and ended in a stalemate, letting Texas remain sovereign.

John gave up and pulled himself out of his chair. A twinge in his back made him wince, and almost regret offering to work extra the next day. He went to the kitchen and put on a pot of coffee, one of the few luxuries available to them, and turned on the back porch light, a light that much of the neighborhood was watching for. Like moths to the flame, several people that lived near would be drawn to this beacon in the dark.

Chapter 3

I remember the day they removed the Constitution from its resting place, and sealed it away in some secret archive. Our President believed that the document was flawed, outdated, and no longer necessary to protect the rights of citizens. He gave a speech in which he told us how our founders did not allow for the natural evolution of our society, and how the document was great for their time, but incompatible with ours. Shortly after the speech the President signed an executive order banning the owning or display of a copy of the Constitution. I still have mine, safely tucked away until it is needed again, someday.

-Excerpt from the journal of John Evermann

"So what did happen to Jerry?" Steve asked, looking about the room.

None of the fifty-five men and women assembled in the small basement of John's house had an answer. Looking back at Steve were the faces of his friends, light and dark, young and old, small and large, all bonded by the same ideals. Everyone looked worried. As far as anyone knew Jerry Hernandez had disappeared without telling anyone where he was going.

The basement, like most under older homes in the Midwest, was more about storm safety than aesthetics. A rough cement floor was bordered by brick walls and a low ceiling of exposed beams capped it. Everyone sat on boxes or stood around the perimeter of the room.

"It doesn't matter," John said, "He's gone. We just have to hope he made it to Texas. Now, I was approved for my travel permit last week so it's Steve's turn."

John looked at Steve who nodded.

"I have my paperwork ready to go, and I have an appointment to see the judge tomorrow about it," Steve explained.

"Good. Once Steve has his permit we will start leaving in the same order we got our permits in, so Ed you will be first," Ed nodded but kept silent, "Remember, we each have different routes for a reason, don't be tempted to take a shorter one. Any deviation could jeopardize everyone else."

Toward the back of the room Carl stood up, scratching at his stubbled chin. He looked nervous with all eyes on him.

"What is it Carl?" John asked.

"Well, I was thinking. Wouldn't it be safer if we just stayed?" There was some angry muttering. "I mean, we have everything we need. As long as we don't break the law they leave us alone."

"Carl, you don't have kids," John started, "You don't have to hear what they talk about in school, or try to explain to them why they are being taught that Lenin and Mao were just misunderstood. You don't have to sit by while your kids are being taught that family is unimportant, just a place to raise kids so they can grow up and contribute to the collective."

Carl looked down and took his seat again, "Forget I said anything John, you're right."

John and Steve exchanged a worried look.

"Are you committed to this, Carl?" Steve asked.

"I am." Carl looked up and met Steve's eyes. "Just scared now that we're here I guess."

"We all are. It's all right to be scared," Steve said. Everyone nodded or murmured their agreement.

"Does anyone else doubt our plan?" John asked, "Here in my house, just like in your own, you are free to speak your mind."

John looked around, but no one spoke. Some shook their heads and others just watched him. As a group they had determined to leave their homes and try to make it to a new life in Texas. As a group they stood with John, willing to do anything to make sure that as many of them made it as possible. John imagined that was the look in the eyes of the founders when they wrote the Declaration of Independence, when those men signed their names to their own death warrant.

Everyone in John's basement came from different walks of life, different backgrounds, both economic and ethnic, but they all had one thing in common. All of them wanted a life where their hard work was compensated fairly, where they could do or say what they liked as long as they didn't hurt anyone else. Those that were old enough remembered a time before all the changes, and they were all good people who had volunteered where they could, or donated money when they had no time. They all believed in helping others, but none of them believed in being forced. Not one of them wanted to be forced to rely on their fellow man, nor did they want anyone but their families to rely on them. That was why they gathered, and that was why they were all leaving as soon as they could.

The meeting soon broke up as some left, but others stayed to talk. Small groups formed to discuss everything from politics to the war, their kid's school, or work. John looked on in silence, not really in the mood to participate in any kind of discussion or debate. His wish wasn't respected for long though as Steve came up to him.

"Can we trust Carl?" Steve asked.

John looked down in thought, rubbing the stubble on his chin. He sighed and looked over at Steve, "I think so. He is just scared, like most of us are. I don't think he would do anything stupid"

Steve didn't seem so sure, but he accepted John's answer. Truth be told, John was not so sure either, but if Carl were thinking about doing something like running to the feds, there wasn't much anyone could do about it.

John avoided conversation the rest of the night and before long he was saying goodbye to the last of his neighbors. John helped Amanda clean up after the meeting and make sure there was no evidence of the large gathering of people. They didn't talk much. John was more worried as the time for them to leave approached, and Amanda left him to his thoughts. They both headed to bed when everything was put back in order.

John lay awake for what seemed like hours after the meeting was over. He couldn't seem to banish the thoughts of their missing member from his mind. Jerry could just as likely be in the hands of the authorities as in Texas. If they had Jerry then his family was in danger. Carl was a question as well. If he just got scared and backed out then they had nothing to worry about, but what if he betrayed them? The government paid extra rations and even some luxuries to informants, but Carl hated this government as much as any of them. John just could not believe that any of their group would do that.

John was staring at the ceiling, trying to calm his thoughts, when he saw the faint flash of red and blue lights mar the pristine white of the surface he was focused on. With his heart fluttering John leaped out of bed, and stumbled as the tangled sheets kept hold of his foot. He made it to the window and carefully drew aside the curtains. His worst fears were realized when he looked up the street. At the end of the block a large black van and several police cars were parked. He could see several officers in riot gear forming up, and one officer starting to point to houses along the street, including John's. John was worried someone had talked, and the Federal Police were here to arrest him and his friends.

"What is it dear?" Amanda asked sleepily.

"Feds," John watched as they knocked on the door of an old woman who was not in his group.

He realized they were just doing a standard search, since they weren't going directly to the homes of other members of his group. He pushed away from the wall and rushed down the stairs. It was just like the Feds to do this search in the middle of the night so no one had time to hide anything. For once John was thankful for insomnia, and his obsessive checking for contraband laying out, but he didn't want to take any chances and was going to give the house a quick once over.

"John, what's going on?" She asked.

"Contraband search. I have to make sure it's all put away," John called back.

John reached the front door and checked the lock. He could hear Amanda upstairs, probably looking for anything that might be considered contraband. He quickly searched the living room and kitchen. He then checked the loose panel in the back closet. Behind the panel were his books, an old flag, and his copy of the Constitution. It was a copy of the Constitution bound in a little book along with the

Declaration of Independence and sold in museum gift shops years ago. He also kept their travel permits in the compartment. Once satisfied he closed it up and made sure it was concealed properly.

Susan was standing in the middle of the hall when John went back upstairs to check on everyone. He could see she was terrified, but trying not to cry. Amanda was checking their rooms for anything that could be considered illegal.

"Thomas, do you have anything you aren't suppose to have," John asked as the boy appeared in his bedroom doorway, rubbing sleep from his eyes.

Thomas shook his head and John reached out for Susan, she reached up to him and he swept her into his arms, trying to comfort her.

A loud pounding on the front door downstairs startled them all.

"Open up, Federal Police Officers!" A man shouted outside.

"Quick, back to bed," John whispered, ushering his family back to their rooms. The pounding on the door grew more insistent, but John took his time. He wanted it to seem as if he'd just woken up.

John answered the door and four Federal officers, dressed in black fatigues, pushed their way past him. One of the officers, holding a clipboard, stopped and turned to John while the others began to search the house.

"John Evermann?" The officer with the clipboard asked.

"Yes," John nodded.

"Your file shows one other adult, your wife, and two children reside here. Is there anyone else in the house that is not authorized to live here?"

"No, it's just us," John replied.

"Are we going to find any unauthorized materials on the premises?"

"No," John replied.

The officer nodded and made a few notes on the clipboard.

"Please bring your family down here," the officer ordered.

John started to call up, but Amanda and the kids had been listening. They came down quietly and stood next to John. Susan took his hand and stood staring at the officers in fear. They could hear the men ransacking the house in their search. The one in charge looked at each of the Evermanns in turn, nodding and making marks on his clipboard.

The house was not large and the Evermanns didn't have much, but the officers went through everything. John didn't react when they searched the closet, or broke another one of the kitchen chairs. After what seemed like an eternity the other three officers reported that the house was clear. The man in charge made another note on his board and then put his pen in his pocket.

"Thank you for your cooperation Mister Evermann," with that the four officers left the house.

Amanda put the kids back to bed while John started to put the house back in order, but he didn't make much progress. He was furious, but tried his best to contain it for his family's sake. He felt violated, and embarrassed.   A man's home was almost sacred at one time.

Amanda joined him soon after, and he could see tears in her eyes. He stopped and took her in his arms. They stood like that, without speaking, for several minutes before finally going to bed.

Chapter 4

When the government took over the grocery stores you would have thought they were offering free champagne and caviar to everyone. People actually held massive block parties and city wide barbeques to celebrate. They were happy that food was going to be free. If they had only spoke the words that I repeat like a mantra. Nothing ever offered by the government, for free, is ever worth a damn.

I have to give the people credit though. They didn't complain when they did get to the new National Grocery and received their ration. Not at first, anyway. People just figured it would take time for the good stuff to be sorted out. It's when the luxury items were destroyed that the people started to realize how it was actually going to be. We get rice, bread, beans, milk and eggs every week. Meat comes once a month, usually chicken, and fruit every two weeks. We have to think about our health after all.

-Excerpt from the journal of John Evermann

The morning after the intrusion John helped get the kids ready for school while Amanda cleaned up the house as best she could. No one talked much as they went about their morning routine which was regularly interrupted by picking up broken furniture and scattered household items. The officers had broken a vase and a picture frame, two of the few special items they managed to requisition. Amanda was trying not to cry in front of the children. John felt like a low burning fire was growing in him, and this was steadily adding fuel.

Once the kids were off to school John helped clean up as much as he could. He picked up the picture frame and held it, looking at the image of his family inside. The broken glass had scratched the picture but it hadn't ruined it. He opened the back of the frame and took the picture out, shaking the glass off into the trash. The scratch was minor, leaving the images of his family unscathed. Damaged but not broken. He folded the picture and stuck it in his pocked, and tossed the picture frame into the trash as well.

There was still more cleaning to do and John considered calling in sick so he could help Amanda. He had as many sick days as he wanted, but he just couldn't bring himself to do it. John felt like he received enough *free* stuff from the government and didn't want to take a free day off unless absolutely necessary. Besides, he'd made a promise to make up for the lost time.

"Have a good day," Amanda said quietly when John was pulling on his jacket. The numbers on the back somehow felt heavier.

"I wish I could do more." John gestured to indicate the mess of the house.

"It's fine, I'll be able to manage the rest."

Amanda had kept her head down, always busy with something so that she didn't have to look up. John went to her and took her by the shoulders, turning her to look at him. She looked up and gave a shuddering breath. John pulled her into his arms and she let herself cry for a minute in the protection of his embrace. They didn't speak, he just held her, and stroked her hair as she let the stress and fear pour out onto his shoulder. After a few minutes she stopped and he held her by the shoulders again. She nodded that she was all right.

"Love you."

"Love you too."

John kissed her and rubbed the tears from her eyes before she gave him a gentle push toward the door.

John started his walk to work with time to spare. He hated being late, but hated breaking his word more. More than that, being late could mean a cut in rations. It was Friday. John hated Fridays. Before, Friday was payday, the start to the weekend and all that. Now it was just a reminder of what they lost. No paychecks, and no weekends. Everyone worked on Saturday.

John took a different route to work in the mornings than he did on the way home. He barely noticed where he went, however. His mind was still focused on those men violating his home. It was no longer illegal to search homes without cause or consent. The houses were government property after all. He just couldn't shake the feeling that his rights had been violated, whether he had rights or not. The people were told they still had rights, but the needs of the community were more important.

John's walk took him through a part of town that once was home to quite a few small businesses. Bookstores, gift shops, and novelty stores among others, were all closed across the country. Their owners were told that their businesses were property of the government. That same government declared all such businesses unnecessary and closed them down. They sent the former owners to work in more productive areas such as manufacturing. That part of town always looked sad to John, but it served as a reminder of what he was risking himself and his family for. Every time he walked through the area it refueled his desire to flee the only home he had ever known for something better. He reached the mill without seeing another soul and entered the building with the resigned calm of a soldier going to war.

After clocking in for his shift John made his way over to the door leading to the mill floor. The scene through the little protective glass window in the door showed him the same thing it always did. The floor reminded him of those old movies where robots worked at the same menial task over and over. The only difference was the robots he saw were people. Everyone had their station and task, and no one deviated. It was all so regimented that the workers seemed to be one with their machine, and the machine part of the mill, like a living thing made up of gears and flesh, muscle and grease.

When he exited the break room into the mill the noise and heat washed over him like a wave. He instantly started to sweat as he put in his ear plugs. He was always struck by the lack of enthusiasm in his coworkers whenever he moved through the mill. As usual some greeted him and he smiled and shouted greetings back. Even those smiles were fleeting as everyone returned to their task, head down, and eyes dull.

The visit by the federal officers the night before was playing over and over in his head. He couldn't figure out why that search, that invasion of his home felt different than all the other times their house had been searched. Despite his frayed emotions he kept his head down, took his federally mandate breaks and lunches, and he did his job to the best of his ability.

John finished out his day as usual, clocked out and started the long walk home. Nothing unusual had happened that day, just like every other day. He walked by the confiscated businesses, the abandoned bar and the classic American houses. He greeted his kids, but they were unusually quiet on the way home. Something had changed in the world his family knew and even the children felt it.

When they got home Steve was waiting anxiously on his own front porch.

"Go inside and start your homework. Tell your mother I will be in, in a minute," John told his kids.

Once the children were inside John walked over to Steve's yard.

"What's wrong?" John asked.

"Jeff and his wife are gone," Steve replied.

"What do you mean, gone?" John asked, alarmed. Jeff was one of the members of his secret group.

"Gone, Jeff didn't show up for work this morning and no one is answering the door at his house," Steve answered.

"Dear God. Do you think the Feds know about the meetings?" John's question was not directed at Steve, and Steve did not answer, leaving John with his thoughts for a moment.

"Maybe they couldn't wait and left on their own," John said, though he didn't really believe that.

"That's my hope, but John we have to assume the worst or we put everyone else at risk," Steve said.

John nodded grimly.

"You're right, we should get everyone together tonight at my place so we can decide what to do," John decided, "We may have to go early."

"Two nights in a row, do you really think that's wise?" Steve asked.

"It's a risk we'll have to take. If the Feds know about us then we might not have much time," John said, "Besides, if they are onto us maybe they won't expect a meeting so soon."

Steve nodded, "I'll make the calls."

The friends shook hands and parted without another word.

John stood on his porch watching the people in his neighborhood. His thoughts were on Jeff, his wife, and others that had disappeared in the past. Reeducation facilities had been in place for years, and were a real fear for citizens who did not acclimate well. It was rumored that anyone sent to them was tortured or even killed. John prayed that none of his friends were facing that sort of horror. After a few minutes of watching the children play across the street he went inside.

The mood in the Evermann house was more subdued while the family ate dinner. John had told Amanda about Jeff's disappearance. They did not want to scare the children so they would discuss it more after they went to bed. Thomas and Susan ate quietly and went about their evening chores without complaint. They seemed to understand the gravity of the situation without being told.

"We are hosting another meeting tonight," John told his wife while they washed dishes.

Amanda did not question him about it. She trusted him enough that if he thought it would be safe then she didn't need to worry.

"There should still be enough coffee," was all she said.

He gave her a quick kiss and put on a pot. Once the machine was going he turned the back porch light on and went down to prepare the basement.

Chapter 5

Government supporters will tell you that the Feds had to take over everything. Capitalism had failed, they will tell you. I argue that capitalism wasn't even given a chance. Between regulation and restrictions, business involvement in politics and vice versa, and government's inability to allow the free market to correct itself, real capitalism never even existed. Not that anyone in their right mind wanted an economy without regulation, but the system's perceived failure was firmly in the hands of the government-corporate partnership that passed regulation to benefit some and punish others.

Bottom line is America hadn't had a true free market for a very long time, if ever, and that allowed greed and government mismanagement to create the environment that led to the Great Recession. Was it intentional, as some speculate? I don't know, but it doesn't really matter now does it?

-Excerpt from the journal of John Evermann

John looked at his friends and neighbors that were gathered in his basement. They all looked worried; some even scared, after hearing that Jeff was missing.

"I don't think we can wait any longer," John began, "If the Feds have arrested Jeff and his wife it may mean that the rest of us are in danger as well. It's only a matter of time as I see it."

"What if that's what the Feds want?" Carl asked. He seemed to be on the verge of panic. "Maybe Jeff didn't talk and they are hoping we will show ourselves."

John sighed.

"Carl, if you are too scared to leave, you don't have to. No one here is obligated to go along with us," John looked at them all as he said the last.

"Sit down and shut up, Carl," someone in the back shouted. The tension was broken by laughter around the room. Carl laughed nervously after a moment.

"On a serious note," Steve, who was standing next to John, started. "We need to make a decision tonight. Two of our members are now missing. Jerry could have left without telling anyone, but Jeff? My vote is to leave starting tomorrow. We leave individually or in small groups and meet at Benny's cabin just like we planned. He should have the supplies ready by now."

"I agree," John nodded.

Everyone else nodded or said "Yes". Even Carl, after a nudge from his neighbor, agreed. They all looked at John, waiting for him to tell them what was next. It made him uncomfortable, but they had come to depend on him.

"All right, remember to pack only what you need. It's a long walk," John advised.

"Everyone review your routes tonight. Make sure all of your families know the way in case you get separated," Steve added, "It shouldn't take anyone more than a day to get to Benny's. We leave from the cabin the morning after next."

"Don't be late," John added. "We can't afford to wait, everyone knows the route. If you get delayed you will have to catch up."

The meeting broke up as it began. People left individually at intermittent times to avoid detection. Those waiting to leave stood around and talked as usual, but the topics of discussion had changed. Before they would complain about how bad things had gotten. Tonight however they were talking about the future. They planned what they would do once they were settled in the Republic of Texas. It made John smile to finally see hope in the eyes of his friends and neighbors. At last they had something to look forward to, a better place ahead of them instead of behind. It was once said that America was the last bastion of freedom. John realized that night that man will always create a place where freedom holds sway.

Steve was the last to leave the meeting. He and John planned on getting their families out after work the next day. They panned to use Steve's work van to get to Benny's on time. John and Benny had already talked before about the possibility that he may have company early if things fell apart, and their group knew to approach the cabin with caution.

Benny was a friend of John's father and John had met the man when they were both younger. As America changed so did Benny, becoming more reclusive and paranoid. The man lived almost completely without outside contact but when he did need something he contacted one of his few friends he could still trust. One of them happened to be John. When he and Steve had started planning their move they contacted Benny right away to see if he would help.

"You ready for this John?" Steve asked before he exited the back door.

"Have to be," John replied shortly.

"Cheer up man," Steve cuffed him on the shoulder, "Everything will be better when we reach the Republic."

With that Steve walked out of John's house, bound for his own. John stood in his kitchen a moment, looking at the things that had made up his world for so many years. He wondered what it was about human nature that made him regret the loss of things, even things that were not really his. He shook his head. That was a question for people who have more time. His family, who were packing upstairs, were more important that any of that.

John went to the hall closet and opened the compartment in the back wall. He took out three things that he was determined to take with him. He took out the copy of the constitution, an old American flag, and his bible. All contraband but to John they all meant freedom.

He carried the burden upstairs to pack with the rest of his things. It was not a burden of weight, but of responsibility. It was a burden he stoically took on. Not that he asked to be responsible for his friends, or even wanted to be, but he was asked to carry it so he did. With every loss of a friend, or change in their plan it just got heavier. It was his duty, one he would not shirk, no matter how heavy it got.

When he reached the top of the stairs the activity had died down. The kids were already packed and in bed, their backpacks, shoes, and jackets by the door of their rooms. It would be hardest for them, he knew. He looked at their innocent faces and felt a pang of sadness and guilt. They didn't understand what was happening, or why they were leaving. All they knew of the world was the one John was trying to rip them out of. They didn't know anything about this new place, only what their parents told them. They trusted him because he was their father, but he knew they were scared.

He could hear Amanda in their room, stuffing clothes into her own pack. Moving to the doorway he saw that she was packing some extra things for the children in with hers. He wordlessly took some of the extras and placed them in the bottom of his pack with his treasures. Even the children had to carry their own packs, but their parents would make it a little easier for them.

"I'm not sure I'm ready for this," Amanda said without looking up.

"We'll be fine, I won't let anything happen to us," John put his arms around her protectively.

John felt her nod against his chest. He gripped her tighter and kissed the top of her head.

"How were the kids with all of this?" John asked her. She leaned back and wiped her eyes before answering.

"Better than I expected. I think they are excited and scared, like they are going on an adventure," she replied.

"Let's hope they keep that feeling," John said, looking out the window.

"Kids are resilient," she said.

She took his chin in her hand and turned his head to look into her eyes. "Besides, they believe in their father."

He smiled down at her, but he felt the weight of responsibility settle more firmly on his shoulders. He pushed away his fears to keep them from showing on his face. He gave her a quick kiss and they both went back to packing.

As they were finishing up their own packing when they heard a loud knocking on the front door. At first John thought it might be one of his neighbors with a last-minute question. That hope was dashed when a loud voice identified the visitors as federal officers.

"Get the kids ready and down to the kitchen," John hissed, grabbing his own pack and rushing down the stairs.

When he reached the entry he quietly checked the lock and chain on the door. The officer knocked again and John could hear others talking about bashing the door in. He picked up a chair and braced it under the door handle as silently as he could. John looked up as Amanda and the kids descended the stairs and rushed into the kitchen. The knocking became more insistent as he followed them toward the back door.

They all pulled up short when they saw a shadow pass across the curtained window of the back door. Amanda hugged her children close as John approached it. He stood a moment, trying to think of something. He knew, from the muffled voices, there were several officers at the front door so decided to take the risk that they had only sent one or two to the back.

He reached out and unlocked the door without disturbing the handle. As John had hoped the officer outside tried the door and found it unlocked. As the door started to open John grabbed the handle and pulled as hard as he could. The unexpected movement caused the officer to stumble inside, hit the kitchen table, and fall to the floor. The officer's drawn pistol clattered to the tile and slid toward John's feet.

The sound of the officer's fall was punctuated by a crash as the front door was torn from its hinges by a battering ram. John only thought about his actions for a heartbeat. He picked up the dropped weapon, and pushed his family past the stunned officer and out into the night.

Chapter 6

    The first year of the President's term saw sweeping changes to our society, and daily life. Opposition was stiff at first but the progressives of both houses started to show their true faces. All in the name of the greater good we were given massive bailouts for failing companies, free health insurance, and climate change laws. We were told that we could not afford to sit idle anymore. If companies failed, the country would fail. If people did not get free insurance, it would bankrupt America. If we did not clamp down on carbon, we would destroy the planet. The irony was all of those programs assured the destruction they were supposed to avert. The country's debt skyrocketed, as did taxes and utilities for families. The country went bankrupt, and its citizens right along with it. It was the last though, the climate change policy, that was the kicker. Those in power had set up companies, years before, to handle the new product that the climate change laws would create. Imagine our surprise when everyone in the country found out that the very same people that put the law into place were selling those carbon credits and green products.

                                              -*Excerpt from the journal of John Evermann*

Lieutenant Ben Casey hated his job. It was the middle of the night in some Illinois backwater and he was breaking down doors because his bosses in Washington were paranoid. They were afraid that there was some revolutionary faction bent on rising up against the government. Casey had already arrested three of the supposed revolutionaries and as far as he could tell they just wanted to leave the country, not fight it. He tried to tell his bosses that, but they didn't want to hear it. The prisoners had been shipped off to Washington for further questioning. As far as Casey was concerned the government should let them go. If they didn't like the way things were let them leave, it would make his life easier, and let him concentrate on real threats.

Casey had been assigned to the Federal Police right out of college. He had tested well for the kind of work they needed him to do. He was assigned to their counter-terrorism task force in D.C. and specialized in sniffing out 'home grown' terrorists; citizens that felt the best way to create change was to attack the government. He was good at recognizing those types of people. He was also good at recognizing those that were not bent on violence. This group in Stewart fit the latter description, but he was worried that if they were handled poorly it could turn violent.

It was his job though, and it was not like he could quit. He would do his best, follow orders, and keep his mouth shut. Let the higher-ups worry about the morality.

His contraband search the night before had cemented his suspicions about the group in Stewart. He knew these people were *purists*, throw-backs to an America that just did not exist anymore, but they weren't terrorists. He had figured out their routine for meeting, and decided his next arrest should be the latest host. He was hoping that John Evermann could be persuaded to give up more information than had the last detainees.

All these thoughts were at the front of his mind while he looked around the deserted house where the Evermanns lived. The front door was destroyed by their ram, and the fragments of a kitchen chair mixed with wood from the door to litter the entryway. Keys rested in a ceramic dish on the hall table, and pictures hung askew on the wall. Everything that had been disturbed the night before had been put back in place. The Evermanns themselves were gone.

"Lieutenant, take a look at this," one of the officers called from the hallway.

The man was standing outside a small closet, pointing at something inside. Casey looked in and saw a panel had been removed from the back wall.

"So that's where they hid it all," Casey said to himself.

"Sir?" The officer said.

"When we were here before, it was too clean. Everyone has contraband of some sort, some heirloom left over from before. People this clean are usually hiding something, you can be sure of it," Casey instructed.

"Yes sir," the officer said.

Casey shook his head in disgust. His expertise was wasted on these grunts. All they understood was doing just enough to get their contract time in and collect their requisitions at week's end. They were all chosen for their strength, loyalty, and single-minded devotion to doing exactly as they were told.

"Have that back wall pulled down," Casey pointed into the closet, "I doubt you will find anything, but search it thoroughly."

Casey looked around the house with little interest. His officers were tearing the place apart, but there was nothing to be found. He had dispatched two vans to search for the Evermann family, but if he had read John correctly the man was smart. They would not be easy to find. He would call off the search of the house soon, and by dawn they would be knocking on doors, questioning John's neighbors. With a sigh of frustration Casey went to the house's kitchen to deal with one last problem.

Amidst the chaos of the search one officer sat alone at the kitchen table holding his head in his hands. He did not react as dishes were broken and the contents of cabinets were swept onto the countertops and floor. The officer just sat staring at the tabletop in front of him.

"Officer," Casey said sternly as he took a seat across from the man.

The officer did react to being addressed by his superior, jumping as if stuck by a pin. He started to stand, scraping the chairs feet on the linoleum.

"Sit down," Casey said, gesturing toward the chair.

The officer reluctantly took his seat, sitting straight backed and fixing his eyes on a point just over Casey's right shoulder.

"A car is coming from the Peoria office to get you. When you get there write up your report on what happened. Be sure it is accurate," Casey stressed that, "Because mine will be. See the quartermaster about issuing you a new weapon and await reassignment. You are no longer on this team."

The officer simply nodded his understanding.

"The car should be here soon, you can wait outside," Casey stood up to leave.

The officer also stood and saluted Casey before turning for the front door. Casey returned the salute absent-mindedly, already thinking about the road ahead.

Chapter 7

Many people were hopeful in the early days of the last President's term. He promised so many reforms, and changes in the way our government did business. What people were most happy about was his pledge to bring all of our troops home, from all over the world. During the President's second term major attacks on cities all over the world rushed the decision. There seemed to be a massive awakening of terrorist cells, and bombings all over Europe, Africa, Asia, and the Middle East. The troops were brought home immediately, for our protection. Not everyone thought this was a good idea. It didn't take long for our fears to become reality. South-east Asia and the Middle East erupted into years of civil conflict once we pulled out. Millions died, but so many in this country did not care anymore, they just said "It's not any of our concern."

         -Excerpt from the journal of John Evermann

After stunning the officer and escaping their house John and his family had fled through their backyard and the one behind. John scooped Susan up into his arms when she stumbled and nearly fell. When they reached the next street they heard the federal officers behind them, calling out to each other to arrange a search. He quietly urged his family to run faster.

John led them down the street, and then cut through several more yards, always moving in the same general direction. Steve and John had agreed on a meeting place in case something happened but they never expected to have to use it. He was headed for an abandoned and overgrown park several blocks from their neighborhood. The trees and shrubs in the park offered concealment from the streets, and the surrounding homes were abandoned. Like many families they had been relocated by the Fair Workforce Act.

They continued to run through the yards and empty lots to avoid being in the open. When they had to cross a street they did it one at a time. Several times they heard shouts or saw the beams of flashlights. The sounds of sirens cutting through the night lent new urgency to their flight. John knew they were getting close to a hiding spot but he didn't relax just yet for fear he'd make a mistake when they were almost clear.

They reached the park, without any signs of pursuit, a little over an hour after their escape. Amanda led the kids through the overgrown field, toward a stand of trees that John had indicated when they arrived. John stayed behind for a few minutes to scan the area for any signs of pursuit. He was thankful the feds didn't appear to have brought dogs with them, and would have to do a search the hard way. He knew it was only a matter of time before they called in canine units though.

Once he was sure that they had not been followed John made his way back to where his family was hiding. He came upon a scene he had wished never to see. His family was huddled on the ground, scared, tired, and in danger. He sat down next to his wife and put his arm around her shoulders and pulled her close. Susan, who was weeping softly, climbed into his lap and he held her too. Thomas sat on the other side of Amanda, stoically staring off into the trees, and doing his best to maintain his fragile young resolve. John looked at them and wondered if this was how all refugees felt.

"We will wait here until morning. If Steve and his family aren't here by then we'll have to go," John said softly.

Amanda looked up at him, "Do you think the officers tried to take them too?"

"I don't know. I didn't have time to see if any feds were at their house. He'll do his best to get his family out," John squeezed her shoulders and kissed the top of her head. They all adjusted as John pulled off his pack and then his jacket. He settled back against the trunk of a tree and his wife and daughter resumed their positions, seeking the feeling of safety in his arms that they desperately needed. John covered Susan, who was shivering with cold, or fear, with his jacket. He sat and listened to his family fall asleep around him, hoping for their sake, it would be soon. Thomas was the last, finally laying down on this side and resting his head on his mother's leg. John settled himself in for a long night, watching the darkness around him.

Chapter 8

The Fair Workforce Act was passed during the President's third term. Of course the National News proclaimed it "The greatest achievement in social justice of our time." That would be laughable if the truth were not more sinister. The new law allowed the government the power to relocate people from one town to another to insure that government businesses had enough workers. People were forced to abandon their homes and move wherever the government told them to. There was no compensation for their homes, the government assumed ownership of all private property years before.

-Excerpt from the journal of John Evermann

John had no idea when he had dozed off, but he was woken up abruptly by someone shaking him and calling his name softly. His first realization was that his arm was asleep where it was holding Susan, and his legs were cold. His second thought was panic. He sat up in alarm, disturbing the rest of his family, but relaxed when he saw Steve's smiling face.

"Sarah and your boy?" John asked, looking over Steve's shoulder. He sighed in relief when he saw Steve's family crouched in the shadows of the trees a few yards away. They were obscured by the fog that had rolled in during the night.

"We all made it," Steve waved his family over to join the others. John's own family sat rubbing the sleep out of their eyes and shivering in the early morning chill. Amanda hugged Sarah when she got close, and the three kids stood looking at their parents. Their looks were afraid and uncertain.

"Did they go after anyone else last night?" John asked.

"I don't know, John. I don't think so. It looks like they were just after you," Steve paused and looked around again, "Do you think Carl turned on us?"

John sat silently for a few moments, thinking about the question. He did not like to think that any of his friends would turn on him, but he was beginning to wonder. They had been so careful to disguise their meetings, using different member's houses in random order. They never discussed the meetings in public, and every member had been watched for months before being admitted into the group.

"I don't know Steve. It doesn't matter now anyway, we have to stick to the plan," John said.

Steve nodded, accepting John's answer. John had been adopted as the group's leader, much to John's dismay. He didn't want to be anyone's leader, and didn't think he was any more qualified to do it than any of the others. The members just looked to him for decisions, even his best friend Steve. Eventually John accepted the role that was thrust upon him.

"We should still be able to get my work van like we planned," Steve said, "We should make it to Benny's in time."

"I'll go with you in case you run into any trouble," John said, standing up and retrieving his jacket.

"John?" Amanda said. All the questions she wanted to ask were reflected in her eyes.

"We'll be fine. You and Sarah wait here with the kids. We'll be back for you soon," John assured her. He gave quick hugs to his family while Steve said goodbye to his own.

With the goodbyes out of the way, and their families safely hidden in the trees of the abandoned park, Steve and John started across town. They cut across several yards until they reached Douglas Street. Douglas would take them close to where Steve worked. They walked at a fast pace, watching for any sign of federal authorities. Many of the homes on the street were abandoned, but not so many that two pedestrians would seem out of place.

They didn't speak as they walked and the silence gave John time to reflect on how much things had changed in Stewart. He had grown up in the small town, like generations of Evermanns before him. He had gone to school, met Amanda, and gotten married where their church used to be. His kids were both born at the hospital down the street from that church. Now they were about to leave Stewart for good, and that, to John, was the worst thing about this whole situation. Things had gotten so bad that people would leave everything they ever knew just to get away.

John's thoughts were interrupted when Steve pulled him into the side yard of a nearby house. They hunkered down next to some green plastic garbage cans. Steve signaled for silence and pointed to the street, and John looked in the indicated direction to see what had alarmed his friend. An unmarked black van rolled slowly by on Douglas. The two friends waited tensely as the van crept along.

John and Steve both breathed again when the van passed without stopping. They both stood up and started to head through the yard to an adjacent street.

"Wait," John said, "If they've searched Douglas already they probably won't be back. We have no idea if they've searched the other streets though."

"Right, let's get going," Steve patted John's shoulder as he passed on his way back to Douglas street.

The two men didn't see any more federal officers along the way. They reached the intersection of Douglas and Fifth and casually looked up the cross street, to the right. Across the street and two blocks away was the *National Upkeep and Beautification Department, Stewart Office*. It was the government's answer to keeping all of their newly acquired property in some sort of decent shape. Much to the men's dismay a black van was parked out front.

The two ducked into the doorway of an abandoned store front to watch the van. John knew loitering would eventually get them noticed, but they had little choice, and less time.

"What do you think?" Steve asked.

"We can't wait around too long. Where's your van?"

"In the garage around back, but the keys are inside," Steve replied.

"If we do get in there, can we trust your boss to keep quiet?"

"He hates the feds as much as we do. He won't tell them anything, but he will have to report the van stolen. He should give us a couple days before he does though," Steve explained.

"Good, by then we can have it dumped somewhere along a different route," John said.

They waited a few more minutes in silence and their patience paid off. Two uniformed officers exited the building and climbed into the van. John and Steve ducked further into the shadows of the doorway and watched the van drive up the street, away from them. After the vehicle turned a corner they walked casually across the street.

Steve held the door for John and they entered the reception area of the building. Steve smiled at the woman sitting behind a metal and wood desk. The interior was cold and colorless and instantly made John uncomfortable.

"Margaret, is Jack in his office?"

"Steve," she said quietly, "What are you doing here? There are some men looking for you."

"Don't worry about that I just need a minute with Jack."

"Sure, I'll let him know you're here," she said.

"Thanks Margaret," Steve smiled and rapped her desk with his knuckles. He led John down the hall toward the back of the building while the receptionist called back to Jack's office to let him know they were on the way.

Reaching a door that bore the simple plaque marked 'manager' Steve knocked and entered without waiting for a response. The office that he led John into was a drab, uninspiring room furnished with a desk, a couple of chairs, and a filing cabinet in the corner. There were no pictures, posters, or decoration of any sort. Behind the desk sat an older man, round in the middle and bald on top. As they entered he shuffled some papers together on his desk and stood up with a cautious smile.

"Steve, what are you doing here?" Jack asked.

"I need a favor boss," Steve started, "We need to borrow the van for a few days."

"Steve, there were agents here looking for you. What have you gotten yourself into?" This time he looked at John, as if he were the cause of all of Steve's problems.

"Don't worry about it Jack. Listen, just give us the keys to one of the older vans and we'll be out of your hair."

Jack looked at both of them, weighing the decision before him. John could see that he was torn between doing the right thing and doing the legal thing. Finally he went to his desk and opened a drawer. Retrieving a set of keys he tossed them to Steve. Jack's hand shook but he looked Steve right in the eyes.

"You be careful Steve," he said, "I will report it stolen day after tomorrow."

Steve smiled and shook his hand, "Thanks boss, you have no idea how much this means."

"Oh, I think I might," Jack said as they left the office.

Steve took the lead again, walking toward the back of the building. John could see some workers, typing or filing in the offices that they passed. It was a disciplined environment, sterile almost. No one talked, gossiped, or told jokes. Every office was bare of any personality. It was nothing like the television shows that John could remember watching as a kid, depicting offices like this as a beehive of activity. Those shows seemed almost like fantasy to him, as if what he was seeing now was the only reality there ever was.

At the end of the main hall Steve opened a steel door that led to a large, dimly lit space. The smell of gasoline, oil, and exhaust washed over John as he entered. Workbenches lined one wall with their tools organized on racks above, a few lockers sat against the opposite wall, and one van was parked on the end of the large garage. The box-like vehicle was white, with two small windows in the double side doors behind the passenger door. Large letters on the side identified it as an N.U.B.D. van.

"Can you get the door?" Steve pointed to a chain hanging on the side of a wide metal door opposite them.

John nodded and Steve climbed in the van and started it up. John slid the spring-loaded latch to the side and felt the door give a little. He grabbed the looped chain and started pulling, bringing the door up toward the ceiling on its rails. Once Steve had backed the van out of the garage John reversed the chain until the door was down far enough that he could grab it. He ducked under, pulled it the rest of the way down, and heard the latch spring into place. He climbed into the passenger side of the van and Steve turned it onto the street toward the park.

"Do you think everyone else was able to get out?" Steve asked after a few minutes.

"I don't know. I hope so," John said.

John took the pistol out of the waste band of his jeans and made sure the safety was on. He then opened the glove box and buried the weapon under the mess of invoices, bills, and work orders he found in the small compartment. When he sat back Steve was glancing at him out of the corner of his eye.

"You've had that this whole time?" Steve asked.

"One of the feds dropped it at my house. Not sure why I picked it up, it just seemed like the right thing to do at the time," John said.

"Let's just hope we don't have to use it," Steve said firmly. John nodded, hoping the same thing.

They drove the rest of the way in silence, on the lookout for federal agents. When they reached the park Steve pulled into an overgrown parking lot on the back side. John looked at the cracked and peeling N.U.B.D. logo on the side after he closed his door. He picked at a piece of the decal, which peeled up a little more.

"You go get the others. I am going to see if I can take care of this logo," John said.

Steve nodded and walked toward the wooded area of the park. John picked at the decals on the van. They were so damaged from the elements that his only challenge was peeling off a piece larger than a couple inches square. By the time Steve returned with their families, though, he was nearly finished. Steve helped him with the last decal while their wives settled the children into the back. There were no seats in the back so they did their best to make it comfortable.

Once they were all settled in and Steve was backing the van onto the road again John looked back at their families. They all looked a little scared. That was what angered John the most, fear in the eyes of his wife and child. Fear caused by those who are supposed to protect him and his family. He smiled reassuringly before turning back to face the road ahead. Soon, he hoped, they would be in a much better place.

* * *

"Sir," an officer stepped through the open door into Lieutenant Casey's temporary office in downtown Stewart. The officer saluted and waited to be addressed.

"What is it?" Casey asked without looking up from his report.

"Evermann's neighbor didn't show up for work today, and his house is empty. There have been other reports of workers not showing up at their jobs. We are currently investigating them as well," the officer said, still standing at attention halfway between Casey's desk and the door.

Casey looked up at the officer, studying the man, and using the time to think.

"They must have used the raid last night as a distraction," Casey said quietly.

"Sir?" The officer had not heard him.

"Sergeant, our targets are already on the move," Casey said louder, "Continue to investigate the houses of those that didn't show up to work, I want a list of the names of those whose houses are empty. Send Foster in on your way out."

"Yes sir," the sergeant saluted again and left the office.

"Sir, you wanted to see me," another federal officer walked into the office and saluted.

"Foster, get on the phone with the Peoria office, and tell them we need more officers down here. Our subjects are on the move and we're going to have to cast the net wider," Casey said.

"Yes sir," Foster saluted and left the office.

Casey pulled out a map of the area around Stewart, quickly outlining the best routes for a group of people to travel north or south. He figured they would head south to the Republic of Texas, but he would leave no possibly unexplored.

Chapter 9

I imagine that the ancients who predicted the end of the world had a much different definition than the one we latch onto today. I think when we left Stewart, that was the end of our world so to speak, the world we knew. It didn't mean we were going to die, or that everything was going to blow up. It just meant that the world as we had known it was going to change forever. Many felt that the end of the world was going to happen in 2012, or the year before, or any number of other times. In a way it did, just not in the way, or time that all the television programs and books said it would. There was even some ridiculous movie about it. It was when our President was reelected a third time. That day some of us knew it, the world would never be the same. That major change to our system, and apparent acceptance by the public's voting for him, gave him the confidence to push more drastic changes. Too bad no one predicted that would be the beginning of the end. We might have been able to avert it if we had known.

-Excerpt from the Journal of John Evermann

"I hope Benny is ready for us so early," Steve said.

The white van was parked at the beginning of a long, gravel drive that led off the highway and back into some woods. They could see part of the drive before it turned and started up one of the large hills that framed the highway. The trees bordering the highway were showing signs of fall in brilliant reds and gold mixed with the evergreens. The two families had been on the road for a little over an hour, using back roads and virtually abandoned state highways to reduce their chances of being spotted by the authorities.

"Only one way to find out. Let's go up and see who has made it so far. Just remember, drive slow so he can see who it is before we get to the house," John said.

Steve did just that, driving up the steep hill slowly. The man who lived at the top was sure to be watching and didn't trust anyone. Only a few yards back from the road the gravel drive appeared to become so overgrown that it was impassable. It would seem, to anyone that did not know better, that the path had been unused for years. Even John had only been up to the cabin twice.

The van reached the top of the hill and crossed a field toward a small log building set just in the tree line. It was the type of place that used to be featured in survivalist and hunting magazines. Self-sufficient, no electricity, wood stove for cooking and heating. It was a perfect image of independence. They could see a man sitting on the porch, with a rifle across his lap. Benny, and a few others, managed to stay off the grid. When the gun bans were passed by the government these men and women held onto their weapons as they had vowed to do all their lives. Since they had no real contact with the rest of the world the government had a hard time finding the survivalists to relieve them of their weapons. Steve pulled the van close to the cabin and John rolled down the window.

"Benny, it's me, John."

"You're early John," Benny said. Benny was one of those guys who would inevitably bear the nickname 'Grizzly Adams'. He was large, hairy, and intimidating to those who had never met him. He wore a thick beard that was streaked with gray, but his dark hair was yet untouched with age. He was dressed in hunter's camouflage and heavy brown boots. Benny leaned his rifle against the wall and stood up.

"Sorry about the change in plans, there was an emergency, and we had to leave early. We were hoping you might have gotten the supplies ready by now," John explained.

Benny looked past the van toward the road.

"You weren't followed were you?"

"No one followed us. We got out of town without anyone seeing us. This place isn't safe anymore though, a couple of our members have gone missing," John said.

Benny nodded, accepting John's explanation.

"We don't have much time then," the bearded man waved toward the side of the cabin, "Your people are hiding in the back. I'll get the rest of the supplies and meet you back there."

Stepping into the back yard they were greeted by the families that had lived around them. Hands were clasped and hugs exchanged. John did a quick head count, fifty-four members of their group, and their families. Everyone who was at their last meeting had made it. John was relieved but he had held out some small hope that his two missing friends would somehow make it as well. This was the last meeting place that the entire group knew about before crossing into Texas. Once they were gone from Benny's anyone left behind would have to find their own way.

Benny handed John and Steve each a large package, wrapped in brown paper and tied with string. He also started passing guns around to the men who looked old enough to have handled one before the ban. John took note of the large pack on Benny's back.

"So, you changed your mind?" John asked.

"Looks like I've got no choice," Benny said, handing John a hunting rifle, "Besides, you city-folk will just get lost."

John smiled when the grizzly recluse turned away without further comment. He turned back to the rest of the group.

"I don't think we should wait for the morning. Last night the Feds tried to arrest me and my family, and now they're searching for us.

I believe that everyone that is coming with us is here, and there is no reason to wait any longer," John explained.

Everyone looked worried, but none spoke. John looked at every face, but no one disagreed with his determination. He simply nodded and turned back to his family. John and Steve opened the packages of supplies and divided the contents among their family's packs. It was enough food to last for several days if they were careful. The rest of the group began gathering their own gear.

"John," Benny said behind him.

John turned to face the bearded woodsman.

"Take them south. I will dump the van and catch up with you tomorrow," Benny said. Steve had heard the comment and started to pull the keys from his pocket.

"I don't know Benny, that's more dangerous now. If the feds come this way, searching for us, you might get caught. I know it was our plan before, but things have changed," John replied. Steve dropped the keys back into his pocket.

"More dangerous to leave it here. Eventually they'll find your trail, but I can at least send them the wrong way first. It should buy us a few days."

John considered the man's plan. Benny had a point, but John hated to risk any of their number. He looked to Steve for some sort of reaction but his neighbor was looking at him expectantly. Steve was waiting for his reluctant leader to call the shots. In the end John accepted the logic of Benny's plan. They were risking one man to give a better chance to the rest of them. Finally John nodded and Steve handed the keys over.

"Stick to the rocky area along the old creek bed. Hard on the feet but it'll cover your tracks. I'll find you tomorrow," Benny said.

John held out his hand and the recluse took it in his meaty paw.

"Good luck."

"Same to you John."

Chapter 10

Some argued that Socialism was the only answer to our country's problems. I argue that Socialism was the endgame to an intentional plan. Welfare, government health care, public housing, the list goes on of things that can't be sustained in a free society if they grow unrestricted. I think the people in government knew these things would bankrupt us. They knew that eventually the system would collapse under its own weight. I think that was the plan all along, to end private industry, private wealth, and gain ultimate power for those in government. What could we do? We sat idly by for so many years, blind to the world around us. We elected politicians, trusting they would do the right thing, but never holding them to it. Discussing politics became taboo among our neighbors or friends. We allowed this to happen by allowing ourselves to be enslaved to the welfare state. Someone said, 'We get the government that we ask for', and it's very true. We may not have wanted this exactly, but we did get what we asked for.

-Excerpt from the Journal of John Evermann

The refugees, as John was starting to think of them, walked the rest of the day in silence. For the fifty four members of John's group, and their families, this was the end of their world. They left behind everything for the hope of a better life elsewhere. They had all agreed though, even a slim chance in Texas was preferable to the life they had before.

The area John was leading them through was hilly and heavily forested. People were helping each other, holding hands over fallen trees, lifting children over obstacles, and generally looking out for one another. Not because anyone told them to, or because it was law, but because it was best for everyone. A fall could lead to a serious injury which would be devastating for the entire group, much less the injured.

Even with the slower children, the group managed to cross several miles of forest south of Benny's cabin. John called a halt when he found a spot that seemed level enough to be comfortable and was sheltered from the air by trees overhead. He guessed they were less than an hour from sunset.

A few of the mothers gathered the children into a water detail, filling bottles and canteens from a nearby stream. The rest of the group set up a makeshift camp. Camping equipment was not as common as it had been in the past so most had to make do with large blankets and a few tarps. The two tents they did manage to find were used by the youngest children to make sure they stayed warm and dry.

John decided they would only have one camp fire out of necessity, but he was afraid even that little bit of smoke would be visible if anyone was out searching nearby. They would have to risk it to boil the water the children had collected.

John was also worried about Benny. If anyone could find them in these woods it would be the bearded woodsman. John just hoped his friend wouldn't get caught out there. He wasn't worried that Benny would talk if he was caught. He just didn't want his friend to wind up in some Federal camp.

It wasn't long before everyone was settled in for the night. John could tell that most were scared, especially the kids, but they did well dealing with it. John tried to sleep but couldn't and figured someone should keep watch. He sat with his back against a tree, looking out at the darkness.

For a time John imagined he was the only one in the world. He tried to turn his mind to the future, but he kept thinking on the days behind. He tried to figure out when everything went wrong. John remembered a quote from someone, something about judging a society on how they treated their unfortunate. When did helping the unfortunate mean bringing everyone else down to that level? Sure, if everyone is the same then no one is really less anymore, but is that the best solution?

John wondered what a world with true freedom would be like. He hoped Texas would be that world for them. Things were not that bad when he was a kid, but he could remember his grandfather talking about the way it was before. He remembered from his own father's stories, and how he used to talk about the American Dream. People would just laugh if John use those words, or report him to the Feds. America used to be a place that strived to lead, John thought, to be different, to try and be a model for the rest of the world. Somewhere along the line the people in power decided that America wasn't special anymore, and that she should follow the lead of others. Somewhere along the line that dream was lost, or stolen.

The night dragged on as John listened to the sounds of the dark forest. He was tired, physically and mentally. He was tired of feeling helpless against the tide of change, change that went against common sense. He was tired of the uncertainty, tired of knowing things were terribly wrong and being powerless to fix it. As his mind drifted so did his eyelids.

Some time later, he didn't know when, John jerked awake when Steve spoke.

"Why don't you go lay down. I'll keep watch for awhile," Steve said sleepily.

"Sounds like a good idea."

Steve reached down and helped John to his feet.

"What's on your mind?" Steve asked when he saw John's troubled look.

"Do you ever get the feeling we're trying to plug a dam with our fingers?" John asked.

"What do you mean?" Steve returned.

"It just seems like more and more people want this," he waved his hand at the world around them.

"People are fighting in the south," Steve started to say.

"Only four states are fighting back," John said.

"Thousands fled and now fight with the Texans," Steve added.

John sighed and nodded. He took a drink from his canteen.

"You're right," John said finally, "Sometimes my mind just goes off on its own. I'm tired Steve."

Steve patted John's shoulder and gently pushed him toward his sleeping family.

"Everything will be better when we get to Texas," Steve assured him.

"I pray to God we make it there in one piece," John said over his shoulder.

Chapter 11

You have to wonder if those who supported the change approve of what they finally got. It's one thing to be lazy and say you want the government to take care of you, and something else entirely to live with it. I tried to figure it out for years, questioning so-called socialists. Most of them thought that it was just a matter of taking money from the rich and giving it to the poor. As if anyone has the right to tell someone how much money they're allowed to make. Very few would accept that it only works in a country where the government has full control. They just don't realize that you can't retain your freedoms and have a government that takes care of you.

-Excerpt from the Journal of John Evermann

John snapped awake when he heard the group packing up their makeshift camp. When he sat up he could hear Amanda calling the children over to eat something. She turned to him as he rolled out of their blankets and stood up.

"What time is it?" John asked before he yawned.

"About seven," Amanda replied, "We figured we would give Benny a little more time to catch up before heading out.

John rubbed his arms vigorously as his body started to react to the chill in the air.

"Good idea," he said, accepting a biscuit and some jerky. He ate quickly and packed his bag before going to look for Steve. His feet crunched through the first fallen leaves of autumn on his way to where his friend was also packing up.

"See anything unusual last night?" John asked as he approached.

"Except for the frogs down by the water it was quiet," Steve replied, rolling up his blanket.

"Good. We're going to give Benny a few more minutes before we leave," John said.

"Sounds good," Steve tied the blanket roll with some string and used straps to secure the bundle to his pack.

John left everyone to their packing and walked off to find a quiet place to relieve himself. He was not sure how far he wandered but he soon found himself at the edge of the forest, looking across acres of overgrown farmland. The prairie had almost completely reclaimed the unused land so that only the linear boundary of trees made it recognizable as a field.

John took a deep breath. Could this be how America looked to the early dreamers that came to this country, he wondered. He could almost imagine some farmer or rancher standing in this very spot. Could that settler have imagined the great nation that would follow, or how that nation would fall?

"That's enough John," he said softly to himself, "It's time to look to the future."

He didn't usually talk to himself, but he thought that saying it out loud might finally snap him out of his melancholy. He took one last look around before he turned back to the forest to relieve himself.

With the morning necessities taken care of, John returned to camp to get everyone ready for the long day. Everyone was packed up and anxious to leave when John returned. He wanted to give Benny a few more minutes to catch up so he gathered some of the men and children together to sweep the campsite for garbage or other cast-offs. He didn't know much about tracking, or hiding tracks, but he figured that making sure they left the place looking as undisturbed as possible would help.

"Still no sign of Benny," Steve said when they finished picking up the last of the trash.

"I don't think we can wait any longer," John said.

"True," Steve nodded. "We heading out then?"

"Yes, we have a lot of ground to cover and none of us are used to this kind of walking. Benny's though. He'll catch up even if we keep moving."

"How long do you think it will take us?" Steve asked.

"Hard to say, depends on everyone here. Best I can figure, it will take ten or twelve days, if we don't run into any problems," John replied.

"Do you think everyone will be able to do this?" Steve asked.

John looked around at their group. The children were still full of enthusiasm, excited about the adventure. The adults looked anxious but determined. He imagined the looks he saw on everyone's face was the same as anyone who has ever fought to be free.

He turned to Steve and nodded. "I do."

Steve smiled and shouldered his pack. He took his son's hand and put his arm around his wife's shoulders, and started walking south. John's family gathered their things and followed, with the rest of the group right behind them.

The second day of the trip was hard on most of the adults. They were tired and sore from the exercise of the previous day. The children took it well, as most children would take an exciting hike through the woods. The kids were so enthusiastic that parents were constantly cautioning them to 'stay close', 'keep the noise down', and 'stop running' for fear of a fall. Regardless of the frustration, every parent in the group was happy to see their children smiling and laughing.

John called frequent breaks to ease everyone into the rough exercise of the trip. He figured that the breaks would become fewer as people grew accustomed to being on the move all day. It was during their lunch break that they heard a popping sound in the trees. They had all stepped on twigs and branches during the day so the sound was already familiar. Silence fell over the camp as those men who had rifles armed themselves while everyone else gathered the children and cautioned them to be quiet. John and Steve quietly approached the source of the noise at different angles.

John's hand gripped the unfamiliar rifle nervously. He had never fired a gun until Benny had given them some basic lessons. The recluse wanted everyone that would carry a weapon to learn how to use it, so a few had gone out to the cabin during the weeks leading up to their leaving. John checked again to make sure the safety was off and hoped that Steve remembered to do the same.

Just as John started to wonder if he was going to have to use that rifle Benny stepped around a bush that grew between two trees that were in his path. John and Steve both sighed in relief and lowered their weapons, resetting the safeties.

"Benny, you scared the hell out of us," John said, shaking hands with the bearded man.

"Glad to see you were prepared to handle me," Benny said with a smile.

John looked down at the rifle in his hand. He was glad that he was ready to defend everyone so easily. He was also surprised to realize he had not really been scared so much as nervous. He clapped Benny on the back with a smile and started to lead them back to the others.

"How far did you take the van?" Steve asked.

"I made it look like it broke down a few miles north on 97. Hopefully when the Feds find the van they'll think you went north. By the time they figure out their mistake we'll have a couple of days on them," Benny replied.

When the three were within sight of the others the group visibly relaxed.

"You want to eat something before we head out again?" John asked Benny.

"No, I can eat while we walk," Benny replied.

John nodded, hoping that his group would soon build up the same endurance as the grizzly recluse had. He signaled that it was time to leave and the group gathered their things, did one last look for trash, and started walking again. Some limped, or grimaced at the pain of cramped muscles, but a mask of determination was the uniform of the day. John was proud of his friends. They may not have been as strong or resilient as Benny, but he was sure they would make it.

The rest of the day was spent in silence, with only two short breaks before they stopped for the night. They had to cross several roads, some still used, but most showing signs of neglect. The roads that were free of overgrowth were crossed quickly, one family at a time. The tension was palpable every time they had to make a crossing.

When they made camp that night Benny approached John as he was clearing a place to sleep in the dark field. They hadn't reached another stand of trees since entering the long vacant farmland so had decided they were safe enough bedding down in the long grasses.

"We'll be near Quincy tomorrow evening sometime," Benny said by way of greeting, "Do you have a plan to get us across the river?"

"I hadn't put much thought into it honestly," John replied. He knew they would have to cross the Mississippi eventually, but his sense of time and distance was not nearly as good as Benny's. "I didn't realize we were so close."

"We should probably try to get through the city at night, in small groups," Benny said.

"Sounds good to me," John returned. He was not one to argue an idea that seemed sound right away, nor too proud to take another's advice when it made sense.

Benny nodded and returned to his own blankets nearby. John lay down and stared into the dark sky. He'd taken to trying to identify constellations when he had a lot on his mind. Tomorrow night would be a real challenge for them. The Mississippi was one of only two major rivers they had to cross, but unfortunately it was the one with the fewest bridges. That meant passing through a city to get to the bridge, in this case, Quincy. John knew Benny was right. Their only chance to get through was to split up and cross the bridge at night. He drifted off to sleep, thinking of all the ways this could go wrong.

Chapter 12

The Selective Population Act, now that was a piece of work. Environmental extremists and global warming nuts had convinced the government that overpopulation was just around the corner, and would destroy the planet, or some such nonsense. Fact is the government already realized that the problem with having total control comes when there are too many people to control. That's no way to frame legislation though so they used the Environmentalists to back a new law. After it was passed families were limited to one child, kind of like China. Once the child was born and safely home the parents were expected to get sterilized. Thank God Thomas was born and Susan was on the way before the law was passed. I have to say though, you look at your children differently when you know for sure they are the only ones you will ever have.

-Excerpt from the journal of John Evermann

"Sir, we found something," the call came over the radio as Casey was driving back from a meeting in Peoria.

Casey picked up the handset and keyed it, "What is it?"

"White van, looks like a government work van but the decals are torn off. It's broken down on 97 a couple hours north of Stewart. Matches the description of the one reported stolen from the Stewart maintenance office."

"Alright, I'll head that way," Casey replaced the handset and reached behind the seat for a roadmap. He opened it as best he could without taking his eyes off the road for more than a second. Looking down at the map and back at the road several times he was able to pinpoint his location, and find a more direct route to highway 97. He attempted to refold the map, but gave up after nearly tearing it in half and tossed it into the back seat of his black sedan.

Casey took a deep breath to calm his nerves. The map was just another in a series of irritants grating on him. He'd just returned from the Peoria office where the station commander had denied his request for more manpower. The commander had added insult to injury by questioning Casey's ability to round up a handful of civilians with the resources he already had, and hinting that failure could mean more than a delay in promotion.

He had tried to explain that it was not a handful of civilians, but somewhere in excess of twenty-five families. Casey believed the number would grow as the investigation continued. He knew for sure that one was armed, but the capability of the other fugitives was a mystery. The civilians had been very careful to hide their activities, so they could all be ex-military as far as the feds knew. The field commander finally admitted that even if he wanted to send more men he just didn't have them. Funding was down, and Stewart was not the only hotbed of activity. Casey would just have to make due.

   Casey arrived at the white van about an hour after the call came through. He climbed out of his car and walked across the brittle asphalt to the abandoned vehicle. Officers were searching the van thoroughly, evidenced by much of the interior lying torn and tattered in the ditch. Other officers were fanned out in the fields on either side of the road, with their heads down and eyes sweeping for clues. Casey approached a sergeant that seemed to be in charge of the search.

   "Have you found anything Sergeant?"

   "The usual so far, sir. Miscellaneous garbage under the seats, papers in the glove compartment, but nothing that gives us a clue about who stole it," the sergeant reported.

   "I imagine we won't find anything," Casey said, walking past the sergeant to look at the van.

   Whoever did steal it had torn off the vinyl decals that identified it as a government vehicle, but Casey could still see the partial outline. It was assigned to the workplace of one of the suspected fugitives, and it had been stolen in the right timeframe. The manager of the maintenance office had reported it stolen two days after the fugitives disappeared, but that didn't prove anything. Mismanagement in government offices was common, even under the new government. The manager was probably afraid to report it until he had a credible story. Casey suspected he helped the fugitives in some way, but he had no proof yet.

The van was parked on the northbound side of the highway, leading anyone to suspect that was the direction they were headed when it broke down. The keys were still in the ignition, and there was gas in the tank, but the hood was open.

"Was this open when you arrived?" Casey gestured to the hood.

"Let me check," the sergeant said. He looked around, attempting to locate another officer. "Foreman, come over here."

An officer that had been searching the ditch on the opposite side of the road looked up and crossed the highway.

"Foreman was the first on scene," the sergeant explained to Casey. He turned to Foreman when the officer got closer. "Was the hood open when you found the van?"

"Yes, sergeant and the keys were in the ignition."

The sergeant nodded and then gestured back to the ditch Foreman had been searching, "Carry on then."

The sergeant turned back to Casey, but the Lieutenant was already over in front of the van, looking under the hood. The sergeant shrugged and went back to overseeing the search.

Casey looked at the engine. He was no mechanic, but it was easy to see the problem. The thick hose from the top of the radiator to the engine was dry and cracked, and there was a convincing tear in it. He crouched down and looked under the van. The pavement was dry, but there was a telltale neon green residue on the road. Best he could tell was that whoever took the rundown vehicle thought it would get them wherever they wanted to go. They headed north, but the van finally succumbed to neglect. They abandoned it, obviously, and headed north. At least he was meant to believe that's what happened.

Casey looked the direction the van faced, then south. He couldn't understand why anyone wanting to escape America would run to Canada. Both had the same laws, the same type of government, and the same kind of leaders. Casey knew, to the fugitives there was little difference between the two. The best option, as far as Casey could see, was south to Texas. However, Casey couldn't afford to ignore any lead, no matter how hard to believe.

"Sergeant," Casey called from the front of the van.

"Yes sir," the officer approached.

"Stop the search here, your men won't find anything. Take your unit and spread the search north. It looks as if they stuck to the road for some distance, you might find where they broke off. If you find anything report it immediately," Casey ordered.

"Yes sir," the sergeant immediately walked to his own vehicle to radio for support.

Casey walked to his own car, and turned it around on the highway. He headed back to Stewart, already formulating a new plan to spread his two remaining squads out to search south and west of the town. He figured something had to turn up soon. That many people couldn't just wander across the country without someone noticing.

Chapter 13

America and Israel had been allies since the end of World War Two. The first sign of a breakdown in relations was how we reacted to the terrorist attacks during the President's second term. Israel was getting hit hard, and they asked for our help. The government told them we couldn't spare any troops. Our priority was to protect American citizens. The Middle East Alliance attacked Israel at the end of that year, and without our help they didn't stand a chance. Jewish people here in America were outraged, calling for the government to send aid. The response shocked everyone, "Not our problem."

The war was short, bloody, and brutal. Over five million Jewish Israelis died, with the rest escaping on ships bound for the west. Muslims living in Israel who died in the war were considered martyrs by the MEA, unless they died defending Israel. The saddest part of the entire tragedy was how we treated those refugees when they arrived. They sailed to New York harbor to seek asylum, but our government turned them away. The government had finally cracked down on immigration and there were no exceptions. I think they found some island to live on in the Caribbean, but I could be wrong.

-Excerpt from the Journal of John Evermann

John crouched in the overgrown park watching the sunset. The temperature was starting to drop and the whirring cacophony of insects was rising in volume. Any other evening John would have enjoyed sitting out and just watching the sunset, but he didn't have time to relax and take it all in.

The refugees had walked most of the day, pushing hard to reach Quincy by nightfall. They skirted the north end of the city to one of the riverside parks that had been abandoned years before. It provided them with the perfect hiding place until it was dark enough to attempt a crossing. They knew the crossing here might be the most dangerous part of their trip besides actually crossing the border into Texas. John knew there was little choice in the matter. They had to cross the river and Quincy had the only bridge for miles. Hannibal was the only other choice, but the city was larger which would be more dangerous.

John had gone over his plan with Amanda, Steve and Benny while everyone was settling in to rest before the crossing.

"We'll go first," John indicated the two men. We'll make sure the bridge is clear."

"Wouldn't the rail bridge be less likely to be watched?" Steve asked.

"I looked," Benny said. He'd gone ahead to scout the crossing before the group got to Quincy.

"Collapsed," the bearded recluse said with finality.

"The line probably hasn't been used in years," John said.

"Right, so we go first in case it's guarded," Steve said.

"Yes, and it most likely will be after the bombings a few years back," John added.

They went over the rest of the plan quietly and then settled in to get a little rest. John, of course, couldn't relax to save his life. Just as the sun touched the tops of the trees to the west he started waking people up.

"You know what to do?" John asked Amanda as she was rolling up the kids' blankets.

"Yes, twenty minute intervals. We go south through the park, quietly as possible, then over the bridge. You three will be waiting on the other side," Amanda recited the instructions.

"Good," John smiled, "I love you." He hugged Amanda and the kids one last time before walking over to where Benny and Steve waited. All three were armed with their rifles, and John had the pistol tucked in the back of his pants. He took one last look at the group and silently wished them luck before following Steve and Benny south through the riverfront parks.

The three men quietly picked their way across the overgrown park area along the river. They watched the distant houses and street for any sings that they had been spotted. This is the easy part, John thought. They weren't likely to be seen crossing an unused park at night. The real challenge would be crossing the bridge. They could see the concrete and steel structure by the blinking safety lights on the twin towers. Several roads cut across their path, but only a few street lights were lit. The pavement was broken and overgrown from neglect, but it was still open ground with no cover. The three made sure to cross one at a time, and as quickly as possible.

After about twenty minutes of walking, the park ended and they entered was replaced area. The old buildings offered better cover than the trees and tall grasses, but walking among the abandoned structures was like walking through a graveyard. The buildings were lined with broken windows and rusted doorways. John imagined he could see people of the past who had attempted to carve out a life with nothing but sweat and a drive to make something better for their families. Ghosts of an era where work had value and you were proud of what you did for a living. As they neared the bridge John realized he had made a slight miscalculation. The bridge was elevated, and there was no way to access it as close to the river as they were. They'd have to walk into the city a couple of blocks to where the bridge met the road.

"Guys, the bridge," John said softly.

They stopped, and Steve looked up at the structure. Benny simply nodded and turned back to John.

"The street probably meets the bridge two or three blocks in," Benny said. There was no accusation in Benny's eyes or voice, simply an acceptance of the mistake for exactly what it was.

"That's going to be a dangerous two or three blocks," Steve said.

"Chances are it's only businesses along that road. They should be closed up for the night," Benny assured them.

"Let's hope so," John said, "One curious citizen could end this entire trip." They stood in the shadows of a building at the pier near the bridge while they discussed the change in the plan.

At one time the building had been part of a marina by the looks of it. It seemed to have suffered the same fate as all other unnecessary diversions. Time and neglect were evident in the sunken roof and peeling paint. Several pieces of the floating wood and concrete dock were rotted and lying half submerged. If any boats were left they had long ago succumbed to a watery grave. John nodded as he came to a decision.

"We can't afford to have anyone stop here too long trying to figure out where we went. Steve, you wait here. I think Todd and Cindy are in the group behind us. Leave Todd here to point everyone else to the beginning of the bridge and explain the situation. Then find a place out of sight near the ramp and point people up the bridge."

Steve indicated that he understood the instructions so far.

"Tell Todd that Amanda and the kids are in the last group. You two come across with them."

John and Benny shook hands with Steve and started walking along the underside of the bridge into town. Their luck seemed to be holding as they entered the commercial district of Quincy. It was just after curfew so the streets were deserted and the businesses closed. No houses lined the street so the two made it to the ramp with no signs of alarm.

With their ears tuned for the sound of sirens or shouts, and eyes scanning everything the two started up the bridge. To their relief everything was silent but for the sound of nocturnal insects and the river below. So far, they didn't see a booth or the lights that one would expect to see if the bridge was guarded, but the two didn't ease their vigilance. Once they reached the point of the bridge that was just above the pier John looked over the side. He could just make out someone he guessed was Todd, talking to the next group that would head for the bridge. Just then they heard a sound they had dreaded their entire journey; the steady rise of sirens blaring in the distance.

John looked down toward the marina to see Todd and the others duck behind one of the buildings in the dim moonlight. Benny ducked down on the bridge, looking into the town of Quincy anxiously. John crouched down with him and a few moments passed as they waited, straining their ears. It sounded like more than one squad car, but with the way sound echoed off of buildings it was hard to tell. The two men could just make out the next group running hard up the bridge in their direction. The group had been waved on by the guides on the ground before they heard the sirens. Once John could see them well enough he motioned frantically for them to get down. The group reluctantly complied. The instinct to flee and hide was warring within everyone.

The sirens were getting closer, and sounded like they were coming from the south. John knew the echo was deceptive and they could just as easily be coming from the other direction, but he couldn't see the lights yet to be sure. It wasn't long before his suspicions were confirmed and he saw lights reflecting off of buildings on the left of the bridge. The squad car, or cars, was moving fast and would soon cross the street that led to their hiding place. John waited, his sweaty hands gripping his rifle tightly. He wasn't sure what he was prepared to do, but at this point he hoped he was prepared to do anything to get the refugees across the bridge.

Just as John wanted to scream with the tension of it all the squad car appeared, rocketing through the intersection at the end of the bridge. It passed very close to where Steve must be hiding, and continued on to the right of the bridge, headed south. John released the breath he didn't realize he'd been holding, and felt Benny relax behind him. John beckoned the group that was crouched several yards away on the bridge.

"Wait here ten minutes. If you don't see anything unusual ahead then follow us across, but be careful," John said when Cindy and the others reached him. She nodded. John and Benny continued on across the bridge.

Chapter 14

The social breakdowns and riots near the end of the President's second term led to the most drastic executive order in history. The President's poll numbers were in the single digits and it looked as if the coming elections would swing away from the him and his party. There was a glimmer of hope for most of us, until January 8th. The President signed the executive order that gave him emergency powers, and halted all national elections. With the stroke of a pen the President secured his office for life, as well as the progressive majority in Congress.

Of course we were told it was emergency powers. Things would return to normal once the riots were over, and order was restored. I guess they never thought order was restored, or maybe 'President for Life' just sounded too good to give up.

-Excerpt from the Journal of John Evermann

John was feeling a little jumpy after their close call but kept alert as he and Benny crossed the bridge. They moved as fast as they dared, knowing more than ever that time was against them. The longer they stayed on the bridge, and near the city, the more danger they were in. The two men could see the outline of a guard house ahead in the darkness. It was a small wooden building that straddled the concrete median and hadn't been visible until the two where further up the incline. A lowered wooden arm blocked each side, and dim spotlights lit each wooden barrier. They could barely make out the silhouette of a man sitting in the building. With a signal from Benny they both crouched down and approached the shack silently.

Soon the two were close enough to see that the man was facing away from them, and by his posture he appeared to be sleeping. As they approached a loud snore confirmed their suspicions. The two men stopped for a moment.

"We will have to take him out silently," Benny whispered, making a motion with his rifle as if bashing something with the butt end.

"No," John said, "As long as he stays asleep he's no danger. I don't want to start hurting people unless we have no other choice."

Benny studied John for a minute, but finally nodded. "What do you propose then?"

"You stay here and watch him. Make sure the groups that pass are as quiet as they can be. I'll continue across to make sure the rest of the way is safe," John said.

"If the guard wakes up before we all cross?" Benny asked grimly.

John sighed, looked at the guard, then back at Benny. "If he wakes up…do what you have to do to ensure our safety."

"Fine."

They both walked softly toward the guard station. The guard was asleep in his chair, a copy of the National News in his lap. Benny posted himself close to the building so he could keep an eye on the guard and watch for their people. John patted him on the shoulder before continuing across the bridge.

John crossed the bridge without further incident and found the other side to be dark and deserted. There was an old building, probably a warehouse, north of the road, and a stand of trees to the south across a field. He waited anxiously for the first group, straining to see anyone moving on the bridge. Alone, in the dark, it was peaceful. John could almost imagine that he was in a different place, just living instead of running to live.

To John it felt like an eternity, but it wasn't long before the first group could be seen moving toward him. When they reached the end of the bridge he directed them to the trees south of the highway. Everyone was nervous, but seemed to relax when he greeted them at the west end of the bridge.

John was trying to keep track of how many had crossed, but he was tired and lost count after awhile. When he guessed they were coming to the last of the refugees he stopped one of the groups.

"How many more behind you?" John asked.

"I think just two more," A man named Jeremy replied, "The Smith's and their group, and Amanda and hers are all that's left."

John nodded and waved them on to the trees. He didn't like how long it was taking, and a small part of him was regretting putting Amanda in the back of the line. He pushed those feelings down though. He had to think of everyone, and as far as he was concerned Amanda was the best choice to make sure each group left the park on time and those remaining stayed undetected. He kept telling himself that everything would be fine, and he shouldn't worry.

Two sounds shattered the calm night, and nearly stopped John's heart. First an alarm went off, punctuated by a bright, pulsating red light at the middle of the bridge. The alarm was followed immediately by a loud crack that echoed through the night. John only knew it was a gunshot because of the practice Benny had put them all through, but the sound seemed somehow louder and more sinister hearing it then. He could feel his whole world turning upside down as he raced for the bridge.

John was met half way to the guard station by the Smith's group. Mrs. Smith had a guilty look on her face as she tried to calm her fussy baby.

"Sorry John," Mr. Smith said.

"Don't worry about it, just get to the trees south of the road," John said, waving them on. He grabbed Carl, who had been part of the group.

"What happened?" John asked when the rest were out of earshot. He already had a pretty good idea but he needed to hear it from someone else.

"The baby started crying," Carl said, "I guess the guard woke up and pushed the alarm when Benny was trying to help them."

"Benny didn't hesitate when the fed reached for his gun," Carl looked a little sick as he said it. "He shot the guard once, then yelled at us to run."

John squeezed Carl's shoulder and told him to get to the trees with his wife and the rest. He ran the rest of the way to the middle of the bridge. Benny was crouched near the guard shack, looking toward the city.

"Do you see them?" John asked. He was straining to see the last group of refugees that should be coming up the bridge. Benny looked at him as if expecting questions, but John didn't ask. They could hear police sirens cutting through the cool night air, and knew this was no time for second guessing.

"No. They should be near the ramp, but with the sirens I doubt any of them would want to try and cross," Benny replied.

The refugees had been on the road a couple of days but that moment made it all much more real for him. John wasn't sure if he had been naive or just too optimistic, but he never actually believed they might have to hurt someone. He'd been through all the practice like everyone else, but to him it had all just been in case they ran into trouble. He stood up and held out his rifle for Benny to take.

"It will be easier without this," John said.

"What are you doing?" Benny asked.

"Don't wait for us. Everyone's in the trees south of the highway, across an old field. Get to them and keep going, we'll catch up if we can," John said.

"John, those people back there need you," Benny said.

"We don't have time for this Benny," the sirens were getting closer. "I know I'm breaking my own rules, but it's my wife and kids. We'll catch up to you."

Benny nodded and held out his hand. John shook it firmly and the bearded man took his rifle. He gave Benny a confident smile before he started running back toward the city, and his family.

John forced himself to look in the guard shack as he passed. For him to ignore it, or act as if it didn't happen felt wrong. The man inside was slumped against the wall of the shack and had slid to the floor. John was no expert but from the peaceful look of him the shot had been clean and the guard had died instantly. John wondered if the man had a family. He knew they'd be taken care of, but he still felt guilty that their path had crossed his and circumstances had led to that fatal moment. He imagined soldiers felt the same way. Even when it's the enemy you're fighting, they are people and it's still a life that ends.

In that brief moment that's how John resolved to deal with it. They were soldiers and he hated that a life was lost. He would carry the image of that guard, and the guilt of his death forever, but he was in a war to save his family and their freedom.

Chapter 15

Public criticism and dissent escalated in the summer after the President seized total power. Opponents of the President and his party called for resumption of elections and criminal charges against the new dictator. A large number of the most influential critics in the media were arrested first, as an example. It was enough to silence most. It also made it easier for the government to round up the ones who didn't get the hint.

There was one hold-out. He was a media personality that caused waves through the entire political spectrum. When the first arrests were made he'd been a target, but he was lucky enough to have warning and go underground. They never did find him. He broadcast his views for a long time in secret, moving from place to place in case they pinned down the source of the transmission. He tried to rally people to speak out, but most who had the heart already left during the migration. Finally, having to admit the country was truly lost, he moved to Texas as well. I hear he lives with his family near Dallas now. Broadcasters in the Republic of Texas tried to get him on the air again, but he just didn't have the heart anymore. He was a staunch patriot had his heart broken by the very people he hoped to save. That's the official story anyway.

-Excerpt from the Journal of John Evermann

John ran as hard as he could for the east end of the bridge. He could see the lights of the squad cars getting closer and he was sure he wouldn't make it to the end of the ramp before they did. He looked over the side as he ran, but it was still too high to jump. He looked ahead and saw that two buildings were very close to the left side of the bridge. It would be an easy leap, but he had to get there first. He pushed himself even harder, knowing that if he did make it to the roof it would be very close.

The sirens were louder, closer, and John could see the red, pulsating light reflecting off buildings a few blocks into the city. They were coming from both directions, but the one coming up from the south end of town would turn onto the bridge road first. John looked over the side again as he ran. The second building looked like a better bet. There were no other buildings close that would allow him to reach the ground without risking an injury. He may not have a choice, but the second roof was his goal.

John had a few more yards to go. The first squad car turned onto the main road leading to the bridge, but its lights were still at street level and not angled to illuminate the ramp. Time seemed to slow as

John ran for his life, and the lives of his wife and kids. The car was speeding toward him as he raced toward it.

The squad car started up the ramp as John jumped from the concrete wall at the side of the bridge. He hit the steel roof of the building hard and fell on his side. The corrugated ridges of the roof bit into his ribs and hip, but he lay still, holding his breath. He couldn't be sure if the car's lights had revealed him before he jumped. His ears strained for any sound. He was sure he was going to hear the car stop and the officer inside come after him. After what seemed like an eternity he heard the sirens pass him by. He sighed in relief and quickly made his way to the ground.

Once he was on the ground John looked around. He was in the middle of an old lumber and hardware supply yard. He could see the building where Steve should have been standing, directing people up the ramp to cross the bridge. No one was there. He walked around the building and headed back toward the pier, staying in the shadow of the bridge.

By the time he reached the old pier he could see the lights of the squad cars in the middle of the bridge's arch, stopped near where the guard house would be. There would be no crossing there in the near future. The rail bridge was out, so their options were very limited. He pushed those thoughts back. It didn't do any good to worry about things that he was unable to change. He would find a way across the river, but first he had to find his family and friends.

John searched the pier, and the surrounding buildings but he didn't find Steve or his family. He guessed they were probably all together. He just hoped they were all safe. He turned and headed back toward the bridge ramp. He figured they had to be hiding somewhere close, waiting for the road to clear.

John looked behind the old store Steve had been posted at. The alley behind the store was empty. The store was part of a haphazard group of buildings on that block. There were several dark alleyways and concealed hiding spots, and John searched them all to no avail. He started walking away from the bridge, hoping that they just went looking for a better place to hide.

He crossed the next street and looked around the narrow block. There was little cover so he moved on, crossing the next street to the north. He found himself in an empty lot between three rundown old warehouses.

"Amanda, Steve," John called as loudly as he dared.

He was confident that he was far enough away from the authorities that he wouldn't be overheard. There was no answer, so he continued the search.

His path led him to the backyard of four houses facing the eastern side of the block. There was nowhere to hide that he could see. While he was deciding whether to continue his search north or cross to another block and walk back toward the bridge the back porch light of the last house flickered to life. A screen door creaked open and an old man peered out at John.

"You look lost son," the old man said.

"Looking for someone," John replied.

Part of John screamed that he should run before the feds arrived, but something about the old man made him hesitate. He was reminded of his grandfather for a moment, and part of him wanted to trust the stranger.

"Is your name John?" The old man asked. John's heart skipped a beat.

"How do you know my name?" John asked.

The old man looked around, making sure John was alone.

"Someone is looking for you," the man said. He opened the screen door further, clearly inviting John inside.

John cautiously entered the kitchen at the back of the house, which erupted into chaos around him. Shouting children greeting their father, and Amanda and Steve trying to shush the kids filled the small room with noise. John was surprised and overwhelmed with relief as he hugged Susan and Thomas. Amanda replaced the kids in his arms, and Steve and Todd shook his hand.

"We heard the gunshot just before we started up the bridge. We weren't sure what happened so we found a place to hide," Steve explained, "When we heard the sirens we thought it best to get away from the bridge. That's when Mister Marlowe found us."

John turned to the old man and held out his hand, "Thank you Mister Marlowe."

"Jacob," said the man, taking John's hand in a firm grip.

John nodded, "Thanks Jacob."

The old man waved them toward a table and went to get a cup of coffee from the steaming pot on the kitchen counter. The kitchen was a small eat-in type that was fairly common in older homes. Cracked linoleum floors, faded wooden cabinets and a green laminate countertop with a metal edge reminded John of his grandparent's house they used to visit. Jacob pressed the cup into John's hands.

"Did everyone else make it through?" Steve asked after they were all sitting at the kitchen table.

"Everyone," John said, smiling at Steve's sigh of relief, "I sent them ahead with Benny. The guard woke up and hit the alarm. Benny stopped him before he drew his weapon. It won't go unnoticed by the feds for long though. Once the locals call it in they'll send a team to investigate."

"It won't take them long to get here. If the feds are looking for you it's best we get you on your way," Jacob said.

"We have no way across the river," John started.

"I do," Jacob interrupted him before he could go any further.

Chapter 16

Benjamin Franklin said that the founders gave us a Republic, if we could keep it. Keeping it is the key. You can't just sit back, vote for whatever politician sounds good, and hope for the best. We're where we are, because people got complacent. People stopped paying attention to what was going on. They stopped talking to each other, and allowed politics to become some sort of taboo. It's my hope that if America is ever restored, people will remember how easily she was lost.

-Excerpt from the Journal of John Evermann

"Sir, I think you should see this," Foster called from a few feet away.

Lieutenant Casey was overseeing the search of a small, abandoned park in Stewart. The sky was overcast so he was pushing his unit to complete the search before a heavy rain washed away any evidence. His men had finally tracked the path of the van from the NUBD office to the overgrown lot. The impressions of the tires were clearly visible in the flattened grass where the vehicle's tires rolled over the dew-softened ground. Casey was close to piecing together the entire timeline from the escape of the Evermann's to the van being abandoned. There was one more lead to follow, some vague clue about a cabin in the woods near Stewart, but he was confident they would have the whole story soon.

"What is it Foster," Casey said without looking up from the section of ground he was searching.

"A strange report out of Quincy. Locals called into the Peoria field office about a shooting," Foster reported.

"A shooting?" Casey looked up in surprise.

"Yes sir," Foster flipped through the pages he was holding, "Here it is, last night a homeland security officer was shot and killed on the Bay Bridge in Quincy. Seems he was able to set off the alarm at his station, but when the local officers arrived all they found was the body. It's believed that whoever did it crossed to the west side of the bridge and escaped."

"Might be our fugitives," Casey said excitedly, "Have they searched the town yet?"

Foster flipped to another page.

"Yes sir, they searched the immediate area around the bridge that night. A more thorough search of the town is underway, but they haven't found anything yet."

"Have our squads found anything north of the abandoned van?" Casey asked.

"No sir, nothing that leads me to believe that four people are on foot walking north, much less more than fifty."

"Call them back in," Casey said, "They won't find anything. Tell them to drive on through to Quincy, we'll meet them there."

"Yes sir."

*   *   *

The sun was starting to set while John and the others sat nervously in Jacob's living room. Todd and Steve watched the street from different windows, and Amanda did her best to keep the kids occupied during the wait. Everyone was tired, having only managed to get a little sleep during the day.

No one was able to relax, however, since the local police had come knocking. The officer questioned Jacob about whether he'd seen anyone suspicious or not, but thankfully he wasn't interested in searching the house. The entire group was on edge the rest of the day.

"Jacob, you should come with us," John suggested while they waited for Steve to tell them it was dark enough to move. He'd already offered once but the old man refused.

"Bah, I'm too old for all of that, I'd just slow you down," Jacob said seriously, "Besides, the boat's already gonna be overcrowded."

"What if they find the boat and track it back to you?" John asked.

"I'm not that stupid son, that boat's not registered to anyone," Jacob explained.

"You've put your life on the line for complete strangers, isn't there anything we can do to repay you?" John asked.

"Consider it the last bit of fight in a tired old man," Jacob began, "That's what I am, tired and old. I've fought all these battles already, and I just can't do it anymore."

John nodded in understanding. He couldn't fault Jacob for wanting to be left out of it now. Fighting against something that you know you can't change takes a lot out of a person.

"I think it's safe to go," Steve said from the window overlooking the street.

The small party collected their packs and gear, and Jacob led them to the back door. John took another minute to look out the window into the back yard and surrounding lot. He didn't see any movement so he opened the door and directed the others to the heavy shadows behind a nearby building. Before joining them John turned to Jacob.

"Thank you," John said simply.

"Thank me by getting that family of yours somewhere safe." Jacob cuffed John on the shoulder and held out his hand.

John shook the offered hand, "If you ever find a way to Texas, look us up."

"Will do. Now, head straight for the river. The old boat is hidden in the overgrown brush by the water. Should be plenty of gas in the motor to get you across," Jacob said.

John nodded his understanding.

"Go north around the island, there is a narrow cut just this side of the old rail bridge. From there it should be easy to find your way," Jacob finished.

John nodded and turned to join the others. He led them to the river without looking back. He felt guilty about leaving Jacob, after all the old man was doing for them, but Jacob was right. John had more important things to worry about than one man who had already made his decision. He couldn't force Jacob to go, and John's family and friends needed all of his attention to get them to safety.

They walked for several minutes in the dark, carefully navigating the abandoned industrial area between Jacob's house and the river. The streets they crossed were dark and empty. With the normal curfew, and the added tension of police searches all day, the city was quiet enough that they felt like the only people in the world.

It wasn't long before they heard the sound of small waves lapping at the rocks along the bank of the river. The group crossed several sets of railroad tracks into the small park that bordered the water. Much of what had once been beautiful landscaping was overgrown into a small, wild forest.

John's group searched for several minutes but saw no sign of the boat. In a brief moment of panic he looked around, wondering what they would do if the boat had already been found and confiscated. They couldn't swim the river, and crossing the bridge was out of the question. Perhaps they could cross at Hannibal, but it would be more dangerous.

"Dad, what's this over here?" Thomas called from a few yards away.

John ran over, and found Thomas pointing into a large tangle of ivy and shrubs. The corner of a flat-bottomed fishing boat was protruding from the overgrowth.

"Well done buddy," John patted his son on the back. Thomas beamed at the praise.

"Todd, Steve, give me a hand with this," John called softly.

The three men pulled the small boat out of the brush. They looked it over for holes, but didn't see any. None of them knew a thing about boats, so they couldn't be sure, but it looked like it was in decent shape. John took a look at the motor, and realized it started up much like a lawn mower.

"I think this will work," John said to the others, "Let's get it into the water and see if it leaks."

They carried it to the water, and John climbed in while the others held it near the shore. John used the dim moonlight to inspect the inside of the boat again. He noticed a small trickle of water coming in at the bottom but he guessed it wouldn't be enough to worry about.

Jacob had been right, though, when he said the boat was small. It would be a tight fit for all six of them.

The rest of the group climbed into the boat, except for Steve, who held it in place while John figured out the motor. A few minutes of poking around revealed the release to lower the propeller into the water, after which John got started on the pull cord. It was a bit harder to start than a lawn mower, but after a few tries he got it running. The sound of the motor firing was louder than John expected, and they all looked to the city in alarm.

"Get in, quick," John said to Steve. He was sure that someone had heard the motor start up.

Steve pulled himself over the side of the boat, nearly capsizing the craft. They managed to shift their weight to account for the sudden dip, and Steve tumbled into the bottom of the boat without further incident. John pushed the lever on the motor to turn the nose of the vessel north. He kept the bow aimed to cross the narrow channel as Jacob had directed, keeping it close to the island they could just see by the dim moonlight.

Several minutes passed before they saw the bulk of the old rail bridge rise out of the dark water. They were close to the point where Jacob had told them to cross, and John glanced back at the city. He could easily make out the red and blue lights of patrol cars near where they had entered the river. His anxiety was relieved a little when he realized that the channel and the buildings in the city were creating an echo that would make it hard to determine exactly where the sound of their motor was coming from. He hoped they could get across the river and away from the boat before the local police pinpointed where they were going.

Chapter 17

The environmentalists got a rude awakening during the early part of the transformation. All of the years of eco-terror, protests, and property damage were largely overlooked before, due to all the money and votes fed into Washington. Once the government had total power they didn't need the votes anymore. Soon they wouldn't need the money either, but that was a surprise of a different color. When all the other lobbies were kicked out of Washington the environmental lobby thought they were still in tight with the politicians. They found out they were wrong when they got the boot as well. You see those 'green planet' politicians who flew in private jets every week really only believed in one thing. They wanted votes, and as long as they had a following of people that believed they were going to change the world, they would get those votes. Once there was no need for votes, there was no need for the act.

-Excerpt from the Journal of John Evermann

It didn't take long to cross the river in the boat. As Jacob had advised, John steered the old craft slightly upriver so they wouldn't drift too much. Once they reached the other bank they all climbed out. John and Steve pushed the boat back into the current, something Jacob also advised. John had argued that they could hide Jacob's boat so he could retrieve it, but the old man had waved that off as nonsense. He had said the boat did him no good anymore, and it was best served as a distraction somewhere downriver.

They ran west as fast as they could in the dark. John wanted to get as far away from the river and bridge as they could before turning south. He didn't know how far the feds would expand the search and would rather push hard to catch up with the main group than risk capture west of the river.

A few hours after leaving the river and turning south they came close to the highway that led back into Quincy. John left the others in the trees and crossed the ditch to the old stretch of blacktop. He stayed low, exiting the tree-line and crossing the overgrown ditch. He leaned against the embankment and concentrated, listening and straining his eyes in the direction of the town. They were too far away to see the lights on the bridge, and John didn't see any headlights coming their way. He waved the others up, and started them across the highway one at a time.

The crossing didn't take long, but for John it seemed like an eternity. He was anxious every time he waved someone across, watching the highway, and praying that none of the local police decided to look this far from the city. Finally, when everyone was across and in the opposite ditch, John stood and started to rush across himself. Something seen out of the corner of his eye made him stop and look back toward Quincy. He thought he saw a slight flash of red and blue over the hill to the east. He froze for a moment, not wanting to believe what he was seeing. His lapse passed and he ran to the others and dropped down into the ditch with them.

"What's the matter?" Amanda asked.

John was looking out into the fields south of the highway, looking like a rabbit that has been spotted by the hounds. He soon saw what he was looking for, and stood up, pointing toward a barn a hundred yards away.

"There," he said, "Run, we're not out of this yet!"

None of them needed any further urging. They were starting to hear the sound of sirens in the distance closing fast. The adults each grabbed one of the younger kids with them and the group ran for the barn in the distance. The ground was flat with no cover. John prayed the officers didn't use their search lights.

The patrol cars passed by on the highway as the refugees ran for the barn. When John's group reached the old building they were all out of breath and their muscles burned with the exertion. Todd found them a way in, and they all collapsed on the dry hay that was piled in a corner. The odor of musty air and rat droppings permeated the building but the protective walls and warm hay were comforting.

"We'll stay here until tomorrow evening," John said when had caught his breath, "Get some sleep, I'll keep watch first."

The others just nodded and made themselves more comfortable. John kissed Amanda and his kids and took Steve's rifle. He moved toward the side of the barn facing the road and found a small hole in the wall that gave him a view of the highway and the field between it and the barn.

* * *

"What have you found out," Lieutenant Casey was standing in the dingy office of the Chief of Quincy police. He didn't much care for local law enforcement, nor could he understand why they had not been absorbed into the federal police force.

"The search of the town has turned up nothing," the balding police chief said. He shuffled some reports in his hands, "Every house within a few minutes of the bridge has been searched. No unauthorized inhabitants."

"So you have nothing to report," Casey was barely holding onto the leash that kept his temper in check.

The chief looked a little uncomfortable answering to a federal officer about the abilities of his men.

"There is a report here; a motor was heard on the river during the night. There was no visual identification, but the officer is pretty sure it was a boat," the chief read a few more lines of the report to himself before continuing. "The boat was found a mile down the river this morning, on the western bank. There were no prints in the area and the boat was empty."

"So is it the policy of this department to assume that boats start up their own motors and cross the river themselves?" Casey could no longer contain his anger.

"Of course not," the police chief was taken aback.

"Are your men searching the bank on both sides of the bridge?" Casey asked hotly.

"Well, no, but the boat," the chief stammered, "They found the boat on the south side of the bridge."

"Idiot," Casey exploded, "Get your men and search the banks, up and downriver. I will coordinate a search of the residences on the west side of the bridge."

Casey didn't wait for a response. He pulled his jacket on and stormed out of the office. On his way through the lobby of the police station he signaled his men to follow him out to the van. He climbed into the passenger seat and immediately got on the radio.

"Foster?" Casey said after he keyed up the mic.

"Yes Lieutenant?"

"Split the men into groups of two. Commandeer whatever vehicles you need and get them across the river. I want every house, barn, and grain silo searched for the fugitives. Some of them crossed the river last night in a small boat so there won't be many."

"Yes sir," Foster responded.

"Let's go, take us across the river," Casey said to the officer in the driver's seat.

* * *

"John," he was being shaken awake.

"What is it?" John sat up and shaded his eyes against the bright sun coming in through the cracks in the barn's walls.

"I think we better get out of here," Steve said quietly. He turned and pointed to the wall of the barn facing a house across the field.

John crossed to the wall, stumbling a little in the deep hay, and looked out through a large crack. Parked in the driveway of the small farm house was a black van. A man in a black suit was talking to a little old lady who was still wearing her white housecoat. John couldn't hear what they were saying of course, but he had a good idea what they were talking about. He knew there was no time to figure out what was going on. He had to get everyone out of the barn and away from the farm right away.

John rushed to the opposite wall and searched frantically for some way out of the barn that couldn't be seen from the house. It didn't take him long to find a loose board that had been broken sometime in the past. The others were starting to wake up. John tried to calm himself down but his sense of panic was already noticed. Amanda looked concerned and the children were getting anxious.

"Quickly, over here," John called urgently, but quietly.

Steve grabbed their packs, and handed them to their owners, pushing each member of their small group toward John.

"You first Todd, make sure it's safe," John gestured for Todd while he pushed out on the board, making the hole big enough for the man.

They all waited nervously after Todd crawled through the small hole. Finally, after what seemed like an eternity, he came back and whispered that this side of the barn was safe.

"Go, run for those trees as soon as you are out," John gestured to Amanda, "You kids follow your mom."

Steve, who had been watching the house, came rushing over to John just as Susan was getting through the gap.

"We gotta hurry, the feds are coming this way," Steve said.

"You're next, Steve," John said to his friend

Steve didn't hesitate. He dropped low and pulled himself through the gap. John saw his hands take over pulling on the board from the outside, and he followed his friend as fast as he could. Once they were through, the refugees made a dash for the trees.

Chapter 18

Conspiracy theorists, fear mongers, peddlers of hate, and snake oil salesmen were just a few of the accusations laid at the feet of people who tried to warn us about the government. They were attacked by other who were blind, complacent, or complicit in regards to the changes that were happening right in front of us. I could excuse some of the people. Human nature has a way of accepting unpleasantness for a long time. Many I couldn't excuse though, because once they realized what was happening they turned on the same people that tried to tell them. They demanded to know why someone didn't try harder to warn people. Why didn't anyone make it easier to see, or simpler to understand? They wanted to blame everyone but themselves, and for them I say, you get the government you deserve.

-Excerpt from the Journal of John Evermann

While John and the others were stuck in Quincy, Benny pushed the refugees through that first day after crossing the river, and well into the night. When they finally stopped everyone was on the verge of collapse. During the day's walk they heard sirens far to the north, near the highway and the bridge. Everyone was nervous and constantly looking back. Benny knew they didn't fully trust him, and the shooting on the bridge only served to strengthen that distrust. He urged them on anyway, knowing John was depending on him to get everyone to Texas.

After they stopped for the night, and settled in, Benny noticed a group standing together and talking excitedly. The way they kept looking over at him gave Benny a pretty good idea what the subject of their conversation was. He acted as if he didn't notice, letting them gather the courage to say whatever it was they wanted to say to him. He sat where he was, chewing on the jerky from his ration pack. It didn't take long before the group approached him.

"Benny, we've been thinking," the group's spokesman started, "We think it's a good idea to wait for John. It's what he would do for us."

Benny looked at each of them in turn, measuring their resolve by whether they looked him in the eye or not. None of them did.

"Carl, right?" The man nodded. Carl was their appointed spokesman but Benny could tell he didn't want the task. "John had a rule about waiting for anyone when you got to my cabin right?"

"Yes, but we were all there so we don't really know if he would have stuck to that," Carl said.

Benny nodded, and Carl relaxed a little, thinking that Benny was seeing his point. Benny stood up, and Carl took an involuntary step back. The grizzly recluse was a head taller than anyone there, and an intimidating figure even under the best of circumstances.

"How long do you intend to wait?" Benny asked.

"Well, we figure that John could only be a couple of days behind us at most," Carl said, more unsure of himself now.

"What if they were caught?" Benny asked. "How long do you intend to put your friends in danger by sitting in one place?"

Carl looked down at the ground, his hands, anywhere but at the bearded man questioning him. Finally he asked, "How can we just leave him behind?"

"We do what we have to, everyone else is counting on that," Benny put his hand on Carl's shoulder. "They are counting on you Carl, they don't trust me. We can't risk everyone here for just a few people."

Carl nodded and looked up at the bearded man's face. Benny nodded and cuffed his shoulder.

"Go pray for them Carl, and have a little faith in John. I believe the man upstairs is looking out for him," Benny said.

Benny watched the group disperse and go back to their sleeping spots. He said a little prayer himself, hoping that John and the others were safe. He was worried about them, but the rest of their group didn't need to see it. They needed a confident leader to take John's spot, and get them safely to Texas. He settled back on his blanket, looking up at the trees, and finally drifted off to sleep.

*   *   *

"Stop, Federal Police!"

The shout rang out across the fields, chasing John and the others into the trees. They all ran faster, but John knew it was only a matter of time. The Feds had the trail, and they were too close. Steve seemed to realize this at the same time John did, and he turned back toward the officers and raised his rifle. He fired a shot that went wild, and the officers raced for cover behind the barn.

"What are you doing?" John asked, reaching for Steve's rifle.

"Go John, I'll buy you some time," Steve pushed John away and took aim at the barn. He fired a shot that barely missed the officer that was peeking around the corner.

"Dammit Steve, they're too close. We won't be fast enough with the children," John reached for the rifle again, and got a grip on the barrel. The two men struggled over the weapon, but Steve proved the stronger and pulled hard, taking control of the it again. He stepped back and started to turn toward the barn, waving John off.

When the next shot went off John wondered why Steve had fired without taking aim. Time slowed as realization set in, and John ran toward Steve. He wasn't sure what he was going to do, only that he had to save his friend from what he knew was coming.

The first shot hit Steve in the left shoulder. John found himself horrified, and fascinated at the same time, as the sun shimmered through the mist of blood that followed the bullet out of Steve's back. Steve turned slightly toward his friend, a look of confusion on his face. The second round hit Steve in the chest before he even started to fall. John saw his friend convulse slightly when he was hit, and a dark spot blossomed on his shirt just under his right collar bone. John reached out, but there was nothing he could do to stop Steve from falling to the ground.

Time sped up way too fast for John at that point. He hit his knees beside his best friend, reaching frantically to stop the bleeding. He pressed on the chest wound, but he couldn't keep the blood from coming out, and the pressure just caused Steve to cough blood from his mouth. John could hear the officers running in their direction, shouting something but he couldn't hear them over the roaring in his ears. Someone was screaming far away, but he couldn't tell who. His attention was on Steve, whose eyes were focused on something far away.

"Come on buddy, hang in there," John said. He repeated the words "Hang in there" like some sort of prayer, as if saying them over and over would help. Steve finally seemed to react to John's presence, turning his head toward the sound of his voice. Their eyes locked for the briefest of moments, and Steve smiled slightly, as if all the pain and suffering had left him in that instant. Then it was all gone, the spark that told John his friend was still alive was gone.

The world came crashing back to John as he was knocked to the ground. One of the officers had pushed him into the dirt and had a knee on the middle of his back.

"Put it down!" The officer above him was shouting. John could hear his wife sobbing, and Susan was screaming. He couldn't see the scene with his eyes, but he didn't need to.

"Todd, put it down!" John shouted from his position, his voice raw from the tears he now felt running down his face, "For the sake of the children, put it down."

Chapter 19

Most people didn't believe in the reeducation camps. They didn't want to believe that our government would round people up and send them away. Some of us believed it though, it happened before, why not now?

Once the government had full control of the country they didn't feel the need to hide their dirty little secret anymore. They even tried to make it sound like a good thing with advertising. We started seeing posters, and ads claiming that the camps were just schools, making people better citizens for tomorrow. The abductions were just shrugged off as the government trying to help people that wouldn't help themselves. The magic words were spoken, people would accept just about anything if it was for the greater good.

-Excerpt from the Journal of John Evermann

The interrogation room was stark and cold. Drab gray walls, stainless steel table and chairs, and a large mirror were the only points of interest. John was alone in the room, hand-cuffed to the table. He'd been separated from the rest of the group so he had no idea where the others were taken. He hadn't felt so alone at any other time in his life and the idea that Amanda and the children might be feeling the same angered him.

John had been sitting alone long enough for the cold floor to chill his feet, and the hard metal chair to hurt his back. He was sure that everything that was being done to him since being brought back to Quincy was intentional. He sat straight in the hard chair, staring down at his hands clasped on the table. He was determined not to show any signs of discomfort.

John kept playing the last moments of Steve's life over and over in his head. The look on this best friend's face would haunt him forever. He felt responsible for what happened, and he hated himself for thinking that being captured was a blessing. He felt guilt that he was relieved he wouldn't have to tell Steve's wife what happened. He knew it was selfish, but he couldn't help it.

After what seemed like an eternity, but was probably no more than an hour, the room's single door opened and a uniformed federal officer entered. The officer crossed the room and set a folder on the table, along with a cup of coffee. The officer didn't look at John, or even acknowledge that there was anyone else in the room. He simply sat in the only other chair and started looking through the papers in the folder.

John knew he was being toyed with. He resisted as long as he could, but finally his pain and sorrow got the better of him.

"Where's my family?" John asked quietly, barely above a whisper.

"Hmm?" The officer responded.

"I said, where is my family?" John looked up at the man.

"Oh, yes, they are safely locked in a cell where they belong," the officer said calmly, as if he was talking about the weather.

"And Steve?" John asked, unable to hide the catch in his throat.

The officer looked down at the papers, scanning the one in front of him.

"Ah, the one that fired at my men," the officer looked up. "The body was sent to a disposal facility."

John nearly choked on his grief as he imagined the fate of his best friend. He'd once seen a disposal facility, where bodies were unceremoniously dumped into large furnaces and cremated. It was the only legal means of handling the dead. Burying them in cemeteries was deemed bad for the environment, too costly, and too time consuming for the government.

"Listen John," the officer said calmly, "You can make this easy on yourself and your family. Tell me where the rest of the fugitives plan to cross the border and we'll send you straight to the reeducation camp. Otherwise you go to the office in Peoria for thorough interrogation."

"Listen officer," John started to say.

"Casey," Ben interrupted. "Lieutenant Casey."

"Right, Lieutenant. Look, we aren't going to tell you anything. So, you can just do whatever it is you need to do."

"You might change your mind once you get to Peoria, John," Casey rearranged the papers in the file and stood up.

Casey looked down at John for a moment, and John met his gaze coldly. John felt something in that look, but it wasn't malice, or anger. He could see that the officer truly believed in what he was doing and that scared John a little. Finally Casey walked to the door and left the room.

They came for him sometime later. John had no idea how long he'd been left there, but he had finally fallen asleep in his chair. Exhaustion, stress, and the death of his best friend had caught up to him. Someone shook him roughly and told him to get up. With his mind still cloudy, and his body in pain from sitting in the metal chair for so long, he got to his feet and stumbled in the direction the two officers directed.

They pointed him down a long, dimly-lit hall toward a large metal door. Neither of the officers spoke, and John wasn't about to strike up a conversation. His head felt like someone was hitting him in the temple with a hammer, and at that point silence was golden. He couldn't help but feel like he was being led to his own execution.

When they reached the end of the hall one of the officers firmly pushed John against the wall while the other unlocked the door with a key from a large steel ring on his belt. The massive door swung open and the smell of a garage swept into the hallway. The smell of exhaust, oil, and gasoline took John back to the day Steve and he stole the work van and escaped Stewart. Memories, and feelings, he had been trying to bury flooded to the surface again and he was swept away by grief and guilt over his friend's death.

John was pushed, unresisting, toward the back of a large black van parked several feet away. He was sure if he got in that van he wouldn't see his family or friends again, but he was too exhausted to fight the officers. He knew he should fight tooth and nail to get out and find his family, but his body ignored the screaming of his mind. He stumbled once, against one of the officers, and they both took hold of him by the arms. They practically carried him the rest of the way.

When they got to the van one of the guards reached out and opened the back doors, swinging both of them away from the vehicle. John looked up into the dark interior that suddenly became a chaos of noise as several people began to shout. His heart told him he should recognize the voices, but his mind was still clouded with grief. He was becoming aware that they were shouting his name, and holding cuffed hands out to him. The officers lifted him into the van where he collapsed on his knees on the floor. The closing of the doors seemed to snap John awake and he looked up into the faces surrounding him. He just reached up to his family, and they joined him on the floor. He wept freely, in relief, as he held his wife and kids. Todd gripped his shoulder, and they all shared a moment of quiet grief for the lost and relief to be together.

"Is everyone all right?" John's hoarse voice broke the silence. Amanda met his gaze and nodded.

"I'm hungry," Susan said quietly.

John smiled and hugged her again, holding his child he'd feared he would never hold again.

"Me too honey, but we'll have to wait a little longer," John said reassuringly. He turned to Todd, "Did they question you?"

"No," Todd shook his head, "We were all kept in a room together for hours. Once, an officer checked on us, but didn't say a word. His uniform made me think he was in charge."

"Casey," John said and nodded, "He questioned me too, but he wasn't too happy about my answers. I think they're taking us to Peoria."

With that last statement he gave a look to both Todd and his wife that let them know he didn't think it would end well for them at all. He didn't want to scare the kids he stayed silent. They both seemed to understand, and Amanda held Thomas tighter against her.

When the front doors opened they settled back onto the benches which lined the sides of the van. Two officers climbed in to the front seats. The driver got the van started, and used a radio to let the person on the other end know they were ready to leave. The passenger turned and looked back through the grate that divided the front from the prisoner area. He looked at each of them, and John thought he saw a brief look of sympathy in the officer's eyes. When the driver put the radio mic back on its hanger the passenger turned back to the front and made some notes on a clip board. The driver put the van in reverse and turned the vehicle out of the parking garage. They exited into bright sunlight, and the driver turned onto the highway, leading away from Quincy.

This is it for us, John thought, I hope the others make it.

Chapter 20

They said it would never happen again. I can't believe so many people took their word for it. Did everyone forget that it happened before? Maybe people just can't imagine the government of their time can do the same evil as they did in the past. I've come to learn that the government is always the same. The faces change, but the problems are still there. Sometimes they hide it better, sometimes they fool you, but it never really goes away.

They came and took it all, federal officers with orders from the President. Any valuable metal or jewelry, really anything that was worth anything. Claimed it had to become property of the state so everyone could benefit from it. The worst was grandma's wedding ring and grandpa's gold coin collection.

My grandparents were so proud of those things. Grandpa had saved for a year to buy that diamond ring for grandma. A large portion of his retirement went into those coins. He hoped they would insure that his kids and grandkids would never have to worry about the things grandpa worried about when he was younger. I can't imagine how they'd feel if they were alive when it happened. Hopefully part of heaven is shielding them from the evil going on down here.

-Excerpt from the Journal of John Evermann

The rain had been beating down on their heads for hours. The fat drops fell through the dry leaves of the trees, hitting the red and orange carpet of the forest floor. The sound was like distant applause in a packed theater. Benny looked around at the miserable people, huddled under blankets, tarps and jackets. Some were just sitting as close to a tree as possible, having no place else to shelter from the storm.

Benny was irritated at the rain, and at the people around him. He intended to keep going despite the weather, but when they stopped for a break most of the people sat down and refused to get back up. He cursed his luck, getting stuck with people who were used to their comfortable homes in town. Several times he had considered just leaving them, and going on by himself, but they were just passing thoughts. He wasn't a very religious man, but he believed in God. He knew God wouldn't look too well on him if he left these people to fend for themselves.

The wet was going to be a problem, Benny knew. It would be a cold night, and if they couldn't find a way to dry their clothes, especially their socks, the trip was going to get a lot worse. Some people had dry clothes in their packs, but Benny noticed quite a few whose packs had soaked through. Plastic was an expensive commodity, being made from petroleum, so no one had any real waterproofing. He'd scouted a small field a few hundred yards south, and if the sun would break through soon they might be able to dry things out before dark. He hoped modesty wasn't going to be an issue.

"Give them a break, they aren't like you," a woman had approached Benny without him noticing, only serving to irritate him further. She crouched down close, holding a blanket over her damp hair.

"What do you mean?" Benny asked, honestly confused.

"You're sitting here brooding, looking at everyone like a father does a disobedient child. We're all doing our best Benny," she said.

He studied her face for a moment, "They don't trust me, most of them are afraid of me."

"They just don't know you, Benny," she shook her head. "Most of us haven't been away from Stewart since we can remember. We've lost everything, and the feds want to take more. Everyone is scared, and without John we feel lost."

He looked down for a time, thinking on her words, and watching the raindrops striking the leaves at his feet. Finally he nodded to himself and turned back to her.

"You're Steve's wife right?" He asked.

"Sarah," she nodded. At the mention of her husband she looked away, clearly trying to control whatever emotions were boiling in her. He could tell she was worried her husband and the others might not catch up to them. Benny gave her a few moments to collect her thoughts.

"Just give us a break, alright Benny," she said finally, "Whether you realize it or not we're looking to you now to get us through this."

"Good man, your Steve," Benny said as she stood up to walk away, "They'll get back to us soon."

"I hope so," she nodded, smiling at his compliment. He watched her walk back to where her son was huddled down with some other children under one of the few tarps they had.

Benny hoped so too. He wasn't used to being around so many people at once, and he knew he wasn't a good leader. He preferred to be on his own, doing his own thing. He was determined to do his best though, he owed it to John. Benny had made a promise and he intended to keep it, even if it killed him.

* * *

The van transporting John and the others drove through the pounding rain for nearly an hour before the driver said he had to stop and use a bathroom. John's mind worked furiously, trying to think of some way to get his family and friends out of their predicament. The driver pulled the van into the parking lot of a small-town gas station. John knew they would be in Peoria soon, but he couldn't think of any way to get them out of the van. The officer in the passenger seat kept looking back at them, and John did his best to seem as if he was still occupied by grief. He was, but the need to escape was growing more powerful by the minute.

Without warning the officer in the passenger seat opened the door forcibly and got out with a softly-spoken curse. John lost sight of him until he appeared at the back window of the van. John could hear keys scraping in the lock. They were all surprised when the officer opened the back doors and climbed in with them. Without looking at them he started unlocking their cuffs. John watched him in complete confusion.

"Look," the officer began, "I understand what you're doing. I was assigned this job, but I don't like it. I can't leave the country though, my sister is out there somewhere and I have to find her."

He looked John in the eye and the two shared a moment of understanding. Love of family would drive a man to do things that would ruin him. A man would jump into hell if there was some chance that he could save his family. John nodded and shook the man's hand after his own was free.

"Quickly now," he pulled John out of the van. The others started to get out but he held up his hand, "You're taking the van, stay in there."

John followed him around to the driver seat and climbed in after the officer opened the door. The engine was still running, and John could see there was plenty of gas. He turned to the officer.

"You could come with us, we could help you find your sister," John said.

"I would if I could. I hate this place, but I can't take the chance of getting caught before I find her," the officer said. "Now, you're going to have to hit me pretty good, otherwise they won't believe you escaped on your own."

John looked at the man in shock as the officer tossed his keys into the passenger seat. The young man seemed to prepare himself as John sat speechless.

"Come on John, you don't have much time," the officer said.

"What's your name?" John finally asked.

"James," the officer replied, then turned his head slightly to give John a good target. "Now, get on with it before I chicken out."

John steeled himself for the distasteful task of beating a man that just helped him and his family. He knew the other officer would be out soon, and this was the chance he'd been looking for. It was as if God had put James in his path to answer his prayers. John pulled back his fist and hit James squarely in the side of the head. There was a painful moment when John thought he had broken his hand, and the officer stood stunned. Time seemed to slow as James stumbled, and reached for his head. His eyes rolled back, and he dropped to the pavement. John could see that James had not been knocked unconscious, but he was clearly too disoriented to move much in his prone position.

"I hope you find your sister," John said quietly as he closed the door and put the van in reverse. He backed the vehicle into the road, and drove away, back in the direction they came from. He saw in the mirror, just as he pulled away, the driver exit the gas station. The officer looked from the van, to his fallen partner in disbelief.

"John?" Amanda asked tentatively, "What just happened?"

John looked back into the faces of his friend and family. They were all in a state of disbelief. He would never know why, but the scene caused him to start laughing. Maybe it was the pent-up grief, or stress, or some other emotion he would never be able to explain. He laughed so hard he cried, and his stomach hurt. The others in the back looked at each other, probably wondering if he had lost his sanity. Finally he calmed down enough to answer her.

"A miracle dear, we've been given a miracle."

Chapter 21

There was a time when equal opportunity and equal justice were the things that most people wanted. There were some who wanted more. Better treatment and special opportunity for a few. They thought it was going to happen during the early years of the Presidency. I imagine they were surprised when reality set in and they found out what equal outcome actually looks like.

The one thing that could be said for the government's progressive agenda is it created a truly equal citizen class. Equally poor, equally oppressed, and equally without voice about their lives, but equal all the same.

-Excerpt from the Journal of John Evermann

The drive back toward Hannibal was nerve wracking for John. He decided early that driving the van through Quincy was too risky. He was sure the Feds would know about the escape before they reached the city, and would be watching for them to return by the same route. He hoped that crossing the river further south would be the last thing

Lieutenant Casey would expect. His next decision was much harder for him to make. Once across the river he would have to decide whether to seek out the larger group, or drive on to the border. He was sure that the van would have enough gas to get there, but once their escape was reported the van would become a target. It may be faster, but it would also be more dangerous.

"What are you thinking, John?" Amanda asked from the back. He looked in the mirror and met her gaze.

"We have to decide what to do once we're across the river," John replied. He saw Amanda look away a moment, considering his words.

"They'll be looking for this van," she said.

"I was thinking the same thing," John said. He looked in the mirror again to see her eyes boring into him.

"Sarah needs to know about Steve," she said simply.

He just nodded, knowing that he owed Steve so much. The least he could do was make sure his family knew how he died. He had hoped to keep his mind on other things, but he could not, and would not avoid that responsibility. He looked back at the road, trying to imagine what he would say to his best friend's wife.

* * *

The two officers walked along the cracked stretch of highway, making their way back to Quincy. Their boots crunching on the gravel shoulder was the only sound on the deserted road for a long time.

"I can't believe he took you down that easily," the driver finally said to James.

John's savior shrugged, touching his swollen lip. "I didn't expect him to be so close to the door. He said he needed a drink, I didn't think he'd try to escape."

"When we get back it's all going in my report," the driver said.

"Don't forget the part where you left the keys in the van," James said with a smile.

The diver fell silent, and neither spoke for the next few minutes. Finally the driver asked, "You think the government will get around to fixing the phone back there?"

*   *   *

The drive through the city of Hannibal stretched the limits of John's calm. He felt as if eyes were boring into him from every window and doorway they passed. At every turn he expected to come face to face with a federal roadblock waiting to take them all back to Peoria. John sat in the front seat, wearing the federal officer's coat and hat, while the others remained quiet and hidden in the back. He had to keep reminding himself to stay under the speed limit, and look like he knew what he was doing.

At one point John saw another federal van coming from several hundred yards up the highway. As casually as he could he told the others to stay down. He didn't think they could be seen from the outside, but he wasn't going to take the chance. John's heart was beating rapidly as the two vans sped toward each other on the split highway. He guessed that they would pass close to each other where the road was at its narrowest point.

When the time came John saw the other driver turn his head, and then he smiled and gave an off-hand salute. John returned the gesture with a smile, but held a sigh of relief until the other driver was out of sight. Both vans passed each other with no more than a buffeting of wind. John didn't quote relax though. He knew he couldn't until they were out of Hannibal and on the highway headed west. He continued driving as casually as possible, looking for the point where the larger group was supposed to cross he highway he was on.

It took them less than an hour to drive to the point where the rest were planned to cross highway 36. John was worried about the large group crossing the regularly used road. The highway was split, and the cleared area on each side was wide. They planned to cross at night, and John guessed it would be at least another night before the group reached that point. John and the others would have to wait until then.

He found an old dirt road near where highway 24 met 36 and pulled the van back into the tree line. He drove the van into the wooded area until the ground became too hazardous, and the trees too close together, to go any further. Finally he broke the silence everyone had unconsciously been keeping since they entered Hannibal.

"We'll have to wait it out here until the rest show up. They should cross on this side of highway 24, so one of us will need to watch the van, and another near the tree line to watch the highway," he said.

"I'll go watch the road," Todd said, and climbed out of the van before anyone could protest. John just nodded and turned to Amanda.

"I'll stay up here, you and the kids get some sleep," he said, giving her a quick kiss and climbing out of the van himself.

He walked a short distance from the vehicle so he could keep an eye on it and the surrounding trees. The silence of the woods was oppressive, only broken by the occasional drip of water from the trees to the leafy carpet. He settled himself on the ground, with his back against a tree, ignoring the damp that soaked through his pants. The earlier rain left behind damp and stifling air on a day that was warmer than usual for autumn, and the atmosphere seemed to settle right on John's chest, like an unwelcome guest.

For John the waiting was the worst part of the journey. Being alone with his thoughts seemed, somehow, to be more torturous than the constant fear of capture. Self-doubt ate at him. He couldn't help but wonder if he was doing the right thing for everyone. They all looked to him to lead, but what did he know? He hadn't even been assigned a management job back home. He didn't know anything about leadership except what people said in books about famous generals, and if you could learn that sort of stuff from a book then anyone could lead, right? He'd made a promise though and he intended to keep it. He would lead them to Texas even if it killed him.

That thought brought his best friend, Steve, to mind. It was ultimately their plan, a shared dream to get their families to Texas but John felt responsible. He imagined that guilt would weigh on his mind forever. He wondered how he could face Sarah when the two groups were finally reunited. How would he look her in the eye and tell her that their dream had cost her a husband? Amanda was right though. Sarah deserved to hear it from him, and sooner rather than later. Just another of the responsibilities John had found himself shouldering, without being told or even wanting it, but knowing it had to be done. He hadn't looked for it; they had all just looked to him.

John looked around the damp woods they were hiding in. This is what he had led them to; running from the feds, hiding in the woods, losing a friend, husband and father. He looked southwest, toward their destination. Freedom, liberty, Texas, he prayed to God it was worth it. A quiet cough from the van brought his mind back to his family. He was risking everything on those ideals, a dream to see his children free to choose their own destiny. His family hadn't questioned him, nor did they have any doubt, and he certainly couldn't show his own fears to them. It was up to him to be strong, confident, and, when the time came, the leader that everyone was expecting him to be.

As night fell in the woods, John let his mind wander and work out any possibilities his subconscious could come up with that might be a problem on their way to Texas. It was something John did frequently when alone, but before it had always been a nuisance. He would be working the line, doing the redundant tasks that were his everyday job, and his mind would just create the most fantastic, or unrealistic situations and how to solve them. Many times they were situations he hoped would never happen like what he would do if his wife became terminally ill, or if one of his children got seriously hurt, or if a major fire broke out in the plant. Now the way his mind worked seemed to be useful. He could work through all the possible problems in their plan to reach Texas, and let his mind work through them ahead of time. As always though, he hoped these were just daydreams, and all the planning was unnecessary.

Sometime after dark, John dozed off against the tree, his head slumped forward, his chin against his chest. He didn't fall into a deep sleep, due to his anxiety and the cold damp under his legs, so when Todd came running back to the van John jerked awake and to his feet. He didn't know it was his friend at first, and was prepared to fight whoever was charging into their hiding spot. Thankfully Todd called out quietly before John had a chance to leap to the defense of his family.

"John!" Todd called when he came within sight of the van. Seeing John a few feet away, Todd changed direction but didn't slow down until he reached his friend.

Seeing Todd rushing to him, out of breath, John knew something was wrong. Todd stopped, put his hands on his knees and bent forward, trying to catch his breath. John gripped his shoulder, "What is it Todd, what's wrong?"

"The others," Todd gasped, unused to running he was having trouble getting his breath, "I saw them…signaled them to follow, but something is wrong." He drew in a deep breath, finally able to stand upright. "They are running like the devil himself is after them."

Chapter 22

Why is it that everyone held to the constitution until violating it helped them out in some way? That theme existed throughout history but it became so much more noticeable in the years leading up to the end of the Republic. Give the government more power, give up more freedoms, as long as it is for the 'greater good'. The worst were the ones who didn't mind taking away someone else's rights as long as it helped them personally. It's ironic that those who talked up the collective mentality, and denounced individual liberty, were just doing it to help themselves in the end.

-Excerpt from the Journal of John Evermann

John rushed back the way Todd had come from. He didn't know what to expect, or what he would do, but waiting where he was wasn't an option. When he broke through the trees he saw the other group running headlong in his direction. He could tell they had been running for a long time and most were beyond their limits. The children were being carried by parents that could barely carry themselves. Fear was all that could push them to such obvious extremes. John anxiously scanned the crowd, and thanked God that everyone seemed to be there. He caught Benny's eye. The big man was near the front, helping Sarah along and carrying Steve's son. When they got close, Todd, who had followed, took the boy and led Sarah and the others to the van. Once out of earshot Benny turned to John.

"Dogs, the feds got dogs on our trail John. Not more than an hour behind us," the reclusive man said gruffly.

"Damn," John said quietly. Without another word he led Benny to the others and the van, his mind already working on a plan.

"Any idea how many?" John asked as they walked back to the others.

"Hard to tell, but from the noise they're making I'd say no more than six of the beasts," Benny replied.

When they returned to the van, everyone else was waiting anxiously, talking excitedly among themselves about what might happen next. As John approached, they turned to him and he could read their thoughts on the faces staring back at him. They were looking to him for guidance, that much was obvious, but he could also see that they were wondering what he would do with the van. Some were hopeful, others were resigned. All of them knew that the vehicle couldn't take everyone.

John wasn't the only one that could read the faces of the people present. Benny patted his shoulder and walked ahead when John stopped. The sympathy in that simple touch was surprising. Benny knew what needed to be done, and how some would react, and was positioning himself to back John up should things get ugly.

"Listen," John started, uncomfortable with how they all seemed to stand straighter and fell silent. "We don't have much time. The van has enough gas to get to Texas, but obviously it can't take all of us."

They were all looking at him with rapt attention, all except Sarah. She was looking around the crowd, obviously for Steve. John cursed their lack of time, ashamed that he didn't tell her first. He saw Amanda move toward her and take her hand as she leaned in close and spoke softly to her. John looked at the others; he had a job to do, and not much time to do it.

"We'll send the children and those unable to move fast enough, ahead in the van."

They all knew that was the most logical choice, but he could see the disappointment in the eyes of some, and the fear in the eyes of others. Mothers held their children tighter, some, he knew, were thinking of excuses to get themselves put on that van. He didn't blame them. With the feds so close behind the trip was becoming more and more dangerous.

"Benny knows which of you were struggling so he'll handle assigning adults to the vehicle. You will be responsible for the kids, and finding a safe place to wait for us once you reach Texas. Everyone knows where we plan to cross the border," John said.

He nodded to Benny who immediately set about organizing the group and getting the children into the van. Most took the news calmly, saying tearful, but quiet goodbyes to children. Kids hugged parents and promised to be brave. Everyone knew time was short and they tried not to waste it. There were a few that looked at the van like they might do something foolish, but Benny singled them out and set them to watching the road, or other tasks to occupy their thoughts. John left him to it and approached Amanda and Sarah.

"Sarah, I'm so sorry. I don't know what to say," John began, but was instantly silenced when Sarah lifted her tear-filled eyes. She just shook her head and opened her mouth to speak, but closed it again. She took a deep breath and finally spoke quietly.

"He knew…we knew this might happen," she couldn't say any more, but nearly fell into John's arms when he moved to comfort her. She shook against him, her tears soaking his shirt as he looked over her head helplessly at Amanda, whose eyes were also red from crying for her friend. He smoothed Sarah's hair and spoke to her quietly.

"He was the best man I knew Sarah, and braver than any one of us. He's watching us now, and we have work to do. I need you to go with Benny and the kids in the van. Get them to Texas, can you do that?"

Sarah took a deep, shuddering breath and stepped back, smoothing her clothes and wiping her eyes. Finally she looked at him with hard determination in her face. She just nodded once. John gave her a reassuring smile.

"Good, we're all counting on you two to get them to safety. Of all of us, the children have to make it to Texas, they're the reason for all of this," John said firmly.

Sarah nodded again, turned to hug Amanda, and then walked toward the van. John could see she was gathering herself, her first steps slow and hesitant, but soon she was walking toward the vehicle with determination in her step. He knew it would be some time before she was all right, but for now she had something important to occupy her. Something she knew had to be done and a reason to push her grief in the back of her mind for now.

"They're all loaded, John," Benny said, stepping close to John and his wife.

"Benny, I need to you drive the van," John turned to him. "I need someone reliable to get them to Texas."

Benny didn't question the decision, he just nodded, taking John's hand firmly in his own large one. "We'll see you in Texas my friend."

"We're counting on you Benny. Once you're there let them know we're coming."

John shook Benny'shand, but the large recluse turned it into a hug, patting John on the back hard. There was no more time wasted on their goodbye. Benny let John go and turned back toward the black vehicle, the van that held the future hopes and dreams of everyone standing in that wooded clearing. John and Amanda walked with him, noting the last two children still standing outside the back doors.

John knelt in front of his own children, wordlessly pulling both of them into his arms and holding them tightly for a moment as Amanda looked on, tears coming to her eyes again. He settled back on his heels, looking at them and wiping their own tears away with his hand.

"Thomas, I need you to look after your sister all right?" The boy nodded, trying his best to be brave and hide the tears he was struggling with. John nodded and shook his hand like a man before giving him a kiss on the forehead and a nudge toward his mother. He then looked at Susan.

"Susan, honey you need to be good for your brother. Listen, and stay close. Can you do that for me dear?" She nodded, not able to stifle the tears like her brother had. John smiled and gave her another hug, "That's my brave girl. Now, go give your mother a hug, there isn't much time."

Susan ran to Amanda, who snatched the little girl up in her arms, carrying her to the back of the van. Once the two were loaded in with the rest of the children, and the people too old or injured to move fast John leaned in close to Amanda.

"I don't suppose I could talk you into going with them?"

He knew the answer, but the protective part of him, the part that made him put his family first, had to ask. Amanda looked at the kids in the van, then at the people standing around waiting to move before the feds arrived, and finally at John. He could see in her eyes that she wanted to stay with the children more than anything in the world, but there was also a determination in them. The same sense that made each one of the members of this exodus put others before themselves. It was that same ideal that brought them all together, the same moral fiber that built the original Republic, and founded the new one in Texas. Amanda shook her head and took his hand firmly.

"Not in this lifetime John. The kids will be fine with Benny and Sarah. I can run just fine and you…they might need me," He nodded at that and closed the back of the van with a small wave to the kids inside. Pounding on the door he walked with Amanda, out of the way, as Benny backed the vehicle out of the clearing and onto the road that would take them to the highway.

They all watched the black van pull away, watched their future, their hopes and dreams slide away into the misty morning. Children that hadn't known anything but the world they were trying to leave. Some of kids had no idea why they had to leave home, why their parents had pulled them out of beds in the middle of the night to run through the countryside, scared, tired and hungry. The ones that did know, the ones old enough to understand the words their parents used to describe where they were going, still didn't know exactly what it all meant. They couldn't conceive of a world where they were free to choose their future, or how they would live the rest of their lives. They heard words like liberty, personal responsibility, republic, and democracy, but those were just words without any practical experience for them. Those kids were speeding headlong into a world that would be alien to them, but it was the chance at that future that made their parents risk it all. It was why they risked everything so that their children would have a better life than the one their parents had. Everyone prayed that, whether or not they made it themselves, the van crossed the border into a new life in Texas, with its precious cargo safe and sound.

Chapter 23

It was late in the President's second term that the government, under the auspices of bringing us all together as 'one nation', absorbed the states into one entity. Most people were shocked, outraged, but what were they to do? The government had all the power, all the control. Statehood was abolished, but not every state was willing to just sit back and let it happen. Texas, New Mexico, Arizona and Oklahoma seceded and formed the New Republic of Texas. The old government didn't have the money to stop them, though the secession sparked a war that would go on for a long time. With the newly formed Republic of Texas being so small, and the old government being out of money, neither could do much in this war except keep each other at bay. A stalemate to last generations maybe?

-Excerpt from the journal of John Evermann

Lieutenant Casey stood at the hood of a black, government issue SUV, in his government issue uniform, looking over an inadequate government issue map of the area that used to be Illinois and Missouri. He had recently sent two officers to Peoria to be reprocessed to the nearest reeducation camp. A fair punishment for losing the prisoners, he thought, but it only served to heighten his already foul mood. He couldn't understand how it was possible for so many citizens to elude him for so long now. His requisition for search dogs had finally been approved from D.C., but he only had them for two days before they were needed elsewhere. Overall this assignment was beginning to irritate him.

The SUV was pulled over to the side of the highway west of Quincy, the last place anyone saw the fugitives. Several other cars and vans were pulled over as well, all part of the team assigned to the hunt. The agents with the dogs had gone ahead, but Casey trusted his instincts more than anything else, and was trying to think like the hunted, to figure out where they would go next. He didn't understand them, or their desire to run in the first place, so he was finding it difficult to put himself in their shoes.

"They'll keep the van," Casey said without looking up. He was surrounded by aides, other officers who were tasked with assisting him. He didn't know why he needed so many or any at all, but it was their job assignment, and he wasn't one to question it. If his bosses thought he needed so many assistants, then that's what he got.

"Do you think they'll pick up any others?" One of the nameless aides asked. Casey stopped caring what their names were, nor had he asked anything about their personal lives. His assistants were rotated out so frequently it didn't seem to matter anymore.

"No, I expect the group that stole the van to keep it. They'll probably head further south before crossing the river, maybe even Saint Louis, we'll let that office deal with them. The larger group, the ones we're following now, have children and old people, they won't be able to stay ahead of us for long," Casey replied, tracing his finger along the route he suspected the fugitives to take.

The idea that one person might sacrifice so much for others was simply beyond Casey. In his world volunteers got paid, charity was compulsory, and people just didn't give anything away without being told to. That arrangement eliminated the need to rely on some vague concept of human decency. In the lieutenant's mind there was no chance that those who stole the van would do anything other than keep on driving and never look back.

"Have the handlers checked in?" Casey asked, finally looking up from the map.

"Yes sir, they believe they're getting close. We should have the fugitives run to ground within the hour."

"Good, let's get moving then, we've wasted enough time on this," Casey said. Leaving the map for one of his aides to take care of he pulled open the passenger door of the black SUV and climbed in. He was impatient to get moving and grumbled in irritation at how long it was taking everyone to get in their vehicles. His superiors were breathing down his neck to get everything settled quickly before it sparked similar ideas in other citizens. None of that motivated the rest of his team however. It wasn't their problem if he was getting pressure from his bosses.

He thought about that as the men and women around him finished their cigarettes, conversations, and whatever else they were doing before getting in their vehicles. Nothing was ever efficient, but it would eventually all get done. He had to keep reminding himself of that. Despite his impatience, it was human nature to take one's time and not overwork. He had a hard time imagining how people of earlier generations could accomplish so much, so fast, and why they would want to. The concept of working for someone else's gain, another man's profit, didn't make any sense to him. He couldn't conceive of how a system like that would drive people to work harder than they did in his generation. In his world people worked for the benefit of their neighbors, their fellow man. As one of the true believers in the new America, Casey didn't understand why that wasn't enough to bring out the best in everyone. Whether he understood it or not, that was the way of things, and no one expected it to change anytime soon.

"Finally," Casey grumbled as the last of the officers climbed into their vehicle and the team was pulling back onto the highway.

"What was that, sir?" The driver asked, not looking up from the road.

"Nothing, take sixty one south, we'll catch the handlers somewhere along twenty four," Casey said.

"Yes, sir."

*   *   *

For James, the ride back to Peoria was too long and too quiet. He was riding in the back of a black sedan, driven by a fellow officer. His partner was sitting next to him in the back seat, and had not spoken a word since they were told of their fate. Not that James cared; he had enough on his mind.

They weren't under arrest in the traditional sense; the back doors weren't even locked. No one expected them to defy orders, but James couldn't get the image of John and his family, out of his mind. He wondered if he had what it would take to simply run. Would he be able to leave everything behind like John did? He believed he could go on the run. One man could easily evade capture, especially if he knew how the Feds worked. He could go find his sister, and try to get to Texas.

Those thoughts were in the forefront of his mind when the car stopped outside the Federal building in Peoria. The driver needed the proper paperwork before taking the two over to the local reeducation and reassignment facility. When the officer went inside, without even looking back at the passengers, James reached out and opened his door.

"What are you doing?" His partner asked.

James looked back at him, knowing he had little time before the driver returned. He pitied the man, his mind lost to the certainty that he couldn't change his life in any significant way. James pitied everyone that chose to stay, and be held as slaves to 'the common good'. He realized that he had pitied himself as well, all the years doing the easier thing, falling in line, never questioning. He was done pitying himself, but he couldn't help feeling sorry for others. Many had just given up, given everything over to someone else. No more self-reliance, or self-determination. It was a perfect world for some, but there was one thing about it James could no longer ignore. No more personal freedom.

The other man could see that James was different. In just those few seconds when they were alone he could tell James had changed. It was in the set of his shoulders, and the look in his eyes. It was a look he didn't understand, but he knew what it led to. He started to speak, to tell James it was foolish, but his partner cut him off.

"I'm leaving," James said simply, before exiting the car and setting off up the road at a run.

Chapter 24

I always hated election years, all the negative ads on TV and radio, the repetitious articles digging up dirt that didn't matter. All of it was so tasteless, so un-American. I never thought I would miss it until the years following the President's declaration of absolute power. After that I would have welcomed the ugliness of it all just for the chance to change things. Some say it wouldn't have mattered, that the next president would have been just as bad as the last. We always heard how they just got worse and worse over the last few generations, that we would have only traded one evil for another. I, for one, would rather have taken that chance. At least then I could say I tried.

-Excerpt from the journal of John Evermann

The sound of dogs baying carried through the woods as the van pulled out of sight. When John heard it he felt that flash of fear that he knew the others had been dealing with all night. His heart seemed to stop and the hair on his neck stood up, but he forced himself to breathe and calm down before he turned back to the rest. He had to swallow his fear for the sake of the group. When he looked at his friends and neighbors he saw his own fear reflected in their eyes. This time he didn't dwell on the fact that they were looking at him for guidance, he just started on the idea that had already been forming in his mind.

Taking a quick, rough count, John started separating people into small groups. He was careful to keep family units together. Once he had a small group separated out he pointed them off in a direction, relatively south and west. He instructed them to move fast until they could no longer hear the dogs, then turn toward Mark Twain Lake that lay in their path south. It was one of the landmarks everyone had been told about. One of the places they would meet if they had to split up or became lost. The lake and its offshoot waterways would be nearly impossible to miss on their way south. It was his hope that splitting up would throw the dogs off enough to get away. Then he moved off to the next group and repeated the process, sending each in a slightly different direction until it was only he and his wife, Todd and two others making up the sixth group. It had only taken a few minutes, but it felt like hours with the baying of the hounds from the north. Again he had tried to get Amanda to go with another group, but she wouldn't hear of it. He couldn't force her so he would just have to live with the danger his plan put them in.

John crouched down to wait after the last of the smaller groups disappeared into the trees. The hounds in the distance made it hard to be patient, but he knew he would have to time it just right if they were going to get away and protect the rest. He looked at the few he kept with him. All men without wives or children, men he believed would be able to keep up and not let fear get the better of them. Then there was Amanda. John could see she was scared, but her jaw was set and she was looking at him, ready to move and determined to remain strong.

"What's the plan John?" Despite Amanda's obvious fear, her voice was even and firm.

"We wait until they're close and let them see us before we run. Hopefully they'll think we're stragglers following the rest," the others looked at him in shock. "If all goes well they won't bother to find the other trails and just chase us."

John could see them visibly wrestle with the rising panic as they realized just how dangerous this was going to be. It was Amanda who broke the tension.

"It's a good plan John, we're up for it," she looked around as she spoke, receiving nods from each before finally looking back at her husband. She could see, in his eyes, how proud he was of her and she couldn't help but smile. The moment passed, however, at the next baying of the hounds. They were close.

"Let's move," John led them across the clearing. He started the first couple of them into the trees, holding Todd back with him. He nodded for Amanda to follow the other two but she hesitated. John kissed her and gave her a quick hug.

"Go with them, I'll be right behind you. I want them to just catch sight of us before we run," she nodded and kissed him again.

Unable to trust her voice, Amanda didn't say a word. She just turned and jogged to catch up to the first two of their group. She looked back once when she caught up, and John saw a different fear in her eyes. She believed she might be looking at him for the last time. John finally turned away when they were far enough into the trees he could no longer see them.

John and Todd were both at the edge of the clearing furthest from where the dogs and their handlers would appear. They both crouched in the ferns, with John clutching at Todd's shirt at the shoulder. When he realized what he was doing John let go with a quiet apology. They were both tense, ready to bolt the moment the feds caught sight of them.

"Don't worry about it, John," Todd said, giving his friend a sympathetic smile.

The two didn't have long to wait, though the anticipation made it seem like hours. There was one more round of excited barking before the first of the leashed hounds entered the clearing, followed by its handler. John waited for the fed to look up, and when the officer's eyes met his and flashed in triumphant recognition John cuffed Todd on the shoulder and the two sprang away into the trees and underbrush. The officer gave a shout and the chase was on.

*   *   *

Sarah sat in the passenger seat of the van, staring out the window in silence. She watched, without really seeing, as the faded white lane markers flashed by on the cracked pavement. She and Steve had both known it would be dangerous to run, but neither of them had imagined anyone would die. As the reality of how wrong they had been settled in she couldn't even cry. She imagined she was still in shock, but wondered if a person in shock would be rational enough to realize it. Maybe she wasn't crying because she had too much to worry about now. She had to think about the kids she and Benny were now responsible for, and her own child, whose future depended on her and how she handled the road ahead.

She knew that's why John had put her in the van. She was mad at him, but she knew she shouldn't be. She and Steve had made their own choice to go and John was doing the best he could to look out for everyone. She just couldn't help feeling like he was responsible for Steve's death. John had known exactly what she needed though. He knew exactly how to keep her going after the loss of her husband. He didn't do it to escape his own guilt, of that she was sure, he did it for her and that too made her mad.

She knew she had to look at the road ahead, forcing herself to physically do just that. Looking out over the hood of the black van, watching the pavement rush toward them she could almost imagine that they were rushing to a better place, taking the children to a promised land down a river of black asphalt. There would be plenty of time to mourn once they reached Texas, but she had to focus on the here and now. She rubbed her face and took a deep breath, steeling herself for the trials they were sure to face in the days ahead.

"He was a good man," Benny said simply.

The recluse surprised Sarah. He rarely spoke, and hadn't said a word since they left the others.

"Thank you," she said softly.

Benny just nodded, keeping his eyes on the road. Sarah turned to look back at the frightened children in the back. Some were crying softly, already missing their parents, some were just too young to understand why they were separated and looked around like they expected mom and dad to crawl into the van any moment. She looked at her own child and forced herself to smile. Looking at each of them again she said, in as cheerful a voice as she could muster, "So, who wants to hear a story?"

*   *   *

As John and Todd crashed through the brush, they realized Amanda and the others had gotten further ahead than expected while the two waited to catch the attention of the Feds. With the feds and their hounds hot on the trail their best chance was to just run and try to lose the agents before meeting up with the others further south. They did their best to run through, or around brush and undergrowth, trying to make themselves harder to see in the woods. No matter how well they did at sticking to cover however, they wouldn't lose the dogs without doing something clever, or a miracle.

"How long do we keep this up?" Todd managed to ask between panting breaths.

"As long as we have to," John said, "We'll split up soon."

Todd nodded and the two ran on. The ground fell out from under the two as they plunged into a shallow ravine. John managed to keep his feet but Todd stumbled and rolled to the bottom, splashing into a narrow stream. John helped him out of the water.

"Can you run?" John asked. When Todd nodded John turned him toward the south, looking down the ravine, "Go then, I'll lead them away."

Todd hesitated.

"Todd, listen, we don't have time to argue. If I don't make it to the lake on the agreed upon time make sure Amanda and the others get moving," John gave him a push, making it clear that it was time for Todd to go. John stood at the base of the ravine, watching the last connection to the refugees run south toward freedom, his boots splashing water with each step. Todd looked back once, and John just nodded to his friend, both wondering if it was the last time they would see each other. Both looked to the top of the ravine when the hounds called out again. When John looked back Todd was gone.

John waited until the first hound reached the ravine and the handlers caught sight of him again. As the canine raised his head to announce his find, John bolted north. He made sure he had the attention of the agents before disappearing into the trees again. As he had hoped, the human handlers followed what they could see rather than what the dogs indicated. When one of the hounds tried to get a scent on Todd's trail the handler just pulled on the lead until the animal turned to follow John with the others. John expected to be caught, but he hoped it would give the rest enough of a lead to get away from the feds.

*   *   *

Amanda and the others ran hard for a couple of miles before turning south toward the lake. The sounds of pursuit had faded long before and they felt safe enough to head for the meeting place. She prayed everyone else stuck to the plan. It was simple enough, but required courage. "Meet at the lake, unless you are followed. If you can't shake the Feds, whatever you do, don't lead them to everyone else.

Wait until dawn tomorrow, and then keep going. Don't wait for anyone," John had said.

While they were running he was leading the agents on a chase with Todd, to give them all time to get away. She knew he wouldn't even think about going to the lake until he lost the Feds. She wondered if she had the courage to leave at dawn if John didn't make it in time. She just kept picturing her children, she knew if she thought of them she would be able to do what was necessary.

They began to slow a little, conserving their strength in case they needed to run again. After a short distance through the trees they could hear the sound of water moving over rocks. The bubbling, splashing sound reminded Amanda of her children playing in the bathtub back home.

"We'll stop here for a minute, get some water and our bearings," one of the men said as they stopped at the edge of the ravine. Amanda just nodded, not trusting herself to speak with the memory of her kids so fresh in her mind.

It was one of the countless streams that cut through that part of the country, headed to or from one of the many rivers. They knew that drinking standing water was a bad idea, but water that was moving over rocks might be safe to drink if it was far enough away from anything manmade. They descended the ravine carefully, knowing that a twisted ankle or broken leg might mean the end of their journey.

One of the men with Amanda got down on his knees at the water's edge and dipped his hand in, cupping some of the cold water and brought it to his nose, then tasted it.

"Seems fine, we should probably use one of the tablets anyway," he said, reaching back for his empty canteen. Amanda handed him one of the few water purification tablets their group had been given. Benny had kept one box of the tablets stored away with his other survival contraband, not many for such a large group. John didn't think they would be relying much on natural water sources so they thought nothing of it. He had distributed the tablets among the group, trying to make sure if he had to split anyone up they would always have someone with them that had one.

While they waited Amanda stood near the stream, looking north. John was somewhere in that direction, doing his best to protect them all. She forced herself to think of something else before she started dwelling on the grim possibilities. She tried to picture their future home in Texas, where the kids might go to school, and John working at a job he actually felt proud of. The images were so clear, so much so that she imagined she could see John running toward her in the stream. It took her a moment to realize it wasn't her imagination, but her hopes were dashed the moment they started to rise. It wasn't John, but Todd running toward them. There was a slight limp to his step and he was holding one arm close to his body. He was hurt.

When Todd saw them it seemed to lift his spirits and he picked up the pace a bit. Amanda and the others rushed to meet him, all else momentarily forgotten upon seeing their friend. She got to him first and took his good arm firmly to help support his weight. He was out of breath, and she could feel the heat rolling off of him. He was wet from sweat and the water he had been running through. Her concern for Todd warred with her fear for John.

"Where's John?" She asked, trying to keep the fear out of her voice.

"Back there, leading them away," Todd said, trying to catch his breath.

Amanda made sure the others had Todd before she stepped away and started walking back the way he'd come.

"Amanda, you can't go after him," Todd said, turning and reaching for her.

"I have to find him Todd, I can't let him do this on his own," she stopped, knowing that Todd was right.

"The kids Amanda, he said you had to keep going no matter what. He told me to make sure you kept going," Todd said, pleading with her to see what she already knew.

"Damn you John," she said, too softly for the others to hear, and with no real conviction. She turned back and helped the others get Todd to where they left the water and their packs. They split up Todd's gear to lighten his load, and started south along the bottom of the ravine, toward the meeting place.

Chapter 25

If any decent outcome can be attributed to the changes we've seen over the last twenty years, it would be the decline in drug and alcohol use. At first people were surprised. Drug legalization advocates thought the progressive government would lift the prohibitions on drugs, and they did, early in the President's second term. They also legalized prostitution on the same bill, the Redefining of Family Morals Act. What supporters didn't realize, and the government didn't bother to share, was that it would all be pointless. With no real cash in circulation over the last few years the dealers and cartels saw no profit in American addicts anymore. With alcohol now rationed and classified as a luxury item people began to find other ways to get a drink, but no one was drinking as much as they had before, except maybe those who lived in secluded areas where bootlegging was still a tradition. I guess it goes to show, nothing ever turns out like you expect when you're counting on the government to do it for you.

-Excerpt from the journal of John Evermann

Lieutenant Casey was looking over the area where the fugitives were believed to have all been together last. He could tell they still had the van, and there was a radio call out to find it, but he didn't have much hope for that. The group's plan to split up had been well thought out. Whether the fugitives had known it or not, Casey didn't have enough men to split up and follow them all. He was gaining more respect for these people, he had to admit. Where once he believed them to be nothing more than disgruntled citizens acting out, he'd come to realize they had planned this well and they were dedicated to their cause. All of that, along with lack of support from his superiors, was going to make his job more difficult.

Besides the tracks in the mud there was little evidence the fugitives had been in the area. Most people didn't think twice about throwing garbage on the ground for the National Waste Management to take care of, but there wasn't even a scrap of paper on their trail from Stewart. No food wrappers, empty cans, or litter of any kind. Casey found it hard to believe that anyone would be so mindful, figuring they must have been coached to pick up after themselves.

The few agents remaining with him had narrowed down all of the routes the various groups used to get away, but it didn't help much, he would have to be satisfied with capturing the ones they had seen when they reached the clearing. He was also running out of time before he lost some of the agents he'd been given. The government's definition of efficiency, use only as many people as needed to do the job, meant there weren't enough agents to go around. It was getting late in the day and still no reports from the handlers.

When Casey stood from inspecting the van's tracks he noticed several officers climbing into vehicles, some already driving away. He grabbed the arm of one agent who was headed toward the SUV Casey had been using.

"What's going on agent?" he asked, "I didn't give the order to pack up."

"Hours sir, most are capped out. Peoria might send relief," the agent replied.

Casey let go of the man's arm, sighing in frustration. Time had passed quicker than he realized. He'd been so worried about getting word the handlers were being recalled he completely forgot about the other agents and their contract regulated time. He should have put in a requisition for relief shifts hours ago.

"Leave the truck," Casey said angrily, quite sure that if he didn't there was a good chance they'd all strand him there. The agent shrugged and headed for another vehicle, leaving the black SUV for Casey. The lieutenant walked over and leaned on the door of the vehicle in case anyone else thought of taking it.

"Lieutenant, there's a message from headquarters. Canine unites are to be recalled for allocation elsewhere," Casey turned to see his aide reading from a piece of paper, obviously someone's hastily written message.

"What could possibly be more important?" Casey asked, wondering why the message had come two hours before it was expected.

"I'm not sure sir, but I did catch a report about a National Official's child missing," the aide answered.

Of course, Casey thought, no one really knows about the fugitives he was hunting, but a politician's child missing would be national news, embarrassing for the government. He imagined if he'd have all the dogs and agents he could ask for if someone leaked the story of these fugitives to the media.

"Fine, fine, radio the handlers, bring everyone in," Casey ordered in frustration.

"Sir?" The aide was looking at him like he wanted to ask a question he was sure to get yelled at for.

"Yes, after that you're dismissed. I wouldn't want you to violate your contract with overtime," Casey said. The agent looked relived and nodded, going to carry out his final orders before finding a ride back to Peoria.

Casey watched the last of the officers leave. He couldn't believe how the operation was turning out. He knew that in years past police and investigators talked about duty, solving the crime, getting their man, but for his colleagues duty only went so far as their contract said it had to. Even he should be heading back but something in him refused to give up. He would be reprimanded, but in the end, the same contract that said he couldn't work overtime also said he couldn't be fired without good reason.

Looking around the empty clearing every fiber of Casey's body wanted nothing more than to lash out at someone. Every officer involved in this investigation would be off until the next week. Three days until he had help tracking the fugitives again, three days for them to get further away, closer to Texas. Most of the department had already written off ever catching the fugitives, knowing that the trail would be nearly impossible to pick up after the weekend. Casey knew it too, but at least he had a chance to stop some of them. They had split up, and by the last report there were a few on their own, quite possibly their leader, John. If he could catch John, and somehow let all the others know, he might be able to stop them from leaving the country. He couldn't imagine they would leave one of their own behind. He had a hard time imagining these people would be that desperate.

*   *   *

John lost his way after he separated from Todd, but he could hear the dogs behind him for hours. When he thought he wasn't going to be able to run any longer something changed. He stopped to catch his breath, and to figure out why the sound of the dogs was different. For what seemed like hours the baying and calling had followed him through the woods, always close, and echoing through the trees in every direction. Then, without warning, the sound changed. The baying of the hounds seemed quieter, further away or pointed in a different direction. The calls of the handlers were also different, and he was confused. Had they given up on him, he wondered. Had the dogs caught the scent of Todd, or the others? John turned around and headed back, determined to find out what was happening, and make sure no others were in danger of being caught. Exhausted, worried, and sore, John climbed out of the creek bed he had been running through and headed back toward the highway.

He hadn't gone far when he realized that the feds weren't chasing anyone else. The sounds went back to the clearing where the chase had started, and the hounds weren't calling out as they would if they were on the hunt. He picked up the pace, to get closer to the agents, and try to hear what was happening. It was easy for him to catch up, the feds were taking their time getting back, and before long he could hear them talking.

"I was wondering how long we'd be out here, the ride back to Peoria is going to push me into overtime," one of them said, as if sitting in a car an extra couple of hours was going to be the hardest work of his life.

John shook his head, all too familiar with that attitude from the mill.

"Good for you, some of us have to go look into this missing politician's daughter," the second officer said. "I'd file a complaint against my contract if I thought it would do any good."

"Can't go stepping on toes in Washington, Smith, you'd just wind up on the border getting shot at by Texans," the first said.

It reminded John of the few times he'd been asked to work overtime at the mill, knowing he could have filed a complaint, but he never did. The government owned everything, and it was no secret they used the contracts to give people the illusion that they still had rights and protections, but that illusion was dispelled the moment the government needed workers to violate their agreement. A worker could file a complaint, but if they were lucky that's as far as it would go when the government was involved. Complain enough and the worker would find himself relocated, in a worse job, or at a reeducation camp to become a more 'patriotic citizen'.

John stopped following the agents before they reached the clearing. He'd heard all he needed to hear and decided it was time to catch up to the others to share the news. All of the feds were being recalled, either due to overtime concerns, or because of a missing child. He would never have wished anything like that on a kid and he hoped she had just become lost and would be found right away, safe and unharmed.

Hearing about the missing girl had turned his thoughts to his own children, lost in a world that didn't even make sense anymore. They were all lost, he believed, every last person that lived in America, trudging along in life with nothing to look forward to. Years before the change people talked about the American Dream being dead, something only rich people could attain, or just a myth to start with.

John didn't believe that was true, and neither did his father, or grandfather. They'd never been rich, but John's father had a better life than his own father had, and John's childhood had been better than his father's. Apparently that wasn't enough for everyone, or even for most. Now the American Dream was truly dead, like some self-fulfilling prophecy, enough people believed it for long enough that it finally became true. Equal opportunity wasn't enough, a level playing field wasn't enough, in the end people wanted it handed to them on a silver platter. Like everything else though, the things given are never worth as much as those earned, and in the end everyone did wind up the same. John wasn't sure if it was what all those people wanted, but it's what everyone got.

John picked up the pace, unaware that one agent was still tracking him. He knew the group was only going to wait until dawn and if anyone was missing when the sun came up the plan was for everyone to keep going. He was about eight hours from the lake and another three or four to their meeting spot on the west side of it. He was already a couple hours behind the last group and approaching evening, which would slow him down. He would be hard-pressed to find them by dawn.

* * *

Amanda and the others made good time, reaching Mark Twain Lake before it became too dark to see. After that it wasn't difficult to follow the lake shore to the western edge where they were all supposed to meet. There was an abandoned house just off highway 24 that Benny had told them about. The place was hidden from the highway by trees and the access road was overgrown from disuse. It was the closest place to hide for the night near the bridge that crossed the last waterway on the north side of the lake.

Once they reached the lake it was just a matter of keeping the water on their left until it cut back to the south. Benny's directions led them to an old shipping yard. From there they would follow some old and mostly overgrown country roads west until they hit the highway. Then they could follow that to the house. At that time of night highway 24 should be deserted, but with agents out looking for them they weren't going to take any chances. Once they reached the highway they stayed about thirty yards back, walking along the tree line until they reached the bridge.

Todd was doing better, his limp nearly gone, something they were all thankful for. No one wanted to imagine what would happen if one of their group was injured and unable to continue. When they reached the bridge they had to get close to the highway since it was the only way across for miles. From what they knew the bridge was long and the crossing would leave them exposed for more time than any of them were comfortable with. Todd had already said he would cross last since he was the slowest. Crossing the bridge wasn't quite half way to their goal, but it felt like it all the same. It was certainly a milestone in the journey for all of them. A tangible landmark, the first place they knew to meet if they all got separated. Amanda helped Todd to his feet and the little group pushed on.

Chapter 26

I was fairly young when the President was re-elected to his second term. I didn't really understand everything that was going on, but I could tell the world was changing. My parents were worried, and disappointed in how things turned out. I remember the news talking about more people without jobs and a lot of anger directed at the government. Some people thought things would calm down after the election but they were wrong. I would find out later, when I was more able to understand, that this is when the rumblings of secession started as well. Several states were already sharing ideas about how to form a Union more perfect than the one before. I guess no one thought it would actually happen at the time.

-Excerpt from the Journal of John Evermann

John ran as fast as he dared in the dark. His pants and boots were soaked from the wet grass, mud, and crossing the streams that fed Mark Twain Lake. He was cold, and tired, but he knew his time was short if he was going to catch the others. He had faith that they would move on at dawn, with or without any stragglers, but a part of him hoped they would wait just long enough. He knew it was a selfish thought, but he couldn't help it. Instead of letting the thought wear on him he used it to push himself. He prayed that he wouldn't fall in the dark, and prayed that the others were safe. He prayed that no matter what happened to him, his family would reach freedom and that his children would grow up in a world where they had a chance to be something. He wanted, with all his heart, to be there with them and that thought, more than anything else, kept him on his feet and running.

He could see the lake to his left, and the moon reflected on the water, but the light wasn't enough. He had to keep his eyes on the ground, watching for darker shadows in the dark that would tell him there was a ditch or hole ahead. That didn't mean he missed all of them. Several times he stumbled or fell, stepping on empty air when he expected solid ground. Each time he managed to fall to the side and land on his shoulder or back. He couldn't afford to take the weight on his ankles or knees and hurt himself.

As he ran John kept going over their hopes for Texas. Their kids would go to a school that actually taught them to think for themselves. He could find a job, any job he wanted and had the skill to do, or learn a new skill. He could earn money to take care of his family with his own sweat and blood. He would be able to look at his family, and all they had, and know pride for the first time. Pride in doing something, working hard, and seeing the fruits of those labors enjoyed by those he loved. They could eat what they wanted, not rations issued by the Sustenance Department. They could watch, read, learn, and speak what they wanted. They could worship openly without having to listen at basement windows for federal police. The thought of it all was overwhelming.

He didn't know if he, or Amanda, would make it to see Texas. He did pray that his kids would though. He prayed that everyone's kids would make it, especially Steve's. His friend died for all of this and it would be for nothing if those kids didn't see freedom for it. John realized too late that his wandering thoughts had distracted him from the task at hand. The ground dropped out from under him suddenly and he was tumbling down a muddy embankment. It all happened so suddenly he didn't have time to stop his fall, or turn it into a less punishing roll. Something in his hip pulled, his shoulder struck a rock painfully, and finally his head slammed against a log right before everything went black.

* * *

Amanda and the others reached the bridge without incident. The highway was dark and empty as far as they could see. They watched the open stretch of road for several minutes, but didn't see any headlights or hear the sounds of a vehicle in the distance. She turned to the little group after she was satisfied.

"One at a time, and be quick about it."

She handed the small flashlight she had to the first to cross. "When you get to the end, click it on twice and leave it for the next, on the south side of the road. Then get into the tree line and wait."

The man nodded and headed for the bridge. They still had a couple of hours before daylight but they all felt like the hounds were still at their backs. Once the first of their group was on the highway Amanda turned to Todd.

"Are you sure about this? I can go last to make sure you get across safely."

"No," Todd said, "I'm the slowest. If someone else gets caught because I held up the line I'd never forgive myself."

She nodded and gripped his shoulder, not liking it at all but knowing he was right. She looked toward the bridge just in time to see a tiny light blink twice in the distance. She tapped the second man who nodded and started for the highway at a jog. They all wanted to sprint across like they were being chased by the devil himself, but it was too dark to do that safely. With only one light in their group and the moon behind the clouds for the moment they had to play it safe. Amanda wished the moon was out again to make the crossing safer, but she was also thankful it wasn't. She felt like God was watching over them, knowing it was better they be harder to spot on the open bridge than being able to see where they were running. She was just glad they could all see well enough in the dark to not jog off the side of the bridge.

Amanda looked back the way they had come. She knew it was too early for John to be catching up to them, but she held out hope that he wasn't far behind. Todd followed her gaze and sat in silent vigil with her for a few moments.

"He'll be fine," Todd finally broke the silence.

"I know," but she didn't. She couldn't keep the worry out of her voice.

"He's smart, Amanda. He learned a lot from Benny before we left. Besides," Todd pointed to the dark sky, "We have Him on our side and they don't."

She nodded and forced a smile. Todd could barely see it in the dark and patted her shoulder to comfort her. She knew in her heart that Todd was right. She had faith that John would be fine. She just wished he was there with them. It was hard enough worrying about her kids. Worrying about John too was agony. Her thoughts were broken when Todd squeezed her shoulder.

"Amanda," he said softly, nodding toward the bridge.

She turned in time to see the second flash from the other end of the it. It was her turn to go. She turned to look up the highway, back toward the east. The roadway was still devoid of lights and there were no sounds except for the animals in the night.

"I'll be quick," she said as he helped her to her feet. She shook her head and smiled a little. Todd was the one that was hurt, yet he was still making sure she didn't slip in the wet grass.

"Just be careful," he said. She nodded and climbed the embankment to the highway.

Once she felt the hard road beneath her feet she set out at a jog. She could barely see the bridge ahead. It was long and flat, with no supports over the top. She knew the sides had a short, concrete railing but she could only see the slightest hint of them in the dark. She was able to make out the light posts, painted gray and showing up as lighter objects in the dark. Those posts had once lit the bridge but with the national curfew there was no need to waste money lighting roadways at night so the bulbs had been allowed to burn out without replacement. She kept herself as close to the middle as she could guess and jogged toward the end of the bridge. She was glad it was straight, and prayed that there were no large cracks or breaks in the pavement to trip her up.

Amanda reached the other end of the bridge faster than she expected. She felt along the end of the concrete railing and found the small metal cylinder that had been their only means of communication across the bridge. She looked up the highway for a moment, and listened intently, but the road still seemed to be clear so she gave Todd the signal to move. She stepped back off the road and carefully made her way down the embankment to the tree line where the others were waiting. They all crouched in the undergrowth watching the bridge.

They couldn't see Todd, or much of the bridge other than the large blocky shape in the night, but they watched anyway. After a minute of waiting breathlessly a flash of light from the north east caught their eyes. Amanda stood up.

"John?" She said softly, having only seen the light briefly before it disappeared.

She thought it had been a flashlight in the woods back across the bridge. A moment later the light reappeared and became two as a vehicle came around a stand of trees to the east. The headlights were moving toward the bridge at an alarming pace. Only federal agents would be out after curfew, and driving like that. The highway ran straight for some distance and they would be able to watch the car all the way to the bridge.

"Dear God," Amanda gasped. She moved toward the bridge with the flashlight still in her hand. She didn't know what she intended to do or how she would warn Todd, but the other two stopped her before she could get too far out of the trees.

"Amanda," one of the men whispered harshly. "Think about this. If you go up there you put everyone at risk. Todd wouldn't want you to do that for him."

The men had a hold of her arms firmly. She knew he was right, and even if she wanted to go anyway they wouldn't let her. She nodded and relaxed. They all settled back into a crouch, watching the bridge and oncoming lights. Each of them whispered encouragement to their friend, not caring that he couldn't hear them.

"Dear God, don't let him fall. Help him make it off the bridge unseen," Amanda prayed quietly.

She knew if Todd didn't make it off the bridge before the vehicle made it around the last bend in the road they were all in danger.

For his part Todd was racing across the bridge as fast as his injured leg would allow. When he was just a few yards across something had made him look back along the highway. He caught the flash of headlights along the road in the distance, but he knew they wouldn't be distant for long. He gritted his teeth and ran faster. He tried to ignore the pain in his leg while he silently prayed that he didn't catch his foot on the broken pavement or stumble too far to the side and fall off the bridge in the dark.

In the tree line below Amanda thought she heard Todd cry out in pain. She knew he must be running now, despite his injury. The headlights were getting closer and she knew it wouldn't be long before the vehicle was close enough for those inside to see what was on the bridge. Her own muscles tensed in sympathy for Todd, her body unconsciously trying to send energy to her friend. She knew the pain must be excruciating for him. She saw the headlights jump as the vehicle hit a bump in the road she knew was right before the bridge, some imperfection in the pavement where the road had buckled. They all tensed.

They waited without breath as a dark truck sped past on the highway. The vehicle didn't hesitate, or even stop and before long the red tail lights were specks in the distance. Amanda looked at the others, confusion and worry on her face.

"Where is he?" She asked as they all climbed the embankment to the road.

Once they were on the pavement Amanda flicked on the flashlight and shined the beam over the bridge. It was empty. They had little time to wonder what had happened to Todd before they heard a groan and the sounds of someone moving on the other side of the road. They rushed to the opposite shoulder, shining the light over the grassy embankment that mirrored their own hiding spot. Todd's muddy face looked up at them.

"Thank God," Amanda said as they moved to help him up out of the wet grass.

"How did you wind up over here?" One of the men asked.

"The last time I looked back I must have veered off to the right. He was too close so I jumped down the embankment just as I reached the end of the bridge,"

"Well it worked," Amanda said. "He didn't even slow down."

Todd nodded, catching his breath while the other two men held him up between them.

"How's your leg?" Amanda asked.

Todd lifted his foot and rotated his ankle a little, then put his weight on it.

"Well enough."

"Good, we should get moving. We all need some rest before morning. If I'm remembering the map right the house is just up the road a little ways," Amanda pointed up the highway, in the direction the vehicle had gone. They all waited as Todd took a couple of tentative steps to make sure he wouldn't need help. He only limped slightly and nodded, gesturing for them all to move on.

Amanda was the last to leave the spot, looking back one more time. When the others were out of earshot she whispered, "Hurry up John."

Chapter 27

I remember a newspaper article some years ago that has stuck with me since I read it. It was one of those signs that our society had dived right off the cliff of sanity. A man killed his entire family in their sleep, then himself. Some part of him just broke one night and he ended everything with a pipe wrench. It was a terrible event, but it didn't end there. After they found his body in the basement they found his suicide note. The man blamed his boss for harassing him at work and the baker for cheating him on his bread ration. He said he couldn't watch his family starve anymore. Would you believe the Feds arrested his boss and the baker? They said that the family would be alive today if those two hadn't driven the man to murder. I believe both of them went to prison as accessories. I remember my father talking about individual responsibility more than once. He said that you only have yourself to blame for your mistakes. I guess we lost that somewhere along the way.

-Excerpt from the Journal of John Evermann

Amanda sat in the middle of the little living room of the house the refugees were hiding in. She hadn't slept at all after making sure Todd and the others were settled in. From time to time she looked around at her friends and neighbors sleeping around her. Some found blankets in the house and had given them to the oldest members of their group to share. Most were sleeping in their coats with their bags held close or under their heads for pillows. So many people clutching at the remnants of their lives and running toward the hope of something better. Mostly she stared at the window near the front door. Her treasures were not near enough to clutch to her chest. John was still out there in the woods somewhere, or in the hands of the Feds. Her children were in a van somewhere between her and Texas, and she could only pray they made it safely.

She'd stared at the window through the night, hoping that John would make it in time. She wasn't sure if she was strong enough to do what needed to be done, but she would do it. Her last promise to John had been to get as many of their friends to Texas as she could and for her to get to their children. She noticed the sky outside was gray instead of black and wondered how long it had been so. She didn't remember the light changing, but the sun was rising and it was time to get the group moving. Some began to stir, either already awake or so used to the sleep schedule they awoke on their own. Others were nudged into wakefulness by Amanda.

Everyone was packing their blankets back into their bags and securing anything they had removed during the night. Several cast looks at Amanda, or looked around the group as if trying to spot someone. Todd crouched close and helped Amanda fold her blanket.

"He'll catch up," Todd said softly, knowing what had been on her mind all night.

She nodded, trying to look optimistic, "I know."

*   *   *

John was exhausted by the time the sky started to lighten. He was sore and bruised from falling and his clothes were heavy with mud and moisture. He hadn't slept at all, having run all night along the bank of the lake. His hazardous run in the dark had been a lucky one. Despite all of his falls he had not broken or twisted anything. He was sure someone was watching out for him and he was grateful. More than once he whispered a thankful prayer after a fall that didn't kill him, or barely dodging a tree that might have knocked him senseless.

He finally stumbled out of the woods near the bridge everyone crossed the night before. The sun was nearly over the trees in the east, and he knew his friends should already be on the road. Tired as he was he put his head down and pushed himself into a steady jog, gritting his teeth at the pain in his legs. His side ached but he kept going, knowing his only chance of catching up was to not stop. The house was a short distance up the road from the bridge and in the trees on the south side of the highway. He hoped that they didn't leave too early and he might catch them soon.

The pavement stretched ahead of him, seeming to go on forever. He couldn't help but imagine that his whole life would be like that. In fact, he hoped his life would be. He hoped that he would always be moving forward, looking to a horizon that held a mysterious future. His previous life had just been the same day over and over. He always knew where he would go, what he would be doing, and that he would do it all over again the next day. Where his past seemed to be one long, gray day, his future was slowly taking on all the color he could imagine. Even their last few days on the road, as hard as they had been, were far better than the life he left behind. He just hoped everyone else felt that way. He hoped Steve had felt that way before he died on this journey.

John crossed the bridge as fast as he could, disliking the exposure of the raised pavement. If anyone were on the highway, or happened to fly over in a search plane, he would be spotted easily enough. The burning need to reach his friends overrode his instinct to stay hidden however. He was across the bridge in no time at all and veered off the highway toward the trees on the south side. He could see, in his mind, the map of the area they had all studied and knew where the house was in relation to the road. He could make a straight line through the trees and get there faster than going all the way down to the access road.

Stepping off the road at the speed he was running proved to be a mistake. John misjudged the steepness of the embankment on the side of the highway and his foot met the ground a lot later than he expected. His knee collapsed under the weight of his body and he pitched forward down the hill. He rolled and bounced the short distance, the side of his face connecting with something hard before coming to rest in the wet ditch at the bottom.

*   *   *

Amanda was packed and ready, waiting outside the house for the rest of the group. It was becoming increasingly difficult to get everyone up and moving in the mornings, especially that one. After the harrowing flight from the feds the day before, and the hours running through the woods, everyone was exhausted. She was anxious to get moving, but a small part of her was thankful for the delay. She felt like every moment they waited increased her chances of seeing John again. She had no idea if he had made it, or if he was captured, but she had faith that he was free and on his way to the house. She'd prayed most of the sleepless night and was confident that he was safe. She just didn't know how far behind he was.

While they waited Todd and a couple others were going over a map of Missouri, planning the next leg of their journey. She listened idly as they talked about the route south toward a little town called Moberly. They were discussing the possibility of having to go around it. From there they would follow an old state highway south. They also talked about the next river crossing that would come during the second day out from where they were. The only place to cross on their route was at a town marked Boonville. It would be a tricky crossing for so many people but until they saw the bridge, and town, they wouldn't be able to plan much in detail.

While Amanda listened she alternated between watching the house where the last few people were getting ready and looking back toward the highway for any sign of John. When the last person exited the little house everyone started walking toward the highway. The group would follow it, staying in the trees as much as they could, until they reached Moberly which was close to a days walk west. Amanda got everyone organized and reminded them to stick together and stay out of sight of the road. She took one last look back to the east and froze. A small gasp escaped her lips.

Those close enough to hear her turned at the sound and a moment of excited panic brought everyone to a halt. They all watched as a lone figure exited the tree-line to the east. He was limping and covered in mud and grass, making him unrecognizable. Some of the group whispered that it was one of the feds and they should run before more showed up. Others were filled with hope that it might be John.

Amanda had no such doubts and didn't need to see the figure with her eyes to know who it was. The set of his broad shoulders, the way he held himself in reserved confidence, and the tired but relieved smile that split the muddy face was all she needed.

"John," she whispered before running toward him.

The single word poured out all the stress and anguish she had been feeling for days. With that release it was as if her entire body had been a coiled spring waiting for someone to release it. She flew into his arms, heedless of the mud that covered him. He braced himself as he wrapped his arms around her to keep his twisted leg from collapsing and accepting her hard kisses on his bruised face. She felt as if she had come home after an eternity lost in the night and realized that was truer now than ever before. Along with their children, John was home, especially since they were all a people with no place to call their own. She sighed and closed her eyes, taking a moment to feel everything she had expected to never feel again until the moment she saw him. She didn't want to let go, but knew she would have to.

"We should move," he said softly after a time, releasing Amanda from his embrace. He looked around at the gathered friends, all smiling and excited.

"We need to get moving," he said more loudly.

"John, you're hurt. We can rest here another day," Amanda said. A few others nodded, but most still looked scared at the prospect of being caught.

"I'll manage. We can't wait any longer," he was firm, and Amanda knew he would not stop now for just himself. She put her shoulder under his arm, picked up her pack, and the two of them led the group west toward Moberly.

Chapter 28

There is a quote from the Declaration of Independence that I've always loved. "All experience has shown, that mankind are more disposed to suffer, while evils are sufferable, than to right themselves by abolishing the forms to which they are accustomed." That basically means we become comfortable and don't like to rock the boat lightly. We will tolerate quite a lot of injustice before we do anything about it. In most cases this is a good thing, a survival instinct. In other cases it is what has allowed so many populations, over the course of human history, to become slaves.
-*Excerpt from the journal of John Evermann*

Lieutenant Casey drove into Moberly late in the morning after the failed attempt to capture the fugitives. It had once been a decently sized Midwestern town, but many of the residents had been relocated to federal farms, leaving only the factory workers and those who ran the federal stores. It was the same story in just about every small town across the country, people were relocated, workers consolidated, and national businesses merged. Casey suspected that in another generation or two all of these towns would be empty. Casey pulled the SUV over and took in the scene for a few minutes while he considered his next move.

Moberly still had just enough activity to make it appear to be a bustling town. People were going about their daily work, cutting lawns around occupied houses, cleaning up trash and fallen leaves, and all the general work that one would expect to find early in the day in any town in the country. Casey looked on the scene, and the order of it all gave him a sense of comfort. Everyone moved with a single-minded purpose. No one stood and conversed on the streets. No one called greetings from yard to yard, or between people passing on the sidewalks. Every occupied house and business had the new American flag flying out front, or on a pole overhead. There were few cars and most of the ones that were moving around the town belonged to government officials.

Every town in the country seemed to have more government officials than average citizens. Business and residential inspectors, federal police, and compliance officers seemed to be needed for just about everything that went on in any little town. Casey saw a few children at play and marveled at the one constant in the world. No matter how things were, how good or bad, or how much their parents were affected by events around them, children always seemed to find the drive to play. Maybe that was why they always seemed to be referred to as a sign of hope for the future.

Casey decided his first stop should be the federal law enforcement office in Moberly. He needed to check in and brief local officers of what was coming their way. He expected them to have already heard about the large group of fugitives moving west, but news wasn't always up to date when the government media was involved. Not that Casey was surprised. If the general public knew about how far the fugitives had gotten it might inspire others to try the same thing. The government couldn't afford a mass exodus of citizens.

The drive through town was short and uneventful. The federal police office was just like every other in the country. It was a short, square, featureless building with a few small windows across the front and double glass doors in the middle of the wall facing the street. Casey knew the back of the building would have garage access, a loading dock and a heavy steel door. He entered the front doors that opened into a simple lobby with a reception desk and a few chairs for waiting. The air had a sterile smell and was cooled to the uniform seventy-five degrees. Even a country focused on the environment wouldn't give up every luxury.

"I need to see the officer on duty," Casey said to the agent behind the desk, the only other person in the lobby. The lieutenant set his credentials on the desk as he spoke.

"In his office, first door on the right," the receptionist thumbed down the hall after looking at Casey's ID.

Casey walked down the hall toward the back of the building and knocked on the door marked 'duty officer', and entered without waiting for a reply. An overweight man, a sergeant by the insignia on his uniform, shot to his feet the moment he recognized the higher ranking officer. A half-eaten sandwich lay on the desk next to a cup of coffee.

"Lieutenant, what can I do for you?" The sergeant asked, obviously surprised. He glanced at the door nervously like he expected more people to come in.

"Relax sergeant, I'm alone. This isn't an inspection," Casey said, sitting down in the only other chair in the room.

The other officer noticeably relaxed and took his seat again. Once he knew he wasn't going to be audited he lost the pretense of formality. He offered Casey a cup of coffee but the lieutenant waved it off.

"We have a problem, sergeant. I suppose you've seen the news?" Casey asked.

"The fugitives? Yah, what little the fed news has made public," the sergeant said.

"Central hasn't sent more than that?" Casey asked. He should be surprised but he wasn't. The sergeant shook his head.

"Well, consider this your briefing. What I am about to tell you is not for public consumption," Casey said. The sergeant nodded and leaned forward, eager for some real news. Casey filled him in about the events since the exodus from Stewart. He left out information the officer didn't need, especially the setbacks. He made sure the sergeant had no doubts that a large group of people were headed toward Moberly and Casey was going to need help stopping them.

"I don't have a lot of man power here lieutenant. We'll do what we can of course but you're talking about apprehending quite a few people," the sergeant said.

"Could we enlist some of the citizens to help?" Casey asked.

"Maybe," the sergeant seemed to shift uncomfortably, "I'll see what I can do on that front."

Casey thought it was odd behavior, but he tucked the thought away for another day. He simply nodded and stood up, determined to have a look around the town and devise a plan to stop the fugitives with only a handful of questionable assistants.

"I'm going to get the lay of the land. It'll be hours before they get this far, but I believe they'll come through here," Casey said.

The sergeant stood as Casey turned to leave.

"Do you want someone to ride with you?" The sergeant asked, seeming nervous again.

"No, I can find my way around on my own," Casey said. He was growing more curious about what had the sergeant so on edge.

Casey wasn't sure if it was his rising paranoia or the sergeant's strange behavior but when he exited the building he looked upon Moberly with different eyes. There was a man and a woman walking on the other side of the street, watching him intently. Was it just curiosity or something more sinister? The shop tender on the corner seemed intent on sweeping the same spot more than seemed necessary, was he thinking something untoward?

He also noticed it was quiet. Towns tended to be quieter than people said they were in the past. There were far fewer cars and people out on the streets. Everyone had somewhere to be and something to do which contributed to less noise pollution. He wasn't sure if it was his imagination but something felt off. He had heard rumors that the closer to the border you went the stranger the people were. Maybe it wasn't just a rumor.

He decided he would drive the perimeter of the town first to spot any potential refuges for the fugitives. He estimated, if they came this way, it would be some time during the night and they might look for a place to hideout until morning.

The outskirts of Moberly were much like all the other small towns in the country. As people were relocated, those left behind were moved closer to the town's center. It was all about safety and efficiency, but also to curb people's sense of ownership over one property or another. It was hard to feel like a house was yours if you knew it could be taken away at any moment. The result, however, were blocks of abandoned houses and businesses that were left to the ravages of nature. In days past these derelicts would be havens for homeless or delinquents, but since everyone was given what they needed that problem was all but solved.

Casey realized that there were far too many places for the fugitives to hide. The best opportunity would be to catch them before they reached the town, but he would need a good plan to stop them with so little help. He knew that if they came through Moberly it would be from the north east so he decided to look there for a place to lay an ambush that might surprise the fugitives enough to capture them.

The drive across Moberly did nothing to curb his uneasiness about the strange town. He was almost relieved to reach the north east end where empty windows, like the vacant eyes of corpses were all that he could see. He drove through the neighborhoods of overgrown lawns and rundown houses, thinking how lonely the homes looked. He knew it was a strange thought but he couldn't help it. There was something almost sad about the emptiness of yards that used to be filled with playing children and homes now devoid of loving families. At least, Casey thought, that part of town was normal.

When he reached the end of the neighborhoods something caught his eye. Set back from the old farm road that headed east from the town was a large, red-brick building. It was about a quarter mile from the east edge of town and surrounded by overgrown fields. It struck Casey as the perfect place for a large group of people to hide for a night. He turned the SUV onto the farm road to investigate the building. The broken pavement rumbled under the vehicle's tires and

Casey put both hands on the wheel after a particularly deep pothole caused the SUV to jerk wildly.

Pulling onto the old gravel drive in front of the building Casey could see the faded paint on a cracked sign marking the place as an antique mall. He remembered them from his youth, places where people sold heirlooms, antiques, and junk from their past. They were a bit like an indoor, year-round yard sale. With the nationalization of the economy these places became obsolete and they were simply abandoned as their previous owners were assigned to jobs that were actually needed. Most of these old places were looted before people came to realize there was no point in it.

The Lieutenant got out of the SUV and glanced around the property. Once he was closer he realized how perfect it would be for the fugitives. With the tall grass all around and the large stand of trees on the north side of the property a large group of people could move through without anyone seeing them. They could walk right into the broken front doors and sleep comfortably with no one the wiser. If they rose before the sun and moved on, the town of Moberly wouldn't even know they had played host to the most wanted people in the country.

Casey walked in through the broken doors and was surprised to find there had been no looting in the building. It looked much like the one from his childhood memory. He found himself standing at the beginning of a maze of cubicle-like booths filled with a plethora of artifacts from the past. The dust was thick, as were the cobwebs. The sun shining through the broken windows created a swirl of dancing motes as his passage disturbed the dust. Most things that had been made of fabric and paper did not stand up to the elements with no one to care for them. Animals had clearly used the building, and recently, as he stepped over the leavings of raccoons and dogs.

Despite the mess and the passage of time Casey could still catch the faint whiff of smells that reminded him of his last visit to a place like this. Oil used to clean a family's prized dining table, and musty old paper from a precious collection of books. He walked down a nearby aisle and smelled a hint of perfume that had permeated a bench that went with an antique dressing table and further along a booth from a house where incense must have been burned every day. He looked at the remnants of the past, and his own childhood returned to him with familiar sights and smells.

All around him were examples of what America used to be. Each booth like a collage of homes and the lives they had held, each so different but all of them so much the same. He touched a porcelain tea service, imagining how proud the family must have been to have a full set. Next to that was a wooden humidor and whiskey decanter. Opening the wooden box he could smell the old cedar mixed with tobacco, more items someone had worked hard to afford. They reminded him of his grandparents, of how his grandfather would take a thick cigar out to the porch and sit in the rocker with a glass of amber alcohol while his grandmother would make tea. His mother and grandmother would sit on a couch with floral print and watch the kids play while his father and grandfather would talk and smoke outside.

They were all just things, and people were taught that to cherish things was wrong. Casey understood though, these were more than just things to the people that had them. These things represented people's dreams and goals. Each person's dreams were different, each goal as varied as the people that had them. It was misguided, but understandable, to value one's worth by things acquired. Those ideas were outdated in Casey's America, an America where everyone's goals were the same, the success of the whole, not the individual.

Casey closed the box and shook his head. He just couldn't understand why anyone would cling to these old ideas. He looked around and felt a little sad that he had to leave, but he knew this would be the perfect place to wait for the fugitives. He had a lot of work to do to prepare. On his way out he saw a small metal toy car on a shelf. It was a bright red sports car, the type that many children had collected when he was younger. He picked up the car and wiped the dust off. It was the very same car he'd had in his own collection as a child. Some impulse he didn't understand made him slip the car into his pocked on the way out the door.

Chapter 29

America has fought many wars over the years. Wars in other countries, wars on drugs and crime, war on poverty and hunger. Some had lasting, positive effects like freeing people from oppression or defending countries against savage aggressors. Some were pointless and costly, like the war on drugs. Others served a purpose other than what it seemed to be, like the war on poverty. We learned that you can't win a war against a disease unless treatment is your weapon, and a war against poverty was really only a means to make some people look good for votes. The most insidious war this country fought was not even acknowledged by one side of the fight.

For many years secular groups fought to purge religion from all public life, using words that are not even in the constitution to justify their argument. "Separation of Church and State" was written by a man who served in a Congress that still had religious services to open each new session of the House. The secularists claimed that they only wanted freedom from religion, but it soon became a fight to tear down every public display of faith whether it be on government property or not.

No one can say when certain government powers realized that religion was one of the things keeping them from taking full power, but it was clear that the current government realized it quickly enough. Shortly after the President took emergency powers, places of worship, holy texts, and the practice of religion were all outlawed. One people, with a shared goal, and shared responsibility had no need for individual faith so they said.

-Excerpt from the Journal of John Evermann

The night of the refugees' mad flight from the federal agents Benny and Sarah looked out from the stand of trees over a blasted landscape. The demilitarized zone that separated the Republic of Texas and America was a swath of bare ground about a mile wide, devoid of anything resembling life. The American side was marked by a high fence that ran North and South, blocking their path. A mile away, in the moonlit darkness would be the fence on the Texas side. While the side they were on was only lightly patrolled and guarded, they knew they would still have to be careful with their timing. They had quite a few children that they would have to herd quickly through a breach they would have to make themselves. Then they would have to cross a mile of open ground without being seen. They would have to leave the Van. It would be impossible to conceal and trying to drive it through the fence would only trigger defenses on both sides.

The semblance of peace between Texas and America had already lasted for a few years, with little interest of returning to the fight from either side. The war itself had been quick and violent but with no significant results and, thankfully, no major damage too far into either territory. There had been a few places where American forces broke through into Texas but for the most part the Texan army kept the Americans out. The Texans only pushed as far into America as was needed to interrupt the war effort. Texas had no desire to conquer land or absorb territory, just to keep American forces at bay. In the end the American government simply didn't have the resources for a sustained conflict, and Texas was more than happy to put up a fence and maintain their own land. America followed suit and did something it had never done in the past, build a secure fence all along its border with a foreign country. Luckily for the refugees looking down at that fence the feds didn't have the manpower to watch all of it all the time.

"Forty-five minutes," Sarah said as they both watched a military patrol vehicle drive along the road that bordered the fence. She put the old watch back into her pocket and Benny nodded.

"Let's get the kids, that truck should be out of sight by the time we get back," Benny said.

He was nervous about the next part. Some of the children were very young and forty-five minutes wasn't a lot of time to wrangle them all through the fence and far enough across the open ground to avoid detection. The few adults in the group were older and not as healthy as those who stayed back with John. All it would take is one mishap and it would be all over for them.

They got to the van and herded the kids out into the night. The older ones helped the younger, some having to be carried. Benny grabbed the old wire cutters and metal wire he had picked up in an abandoned barn a few miles back.

"All right, everyone listen," Sarah said. She knelt down so she could speak to the children on their level.

"I need everyone to stay close and stay quiet. This is the most important part of our mission." Soon after leaving the group she had told the children they were on a secret mission to help their parents. It had the desired effect of keeping them calm and focused instead of thinking about how much they missed their families.

"I need to use the bathroom," a little red-haired girl said, her hand high in the air.

"Be quick Gail," Sarah said, nodding to the trees. The girl rushed off.

"We have to hurry," Benny said urgently.

"Go, we'll be right behind," Sarah said.

"OK kiddos, it's time for us to be sneaky," Benny said, gesturing for the kids to follow.

They all lined up behind the big man like little soldiers on parade. Most were grinning ear to ear like it was some kind of big adventure. Benny envied them their youthful innocence.

They reached the edge of the trees and Benny signaled for them all to wait there and keep quiet. He crossed the gravel road alone with wire cutters and wire in hand. He took one last look up and down the fence line but only saw outpost lights in the distance. He thanked God for the complacency the Feds had fallen into.

Benny started at the bottom of the chain link fence and pressed the old wire cutters against the galvanized link. They were not bolt cutters like Benny would have preferred but he figured they would do the job with enough effort. Even with all his strength however, it was a slow process. The dull, rusty blades on the cutters made it necessary to use all the force he could muster and that made him worry that he might damage them before he was through. He moved slowly up the fence, praying he would have the time to make an opening large enough for them to get through.

"How's it going?" Sarah asked, crouching down next to Benny after getting Gail back to the group.

"Slow, what's our time?"

Sarah pulled the old watch out of her pocket and checked it.

"Thirty minutes since the truck passed," she reported.

"Start getting them lined up, this'll be close," Benny continued cutting as he spoke.

Sarah called the children over and started lining them up near the hole in the fence. She could see that it was already large enough for her and the others but it would still be a tight squeeze for the large man. She looked up and down the road while he worked.

"Benny," she said. Her quiet voice was a little shaky, "I see head lights."

Benny looked up from his work and followed her gaze. In the distance two small points of light were coming along the road. They weren't close enough to illuminate the group but it wouldn't be long. He made a quick decision, dropping the cutters he held open the hole in the fence.

"Miss Sarah, I left Sonny in the van," a little girl said from the back of the line.

"What do you mean Kayla? Who's Sonny?" Sarah asked.

"My bear, he's not here. I need him," The little girl started to cry and Sarah moved to her.

"Hush now child, we can't go back. Sonny wants you to be brave, we have to keep going," Sarah soothed the child.

Kayla seemed to calm down as Sarah talked to her quietly. The woman finally convinced the child that they could not go back, and that they would find a new bear when they got to Texas.

"Quickly now kiddos," Benny said, pulling the first child toward the gap in the fence. "I want you all to go through here and run as fast as you can. Don't stop until you reach the other side."

The children started filing through and ran once they were on the other side. Once the last person was through Benny pulled Sarah toward the fence.

"You need to hurry, I can help make the hole larger," Sarah said.

"No time Sarah, you need to catch up to the kids and get them as far from the fence as you can," Benny said.

"What about you?"

"I'll make sure they don't see the hole tonight. You'll need all the time I can give you," Benny said, helping the stunned woman crawl through the gap in the fence. She didn't resist, as much as she wanted to. On the other side she stood up and grabbed the links.

"Benny, you need to get through here. I need your help," she pleaded with the bearded man.

"You're running out of time, Sarah, those kids need you," Benny was already using the wire to close the hole in the fence.

"Benny, we're so close," she tried one more time.

The man just shook his head, passing her the cutters.

"Time to go Sarah, get those kids home," Benny said.

Sarah gave the large man one last look, her heart in her eyes. He wouldn't look back at her, knowing he had to steel himself if he was going to pull off the ruse to come. Those guards would see him soon and he had to make sure they didn't notice the damage to the fence. He sighed in relief when he heard her footsteps rushing away. He finished wiring the hole closed and stood up. Just as he turned to look up the road the headlights of the patrol truck fell on him. He was relieved to see the spotlight was also turned in his direction and not out across the DMZ.

"Hold it right there," an amplified voice called from the truck.

Benny stepped away from the fence with his hands on his head. The passenger door opened and a soldier in forest camouflage fatigues stepped out, armed with an assault rifle. The soldier slowly approached.

"What are you doing out here citizen?" The soldier asked when he got close.

"My car broke down. Looking for a gas station," Benny said. He gestured as he talked, pointing off into the woods.

The soldier turned and looked where he pointed and Benny bolted. He hoped he could lead the men away long enough to give Sarah and the kids more time. He hadn't counted on the soldier's quick thinking. Benny was fairly sure they wouldn't shoot him, but one was carrying a taser and didn't hesitate to use it.

Chapter 30

I was very young when my grandmother died. She was special to all of us but at that time I felt like it hurt me worse. I imagine everyone feels that way when they lose someone special. She was always in my memories, with a smile and a laugh, looking at her grandkids like they were the most important people in the world. That's how we felt when we visited her. I remember being angry when she passed. I was angry about all the years that would never be, all the things in my life she would miss, and all the things we would no longer share. I directed all of that anger at God, thinking that if He was so good why did he take her from us. I imagine it was difficult for my father, but he set aside his grief to try and explain something as vague as God's plan to an angry little boy. In the end he said that life would always be hard, there would always be obstacles in the way or things that will hurt us, but we must have faith. It's hard to trust someone you don't know, someone you can't see or hear, but we have to trust. When God holds out his hand we must take it and trust that He knows what He is doing.

-Excerpt from the Journal of John Evermann

John limped along with the group, headed west through the trees parallel to the highway. Several times someone in the group suggested they stop so he could rest, but he refused to slow down everyone else for his sake. Amanda only asked once, but even then she knew he would refuse. After that she just kept close, offering her hand or shoulder when he seemed to need it. After Steve's death, and the close calls of the last couple of days, John wasn't going to risk any more of his friends by delaying any longer than they had to.

Recalling the map in his head John hoped they could make it to Moberly before dark. Amanda had warned him about the SUV that passed them and he had a good idea who was driving it. He prayed that Casey would wait there for them so they could skirt the town and get ahead of him again. He knew they had enough supplies so stopping in the next town wouldn't be necessary. He was acutely aware of how lucky they were with their last encounter with the federal agents and didn't want to press that luck anytime soon.

Before stopping for lunch they had to cross to the North side of Highway 24 to avoid the small town of Paris. There wasn't much left in the town but they could still see a few signs of its residents. When they stopped for lunch the groups moved deeper into the trees to reduce the risk of being seen by a passing car. They were getting good at settling down quickly, finding space under trees, or in shadows, so they wouldn't be seen from the air. Everyone knew the routine, silence and efficiency. Eat what they needed, as fast as they could, with no noise. Leaving no trace was crucial so there were always two or three people assigned to sweep the area for missed garbage and to try and disguise any sign they had stopped there.

After the short break they were on the move again, leaving the concealing stand of trees near an abandoned farmhouse. A few people were selected to walk between the groups and the Highway. Their job was to listen and watch for cars on the road. If any were detected they would signal and the entire group would crouch in the tall grass or behind trees. So far they had seen very few vehicles since leaving Illinois. After a little over an hour they came within sight of a town straddling the Highway.

"Madison," one of the spotters reported after seeing a sign.

"Looks like we'll have to go around. North or South, it doesn't look like it matters," John said.

They decided not to cross the highway and continued around the north side of Madison. John hoped the overgrown fields and stands of trees would conceal them from anyone that might be looking in that direction.

Moving through the fields on the north side of town the group was spread out to help avoid detection. John and Amanda were in the lead. John's limp had worsened but his ankle was numb by then. He still felt twinges from time to time but mostly it was a dull ache. They could tell they were getting close to one of the north bound country roads so they slowed down to let the others catch up. John signaled them to wait there and the hand motion was passed down the line. He approached the road on his own.

John walked out of the field slowly, just far enough to see both ways along the road. He spent several seconds watching and waiting. He couldn't see anything moving in either direction so he approached the pavement. When he reached the old, broken asphalt something did move. Under the shade of a tree a hundred yards south of him someone stood up. John thought the person was looking in his direction, but was sure of it when the figure waved. He couldn't run with his ankle and didn't want to lead the stranger to the others so he stayed where he was while the stranger walked toward him.

"Just passing through?" The stranger asked with a knowing smile when he got close enough to be heard. John could tell he was just a kid, no more than eighteen or nineteen years old.

"Yah, car broke down," John lied. He never liked having to lie but sometimes it was the only way to protect others.

"You're John right?" The boy asked.

John was taken aback by the question. He looked around, expecting federal agents to come pouring out of the fields any second. He had nowhere to go and he knew he was in no shape to run. The boy recognized his discomfort immediately.

"Relax, I'm not with the feds. We've been hearing about you all on the radio," the boy said.

"The radio? I didn't expect the feds to make it public," John didn't see the need for anymore lies.

"Not the federal stations, they never tell the truth. We built one that picks up broadcasts out of Texas. You're famous John," the boy said. Now John understood the knowing smile and star struck look in the boy's eyes.

"We?" John asked, on guard again.

"Yah, a few of us got together when we heard about the group that left Illinois. We've been talking about running for months, but when we heard about you on the news we decided to wait. We figured you might come this way. We have kids living in every town near here watching for you," the boy said.

"Watching for me?" John wasn't sure if he should be worried or thankful. There was too much at risk to believe everything a strange kid said.

"Why don't I just show you, the barn's not far. Everyone will be excited to meet you."

John looked back toward the field, unsure which way to turn. This could be genuine providence, or it could be a fed trap.

"John, I know you don't know me, but you can trust me," the kid said, holding out his hand.

John was struck by the scene, and the words the kid spoke. They were words he remembered from his childhood, words that had stuck with him. He saw a fork in their path, and a stranger offering a helping hand. He saw one of the paths was difficult, broken and rough, with a gaping chasm blocking the way. The other path was easy, smooth and led back the way they came. This boy was offering a hand to help along that hard path. Something inside him shouted that he take that hand, trust this stranger. John reached out and took the kid's hand and shook it.

"You already know my name, what's yours?" John asked.

"Jeff," the boy said.

"Give me a minute Jeff, I'll get the others."

John couldn't help but feel a shadow of a doubt about all of this. Despite having just said he would trust Jeff. He knew that is exactly what it meant to have faith, to take that leap despite your doubts. He believed, like his father had, that a person had to trust in something greater than themselves. He valued the importance of self-reliance and independence, but he recognized people could accomplish much more together.

Amanda looked askance at John when he got back to the group. He could see the rest were close enough to hear but still spread out in case they needed to get away fast. He looked at them for a moment, feeling his decision weighing on him. If his judgment wasn't sound he was endangering everyone around him. There was no doubt in their eyes, and that realization humbled him yet again. They knew him, knew his faults and weaknesses and they put their faith in him.

"We're going to meet some people. I think they might be coming with us," John said.

"The kid?" Amanda asked. She had been curious and moved close enough to see them while the two talked.

"Yes, there are others as well. They have news from Texas," John said.

He couldn't have said anything that would have had a greater effect on them. The only news they had of Texas, other than rumor, was the government sterilized propaganda. They were all making the move based on rumor and hearsay. To have real news was more than any of them could hope for.

"You trust him, John?" Todd asked. There was no doubt in his voice, only a straight forward question from a friend.

"Yes, I do," John nodded.

"Good enough for me," Todd said, moving toward the road without another word. Everyone else followed.

The group fell into their usual pattern after crossing the farm road. They were excited to hear the news but understood the danger of losing their discipline. John and Jeff led the group west, across the fields. They could all see the large barn ahead, standing ominous and silent in the middle of the overgrown field. It leaned slightly and was missing its wooden skin in places where time had won out. When they got close the doors opened and several young people, appearing to range in age from fifteen to twenty, stepped out of the building.

"John, they're just kids," Amanda said.

"So it would seem," John agreed.

Jeff approached a girl standing in the doorway, who looked to be the oldest, waving John over to join them.

"Jennifer, this is John Evermann," Jeff introduced him.

At the announcement most of the kids rushed forward to shake hands or hug members of John's group. Jennifer took John's offered hand and shook it firmly. There was a sense of relief among the kids that made John realize how much they had been holding out hope for contact with his group.

"We weren't sure you would come this way. Heck, we weren't even sure the stories were real," Jennifer explained.

"You mean the radio broadcasts out of Texas?" John asked. She nodded.

"We would like to hear them," Todd said from John's left.

"You can, soon. They broadcast in the evening and we can usually pick it up."

While they talked John noticed a few kids running off in different directions and a couple riding off on old bicycles that they must have scavenged and repaired. John became nervous again.

"Where are they going?" He asked.

"To get the others," Jennifer replied. "Jeff told you that we've been waiting and watching for you. We have people scattered all over. We can't leave without everyone."

"Look, Jennifer, we didn't plan on staying. Our kids are waiting for us, we have to keep moving," John said. While he talked he looked around at his own group, and saw doubt in their eyes. When his gaze settled on his wife he knew his initial reaction had been the wrong one.

"John, we have to come with you, we…" Jennifer started to appeal but he held up a hand to stop her.

"I spoke too hastily it seems," John said. "I don't know what I was thinking. Of course, we'll wait and take all of you with us."

Jeff, who had been waiting with bated breath to mount his own bicycle, smiled and climbed on the rusty old bike to pedal away.

"You were thinking about your kids, I understand," Jennifer said.

Looking around at the way the other kids looked up to her he believed she did understand.

"We can't wait long though," John said.

"Don't worry, no one is more than a couple hours away," Jennifer explained.

"If we're staying we better get inside," Amanda said.

"Right, come inside. It's safe and we have some food," Jennifer stood back to let them pass.

The others sprang to action in the excited chaos that always overtakes children when there is a large gathering. They led the adults into the barn with excited chatter and smiles. Some rushed to the back to retrieve ration packs they must have brought from town and fruit found in the area. It turned into an impromptu celebration as makeshift tables were constructed out of hay bales and wooden planks and the food was spread out for everyone. John, Todd, and Amanda followed Jennifer toward the back of the barn where she said the radio was. One of the other children brought food back to them.

The radio was a collection of old electronics, wire, lights and dials. John could see a couple of old books about radio building and operation on the table, and a box of scavenged tools under it. It appeared as if they had gathered every antique electronic device they could find and wired them together into a sort of Frankenstein's monster of a radio. Next to the device was a large metal box with several wires running to the device and a cranking lever on the side.

"We hooked it up to the old antenna on the roof, and that there," she pointed at the box with the crank, "is how we power it."

She moved over to the crank and started to turn it. The task seemed difficult at first, as Jennifer seemed to use all of her strength to start the crank, but once started it seemed to get easier. John could hear a whirring sound inside that reminded him of the old toy cars that were powered by pulling them back to wind up the motor and releasing it to speed away.

"From what I've read I believe the man who used to run this farm was a ham radio operator. One of those books described the equipment and the antenna that we found as the kind of stuff they used to use," Jennifer explained as she cranked the generator.

"Why did you start building this in the first place," John asked.

"For fun, mostly. A couple of the neighborhood boys found the old radio behind a wall in the barn a couple of summers ago. One of them, Jeff, is my brother and he brought me out here to show me. As we worked on it more of the kids came out and before long it was a sort of club," Jennifer said.

She stopped cranking the box and moved to the radio, flipping switches and turning dials. Lights on the displays flickered on and static filled the barn as the radio came to life. The girl adjusted dials and picked up a headset to listen more closely. Her eyes took on a distant look as she concentrated, obviously searching for a faint signal in the white noise. The others kept silent, almost holding their breath as she worked, not wanting to disturb her concentration. Finally, she smiled and put down the headset, moving to another dial to make more adjustments. The white noise had changed. They could all now hear someone's voice low and quiet in the background, buried in the static.

"They never broadcast on the same frequency and sometimes it's hard to get the signal. It's not always the best quality but if I can get this adjusted just right we should be able to hear it," Jennifer said.

"If you can hear my voice Old America, take heart, you are not alone," the voice cut through the static. It was a man's voice, and clearly one accustomed to being on the radio. It was the kind of voice that John remembered from his youth listening to news broadcasts on the television.

"From all reports John Evermann and his people are still free and on their way to the border. Our sources inside the old country have assured me that they have not been captured, and the effort to stop them has met with more setbacks. The agents in pursuit have gone home for the weekend as is their contractual agreement with the government. It's just another example of the problems faced by our brothers and sisters still trapped in that oppressive country."

At the mention of his name everyone looked up at John and suddenly he was embarrassed. He wasn't fond of being the center of attention, even among his friends and family. Even the children were staring at him, though their looks were more along the lines of fans caught up in meeting their idol. He liked that even less.

"I have grand news to share with you my friends. A very special guest is with me today. She has just arrived from old America with a very special package, so to speak," the man continued.

The children seemed excited about the announcement. They kept their cheers subdued but they cheered all the same.

"It's always big news when someone makes it out," Jennifer whispered.

"Miss, I believe you wanted to say a few words?" The man on the radio asked.

"Yes, I," the woman's voice was quiet and she hesitated. It was obvious that she was nervous.

"It's all right miss, no need to be nervous," the man's voice said. "Sit forward and speak normally into the mike."

"I, um. My name is Sarah," all of the newcomers to the barn sat up, suddenly recognizing the voice that went with the name. "If anyone sees John and the rest, or if any of them are listening now."

Sarah's voice caught in her throat as she held back the emotions of her ordeal and the hope that her friends were still safe and well.

"John, if you're out there listening, we made it. All of the children made it with me. We're here waiting for you."

The crowd in the barn erupted into cheers and shouts, but John leaned forward and tilted his head to the speaker. Sarah wasn't finished.

"We made it John, but they have Benny. He made sure we could get away and they have h…" the signal died in static.

Chapter 31

I remember my grandfather talking about the core difference between a progressive and himself. He was speaking to a man at a restaurant about government regulation. The man said the government needed to regulate because people couldn't be trusted to do the right thing. My grandfather asked the man if he believed people couldn't govern themselves and the man nodded. The man pointed out all the terrible things people did out of greed, jealousy, or hate. Grandfather just shook his head and walked away without another word. Later I asked him if the man was right, if people were too bad to be free? My grandfather explained that the man's view was entirely opposed to the spirit of the American experiment. He said that all those bad things were done by just a few, and most people were good and honest. He explained that government is meant to facilitate man ruling himself, not to take the place of that idea.

-Excerpt from the Journal of John Evermann

Casey arrived back at the federal police station to find the place a hub of excited activity. The sergeant and a group of men, the volunteers Casey assumed, were bent over a map and talking about where the fugitives might come through town. The lieutenant walked over to the table and put his finger down about as close to the location of the antique mall as he could guess.

"They'll come through here sometime after dark if they come this way. It's where I would hide out if I were them," Casey said.

"Lieutenant, these are the most reliable citizens that I could round up," the sergeant said by way of introduction.

"Good, we'll want to get everyone out to that site. There's an abandoned building that can be seen from quite a distance. They're sure to see it. We'll station some of you in the nearby fields just in case," Casey explained.

The volunteers filed out of the station to wait for transportation to the property at the sergeant's direction. The sergeant started to leave with them but stopped and pulled a small piece of paper out of his shirt pocket.

"Lieutenant, you got a call while you were out. Some army officer down at one of the border posts."

Casey was thankful the sergeant wrote down the officer's name and number instead of just 'some army officer'.

"Did he say what it was about?" Casey asked.

"Didn't ask."

"Great, thanks," Casey growled in irritation. He waved the local officer off in dismissal.

After the sergeant was gone Casey sat at the desk and dialed the number on the paper. It was answered by the duty officer and Casey asked for Captain Green.

"Captain Green," a deep voice said after Casey waited a couple of minutes on hold.

"This is Lieutenant Casey, FPC. I had a message that you called?"

"Right, Casey. You've been a tough man to track down," Green said.

"What can I do for you, Captain?" Casey asked.

"I thought you might want to know that we found one of your station's vans and one of your fugitives," Green reported.

"Just one? I'm not sure how you could possibly have one of the ones I'm looking for. Can you brief me from the beginning, Captain?" Casey said, completely confused by this turn of events.

Green explained the events from the previous night. He described Benny but could not confirm his identity. They tracked ownership of the van found by the patrol and after a series of phone calls located Casey. From the description, Casey knew the prisoner had to be the one called Bernard Saunders but he couldn't begin to imagine why the man had taken the van to the border on his own unless it was meant to be a distraction. Even as the thought crossed his mind though, he knew they couldn't have timed it so perfectly. Benny's capture, so close to when Casey and the rest should next cross paths had to be pure coincidence. He was sure of it.

"I have something I need to handle tonight, but I'll be down there first thing in the morning," Casey said.

Casey left the station a little less sure of his plan than he'd been before. There were so many things that could go wrong. The appearance of the missing van and one fugitive at the border only served to bring that fact to the forefront of Casey's mind. He couldn't imagine they sent one of their own ahead to distract him, but he had underestimated them in the past.

The volunteers were waiting for him on the sidewalk outside the station. None of the volunteers had cars so they piled into the sergeant's van. Casey led the way out to the edge of town and they parked near an abandoned house so the vehicles wouldn't be seen from the fields. Once out of the van they all gathered around the ranking federal officer.

"You two, I want you over there," he pointed to a spot that would put them about a quarter mile west of the antique mall," spread out and keep your eyes and ears open. They nodded and rushed off toward the indicated spot.

"You," Casey pointed at another man. "I want you about half way between them and the building."

After the man rushed off to his spot the lieutenant looked over the rest, considering the numbers he had to work with. There were trees closer to the east side of the abandoned building so he placed to more men on that side, one at the tree line and one between him and the building. That left Casey, the sergeant, and five others to watch the building itself.

"You two will watch the front," Casey indicated two of the remaining volunteers and pointed at the main doors on the south side of the building. "We'll watch the back."

Casey led the sergeant and the last volunteer around to the north side of the building. There was a back door and a couple of ground-level windows that someone could use to get in. He spread the two men out so they covered as much of the property's north side as they could. The sun was starting to set and Casey settled down to wait out a long night. He pulled a small hand-held radio out of his pocket. Each man in the party carried one just like it.

"Radio check, respond from west to east," Casey said after keying up the radio.

After a few minutes of confusion the volunteers finally understood and started responding to verify their radios were working and on the correct channel. Once they had all checked in Casey keyed his own handset again.

"Stay awake and stay quiet. If you see anything, report it on the radio immediately. Otherwise, keep radio silence," the lieutenant said. He was surprised and thankful there were no responses. They were following orders without question which is more than he could have hoped for.

Alone in the gathering darkness Casey listened to the sounds of the world around him settling in for the night. He couldn't remember the last time he had actually listened to the birds calling to each other or noticed the ebb and flow to the sounds of insects in the evening. He was used to the city and even there he was always too busy to even listen to that. There was a certain peace to the cacophony around him and something buried deep inside relished that.

He leaned back against a small tree and watched the darkening fields before him. His hand found the small metal car in his pocket and his thumb rubbed the enamel paint slowly. It seemed strange to him that he was more relaxed and at peace here, alone, an individual in the dark, than he was anywhere else. He'd been taught to think about the collective, the betterment of everyone as a group, but at that moment all Casey wanted was to be left alone with his own thoughts and feelings. It was a strange sensation, and it made him feel a little guilty, but he couldn't help it.

Through the long hours of the night the lieutenant thought about those feelings. He imagined it was how John and the fugitives must feel and why they were on the run. That realization didn't make it right in Casey's mind, but it explained it in terms he could understand. They were still criminals as far as he was concerned, shirking their responsibility to the state and their fellow citizens. He was sure a few months in reeducation would correct their behavior, once he managed to arrest them. That was likely to be their sentence, though harsher penalties have been used for these cases in the past.

As the hours passed Casey began to worry that something had gone wrong. He was sure they would come this way since Moberly was the next logical place on their route. He figured they would stick close to major roads to avoid getting lost but wondered if they might have risked cutting cross country after their last encounter with him. If they were now avoiding the highway or towns it would make it harder for him to find them.

When pre-dawn started to lighten the sky Casey was sure something wasn't right. Somehow the fugitives had either known he was waiting or they had changed direction as a precaution. He knew there was no point in waiting any longer or searching elsewhere. He could drive every road in the area and never find them. He stood up and went looking for the sergeant.

"Something's wrong. They aren't coming this way," Casey said, handing over his radio. "Dismiss everyone, we're done here. I'm heading south to look for something I can use."

The sergeant took the radio and nodded. Casey didn't wait for any acknowledgement. He made his way to the SUV parked up the road, deep in thought. He had to get information he could use out of the prisoner the army was holding, if it was even one of the ones he was looking for. If it was Bernard, Casey was determined to get him to talk, find out why he was down there on his own, and what might have happened to the others.

Chapter 32

I always wondered when we went from a people that held out our hands to help each other to holding out our hands expecting help from the government. America was a proud nation, built on the idea that we could do for ourselves, and our neighbors, what no one else could. We shrugged off the rule of a tyrant and built a society that other countries used as a model for their own. We made mistakes, some of them terrible, but in the end we built a country that other people wanted to be part of. Somewhere there was a turning point when we stopped standing above our government and looking within when we needed something, and started looking up, hoping the government would do it for us.

-Excerpt from the Journal of John Evermann

While Lieutenant Casey was laying a trap for the refugees, a group of parents were having a subdued celebration after receiving news of their children's safety. The kids from Madison shared in their joy with the knowledge that others near their own age, and younger, had made it to freedom. John, Amanda, Todd and Jennifer were still near the now silent radio.

"What happened to the signal?" John asked.

"When the Feds find it they block it. Sometimes we get more time, but usually they find it in a couple of minutes. The frequency and time are always random and sometimes we don't even find it before the Feds do," Jennifer explained.

John was frustrated that they wouldn't hear more. He sighed and his body sagged a little with how useless he felt, but also relief at the news they had received. It was one large weight off his shoulders.

"They're safe, John," Amanda put her hand on his shoulder. "At least we know that much."

John nodded and pulled her into an embrace. Todd gave him a smile and gestured for Jennifer to follow him so his friends could have some privacy. The two held each other tightly for some time before John kissed the top of her head and leaned back to look down at her.

"More than half our task is done," John said. "We can't let our guard down yet, though. It's going to get more dangerous the closer we get to the border."

"We have to get the rest of them across, and now these children as well," Amanda agreed.

"Sarah said they have Benny. It won't take long for that agent to find out what happened. They'll try harder to stop us," John said.

"Still a long way to go on a long hard road."

"We'll walk it together to the end," John hugged her again.

By the time they joined the rest, the revelry had calmed considerably. It was apparent to John that everyone was exhausted. They had all eaten and the excitement of the last two nights was taking its toll.

"Are you sure no one will come looking for you out here?" John asked Jennifer.

"No, we never broadcast so there's no signal to trace, and we never come straight here to insure we aren't followed," Jennifer replied.

"What about your parents?" Amanda asked.

"Most people in this town support the government. A couple of us don't live with our parents anymore. I was reassigned here when I turned eighteen, but when the mill closed my paperwork must have been lost and I fell through the cracks. A couple of others go to work often enough that they aren't missed," Jennifer explained.

"The younger ones tell their parents they're going to play with friends, and no one questions it. We won't be able to tell them where we've gone," the young woman continued.

"Maybe they could be convinced this is the right thing," Todd said.

"We tried that once. Thankfully we didn't bring Cindy's dad here, but he won't let her out of the house now. We just don't know who we can trust. When we get to Texas we'll send letters back and if our families want to join us it'll be their choice and we won't have to risk being caught."

John looked around at the kids again, realizing that they grew up beyond their years because of the way things were for them. He couldn't imagine what it must be like to want something so much to cause a child to rush out into the world and leave everything they knew behind. He realized, as he looked around, that the youngest of them must be fourteen or fifteen, an age that was considered an adult only a handful of generations ago. Perhaps it wasn't so unusual that these young people were deciding to take their lives in their own hands and fight for their future, even if it meant leaving their families behind.

"They're so young," Amanda said, as if thinking along the same lines.

"There are younger siblings that we have to leave behind. As much as I want to take everyone. I had to draw the line somewhere, and fourteen seemed the most reasonable age," Jennifer explained.

"Fourteen is still young," Amanda said.

"It wasn't so long ago that it was old enough to fight a war or get married," Jennifer said firmly.

"True enough," John nodded. "If these young people wish to find freedom who are we to stop them?"

"We should get back before it gets too late. Some of the others will be coming in later tonight, they shouldn't bother you," Jennifer explained.

"Aren't you all past curfew anyway? You might get caught if you try to go home now," John said.

"The police here don't pay all that much attention. The night officer is probably snoring with his feet on his desk right now," Jennifer said.

John nodded and the kids started to leave in pairs at different intervals. They didn't expect any trouble but they weren't taking any chances. John approved of the wisdom. As a matter of fact John was impressed all around. This group, of mostly children, was showing great discipline and forethought. They would do well in their new home when they all reached Texas.

Within an hour all the children had left and the refugees settled down to sleep. The hay scattered around the barn made for comfortable and warm bedding. With the nights getting colder they were thankful for the added insulation. John noticed that, though the hay bales could have been used to create private areas, everyone lay down within reach of each other. The ordeal they were going through had brought all of these people closer, as if they were one family. They had all struggled, cried, laughed, and grieved together. They each became important to the others over the few days on the run.

John smiled as Amanda and he lay down and he pulled her close. He wrapped his arms around her protectively. Todd was within reach, and he could feel the presence of someone else behind him, close enough to reach out and wake him in case there was need. He finally relaxed and let his mind drift off to much needed sleep. His final thought before losing himself to the whim of his subconscious was of his children. They had made it. From now on, in those moments of self-doubt, when he wondered if this had all been worth it, he could be sure that it was.

Chapter 33

Everyone remembers where they were on September eleventh, that's what they say right? I'm sure it's mostly true, at least that people remember what they were doing when they heard what happened. I don't, probably because I was too young. I think that's a blessing, that children don't remember tragedy like that. Sure they know something is wrong at the time. Our parent's look of horror while they watched the events on television is something a child wouldn't miss. They would have seen the images and known that people were getting hurt, but children quickly forget. Later, before everything changed and our study of history became regulated, I read about the events of that day and the days that followed. There are a few moments in our history, always tragic instances, where things change. It's always fleeting, but for those few days after the towers fell, people were different. We grieved together, cried, and worked together despite all the differences. For those few days no one cared about religion or politics, race or gender. We were all Americans and that was all that mattered. We had been hurt, and we worked together to help each other. Sadly, that moment didn't last. It wasn't long before fingers were pointed, decisions questioned, and blame laid. The same old arguments came back, fights over nothing, debates over nothing. They always say, cherish the moments because they're gone before you know it. I just wish some moments could last.

-Excerpt from the Journal of John Evermann

Casey's frustration mounted as he made the drive south to the border post. He hoped that he would get some useful information out of the prisoner, but he couldn't help but worry because he was driving further away from where he believed the fugitives were. He was certain Benny was a distraction but having lost the others' trail he had no other choice but to find out for sure.

To add to his stress, the closer he got to the border the worse the roads became. Most of the roads out this far were only used by the military and the government didn't see the need to repair roads that military vehicles would just tear up again. That was the official reason but Casey imagined it had more to do with this part of the country simply being out of sight and mind. With the contraction of the populace away from the borders it meant less time and resources had to be spent on upkeep in remote areas. After all, citizens couldn't get upset about a problem if they didn't see it, and a lot of people were happy to remain blissfully ignorant.

When Casey reached the border post he was waved through the gate by a bored-looking soldier. The post itself was a collection of barracks and administration buildings inside a tall chain link fence topped with razor-sharp concertina wire. The western fence line of the compound was part of the DMZ fence with a path between it and another fence wide enough for a truck to drive through, and connected to the patrol road that ran the length of the border fence. The security of the complex was completed by a guard tower on each corner.

Casey drove through the sliding gate that was opened for him by another guard. A third soldier approached the SUV on the driver's side. Casey stopped and rolled down the window.

"You've come about the prisoner?" The soldier asked.

Casey nodded, "Captain Green called me yesterday."

"Pull around to building three, office is straight down the hall from the main entrance," the soldier said, pointing to one of the large administration buildings.

Casey parked in front of the building between two olive green trucks, marked with army insignia, and entered the main doors of the single story building. It was a familiar place, just like all other government buildings. Casey looked at the same grayish-green paint, the same white floor tile, and the same white drop ceiling that was used to construct every federal building in the country. What it lacked in imagination, he always thought, it made up for in putting a person at ease in a new place. It was familiar, like home, and anywhere he went in America he knew he'd find more just like it. He walked to the end of the hall and knocked on the metal door that was identical to the one leading to his own office.

"Come in," said a muffled voice Casey recognized from the previous night.

Casey opened the door. Behind the functional metal desk sat a large black man in a camouflage military uniform. The officer's dress and manner was as meticulous and disciplined as his office. There wasn't a single piece of decoration in the room, and the items that were present were arranged precisely on the desk or shelves. Everything in the room had a purpose, right down paper clips in a small cup within easy reach of the large officer. Casey had never seen another government employee take his job as seriously as Captain Green obviously did.

"Lieutenant Casey, sit down please," Green said in his rumbling voice.

"I'd like to question the prisoner right away." Casey did not move toward the indicated chair.

"You're earlier than I expected Lieutenant. I have to finish this report," Green looked up at Casey. The Captain was obviously used to having his orders followed without question. Casey could respect that, he was on Captain Green's turf and he would have to play by Green's rules. He took a seat, sitting stiffly, and watching the officer as he went back to making notes on the report in front of him.

"Relax Lieutenant, the prisoner is eating breakfast anyway," Green said without looking up.

Casey sat back and resigned himself to waiting until the Captain was done with his work. He looked around the room. It was clear this officer was more than devoted to his job, this was his life. The Lieutenant was used to federal officers, and soldiers, that did only what was required of them, punch in, punch out, and avoid any extra work. The military was different in that they could not go home at the end of the day, but to expect one of them to do more than was in their contract was like asking for a miracle. Casey imagined Green didn't even have a copy of his contract on hand to show anyone that thought to violate it.

Green put a final mark on the last page of the report, put the pages back in order, and arranged it neatly in a plain brown folder before standing up.

"He should be done eating by now, and I have time to take you around," Green said, walking toward the door. Casey stood up to follow.

Outside his office the Captain dropped the folder into a metal bin attached to the wall outside his door. It would be someone else's job to come by and collect the paperwork and drop it off where it needed to be. Green obviously trusted his staff enough to do the jobs that needed to be done. Casey would have delivered the paperwork himself just to make sure it got there. Green led the way down a side hallway away from the main doors.

"Have you had any trouble on the border recently, other than the prisoner you have?" Casey asked.

"Nothing to speak of. We see a few patrols on the other side of the DMZ from time to time, but it's been quiet for a long time here," Green said.

"No one trying to cross from this side?" Casey asked.

"Not since the war. The prisoner is our first," the Captain stopped in front of a locked door and pulled out a set of keys. "The first in my area anyway. If it's happening elsewhere no one is talking about it."

The door opened into a short hall lined on both sides by cells. The cells were nothing more than cages of chain link with a pair of cots in each. The only occupant of the cell block sat on a cot in the first cell on the right.

"Bernard Saunders?" Casey wasted no time getting down to business when he saw the prisoner.

"Everyone just calls me Benny," there was no malice or anger in the response.

"You left Illinois with John Evermann and his group of fugitives?" Casey asked.

"Never heard of him," Benny said without taking his eyes off the bunk across from him.

Casey just nodded. He hadn't expected the man to just start talking anyway.

"We know you disappeared from Stewart about the same time the others did. The van you were found with was the same one stolen from federal agents who were transporting John and others back to Peoria,"

Casey started to lay out the facts to show Benny how futile it was to deny his involvement. He was interrupted by Benny's low chuckle.

"Something about that funny to you?"

"Yah, your agents lost their van to a group of citizens that were locked up in the back. If what you say is true anyway," Benny looked at Casey now and the Lieutenant was faced with the fact that the man was resigned to whatever happened to him. Benny was relaxed, confident, and the laugh was genuine, not nervous.

"Besides, who's to say I didn't steal it from them, or find it on the road somewhere?"

"Why are you down here Benny? Did John send you as a distraction?" Casey didn't expect an answer, but he hoped for some reaction that might confirm his suspicions.

"Road trip," Benny said.

"Road trip?" Casey repeated.

"Sure, you know, drive around the country, take in the sights. Maybe bore my relatives back home with hundreds of slides of gray prison-like government buildings and the like," Benny said with a smile.

"Listen Benny," Casey wanted to regain control of the conversation. "I can offer you a lighter sentence, and your choice of relocation, if you cooperate with me. I might even be able to commute your time at reeducation if I can put on my report that you had a change of heart and helped me."

This did get a reaction but not the one Casey expected. In a flash the large, bearded man was on his feet and inches from the chain link that separated the two men. Casey had already been close to the cage and the size of him, and speed of his movement, made the Lieutenant step back.

"That's your problem, you and your kind," Benny began. His voice was low and Casey could see he was clenching his jaw tight enough to make the tendons in his neck stand out. He continued.

"You honestly believe that everyone is just looking out for themselves. You think we would rather have you feds take care of us," Casey could sense that if the cage weren't there Benny's clenched fists would be reaching for his throat right then. "Some of us believe in taking care of each other by making sure we can all take care of ourselves."

"This is your last chance, Benny. Help me and I can help you," Casey said, but he knew it was pointless. He'd lost control of the situation by backing down, and it was clear that Benny wasn't going to betray his friends.

"That's where you're wrong Lieutenant," Benny backed up and sat on the cot again. "I've done what I was meant to do and there's nothing you can do to me now that'll change that. Only God can help me now and one way or another, I'll be free someday."

The big man sat back against the cage next to the cot and closed his eyes. Whether he wanted it or not, Casey knew the interview was over.

He wasn't foolish enough to think he could get anything useful out of the prisoner. He turned and walked back through the cell block door where Green was waiting in the hall.

"Did you find what you were looking for?" Green asked as he locked the door again.

"No, but maybe the van he was in will tell me something."

"It's in the motor pool, this way," Green led him down the hall toward the main doors.

Casey was quiet as they walked across the compound to the large buildings that housed the installation's vehicles. This group of people he had come to think of as fugitives surprised him at every turn. He was used to people who wanted nothing more than an easy life, and to be left alone. John's people, however, were intentionally making their lives harder, and for what? A life in a country where everyone had to fend for themselves?

Everyone knew what it was like in Texas, or at least what the government said it was like. Casey believed it though. It was like America used to be, people working for money, trying to earn enough to feed their families and pay the bills. You had to search for a job and hope you were good at it so you kept it. He wondered if having that choice was really worth all the effort. He snatched his hand out of his pocket when he realized he'd been rubbing the little toy car with his thumb. Too many of these questions had been filling his mind since starting this case and he didn't like it at all.

"We locked the van in here so it wouldn't be disturbed," Green said, pulling out his keys again to unlock the small garage.

"Thank you, Captain," Casey said when the door was opened.

He stepped through and looked for a light switch. The one next to the door brought the lights overhead to flickering life. The van was parked in the middle of the garage with the doors closed and no sign anyone had been inside or searched it. He walked around the black vehicle, looking for anything that might be readily apparent from the outside.

"No one has touched it except the driver, it's been locked up since we brought it here," Green said from the doorway.

The Captain was leaning against the inside wall, seeming content to wait for Casey to finish his search. He felt like he was being silently criticized by the officer and it made him uncomfortable, like an itch between the shoulder blades he couldn't quite reach. This entire ordeal was an embarrassment to the federal police, especially Casey's division.

"Are you going to hover over me the whole time?" Casey asked, unable to keep the annoyance out of his voice.

"Your van, my facility," Green said as if that were explanation enough. "Don't worry, I won't hover, I'll stay right over here."

Casey cursed under his breath and opened the driver door, trying not to think about his chaperone. There were no readily apparent clues in the front of the van, and after searching under the seats and in the storage compartments Casey pushed the door closed in frustration. He wouldn't accept that Benny had been alone, simply driving around in the stolen van. He moved to the back doors and pulled them open.

At first glance the back of the van was empty as well. Casey climbed in, his frustration mounting, and worked his way toward the cage that separated the back from the front seats. The floor was clear of any trash or debris. Even the step next to the side doors, used to make entry from the side easier, was devoid of anything that might help. He worked his way back, checking storage compartments along the side. He found what he expected to find, tools, a flash light, road flares, and jumper cables. He was about to give up hope when he reached the last storage container at the back. He looked in to find the glassy eyes of a toy bear staring back at him.

The lieutenant was initially struck by how abandoned and sad the toy looked. He knew it was crazy to think like that, but he did all the same. It was clearly a family heirloom, kept hidden during the collection of unnecessary property years ago. It was much better quality than the toys given to children by the government, too good to be lying forgotten in a greasy bin in the back of a van. Casey knew right away, without really understanding why, that this bear had been loved and whoever had forgotten it must be missing it terribly.

Casey pulled the bear out of the bin and closed the back doors of the van. He stepped around it and headed for the garage door.

"I'll call Peoria and have the van picked up, thank you for your help, Captain," Casey said when he reached the door. After a stiff nod he stepped out of the garage and started for his SUV.

"Well, did you find anything?" Green asked. He couldn't have missed the bear in Casey's hand, he was fishing for information. Casey stopped and turned, holding out the toy.

"Everything Captain," Casey said. He started to turn back to his SUV again.

"What about the prisoner?" Green asked. Casey stopped again.

"Let him go."

"Lieutenant?" Green sounded like he'd just been told to learn to fly.

"He's done what he came here to do. He'll be no good in reeducation; I've seen his type before. He'd just be another prisoner costing the state money for the rest of his life," Casey said by way of explanation.

Casey turned back to his vehicle. He didn't stop this time and Green didn't question him further. He climbed into the SUV and set the bear on the passenger seat, looking at it again like it held all the answers. As far as Casey was concerned it answered more questions without speaking than Benny ever would. This is what the man had been doing. He wasn't a distraction to pull Casey off of the others. The big man had a bigger mission. He'd gotten the kids out. This would make Casey's job harder and more dangerous. If the fugitives knew that

Benny had succeeded they wouldn't have anything left to lose. He just hoped they didn't find out before he found them.

Chapter 34

We've all heard that freedom isn't easy or free, but how many of us have really sat down and thought about what that means? When people aren't free they'll fight and die to get it. Slaves and subjects shed blood to break their bonds. Throughout history no civilization became free without great suffering, nor did they keep it without effort. How can we expect to just sit back and hold onto something that is so difficult to get? You don't let someone else do the work, you hold onto it with everything you have. When you put the responsibility for your freedom in the hands of someone else you may think you're free but it's the worst sort of slavery there is.

-Excerpt from the Journal of John Evermann

In the barn north of Madison the last person on watch started to wake people an hour before dawn. The sky outside was just starting to lighten in expectation of the rising sun. Rations were quickly handed out and consumed, and bags were being packed when Amanda found

John outside. He was standing alone in the semi-darkness looking south and west toward Texas.

"I love this time of the day," John said when she stepped close. He put his arm around her shoulders and she leaned against him. Taking a deep breath of the chilly air he closed his eyes and listened as the world started to slowly wake up around them. It had been awhile since John was able to simply enjoy such a morning.

"I know, John. You always have," she fell silent and enjoyed the moment with him. For just a few minutes they could feel real peace before they had to get back to reality.

The air was starting to fill with the sounds of birds getting ready for the day, and the colors of the world were changing with the light so gradually one could easily miss it. To John there are few colors more beautiful than the green of grass and leaves, or the grayish blue sky before the sun is actually above the horizon. This would have been the time coffee would be brewing in the house and John would be doing the things he enjoyed doing in the peace before the day actually seemed to start. He was determined to enjoy those things again in a home of his family's choosing. That's what it would be, when they reached Texas, their home.

"People are slower to get up today," Amanda finally broke the silence, though she kept her voice low.

"They're exhausted. We'll be making less time, though I expect we're only seven or eight days away if we aren't delayed too much."

"We'll get there, John," Amanda said with confidence.

"I just don't want to lose anyone else on the way," he said.

"John, you can't take this all on yourself," she knew he would, despite her words. "You got Steve's family across, I'm sure he's grateful for that."

John knew she was right, but he would never shake the feeling that he was partially responsible for Steve's death. He was determined that he would do whatever it would take to make sure Steve's family wanted for nothing.

"Here they come," Amanda said quietly.

John followed Amanda's gaze and saw the kids from Madison coming toward the barn in small groups. Some of the kids that had come in overnight, and stayed in the barn, were coming out to greet their friends. It made him long for the voices of his own children as he listened to these young people laugh and catch up.

"We're ready when you are," Jennifer said, coming to stand in front of John and Amanda.

"Give us old folks a couple minutes, we're almost ready," John smiled.

Jennifer chuckled and nodded, going to talk to her friends while they waited. Both Amanda and John saw Todd come out of the barn and walk over to join Jennifer. He was one of the youngest of the refugees from Illinois, and the only single member of their group. He'd been a friend of John's since starting at the factory, and eventually started attending their secret meetings. When he got close Jennifer looked at him and returned the smile that was already on his face. Amanda squeezed John's hand and pulled him inside to finish getting ready.

"It's nice to see young love start to blossom in the midst of all of this," Amanda said.

"I couldn't agree more," John replied.

The refugees were ready to leave in a few minutes after the arrival of their new members. Everyone was used to packing up and eating fast. They set out in their smaller groups, and the kids turned out to be fast learners as the older members explained the routine. John also found out that some of them were excellent scouts.

John didn't like the idea of the young people ranging to the side or ahead. He thought it would be more dangerous, but he couldn't refuse them. He reminded himself they had joined the refugees freely, and had to be allowed to make their own decisions. He also had to admit that they knew what they were doing. They were small, fast, and agile, and had spent time sneaking around their town and hiding from the authorities.

The refugees made good time, skirting Madison on the north and following the highway again toward Moberly. Several miles from the next town they crossed the highway, again one group at a time, and continued on. John knew they would be turning south along a new road when they reached Moberly and it would be easier and safer to cross the highway here than closer to the town. Overall the first part of the day was easy, and John noticed that the young people seemed to bring new energy to the rest. When he moved along the line, speaking to each group, he noticed smiling faces that had been exhausted the night before. They were still tired and sore, but the kids were making it easy to ignore the aches and pains.

They stopped for lunch in the woods east of Moberly, getting the young people into the routine of a quick and efficient meal break. The excitement of the trip was making it difficult to get some of the younger ones to concentrate, but John knew they would catch on soon enough. He stepped toward the edge of the trees and looked toward the town that would have been where they slept the night before if they hadn't stopped in Madison.

The woods were on the edge of some abandoned farmland with an old country road that split the fields and headed into town. John noticed a large building sitting next to the road, on the edge of the field. He could see large faded white letters on the side marking the building as an antique mall. He remembered those from his childhood when his grandparents had enjoyed taking the family out on Sunday afternoons after church. They were usually large buildings, built in old schools and warehouses, or sometimes barns. This one looked to have been an old barn that someone had added on to. It was large and would have made a great place for them all to sleep had they actually stopped here.

"What are you looking at?" Todd asked.

"Nothing, just reminiscing," John replied.

"Right, well we're ready to move."

"Let's go then," John said, turning back with Todd to see everyone getting into their groups.

John swept the area with his eyes and was proud to note that no evidence of their presence was left behind, as usual. Even the new additions to their group had picked up on the need to clean up after themselves. He joined Todd, Amanda, Jennifer, and seven others in the lead group and they started out.

"Pretty smart moving in staggered groups like this," John heard Jennifer say behind him.

"Yeah," Todd responded. "Makes sure if one group is spotted the others have a chance to hide or get away."

They skirted Moberly and met up with highway 63 heading south to Columbia. Their timetable was off and John estimated they would be stopping north of the next city rather than a few miles south as he thought before. Columbia was one of the largest cities on their route, and one he knew they would be able to avoid. There was a bridge across the Missouri, west of the city. It would add a few extra hours to their trip, but it was the only bridge for miles that wasn't right in the middle of a population center. The next bridge would be at Jefferson City, which crossed right into the middle of a sprawling town with few places for them to hide. The Quincy crossing had been a risk, crossing at Jefferson City would be suicide. They would reach Columbia in the dark of night, and John felt it would be wise to push on across the bridge instead of stopping so close to the city. He would leave that up to the exhausted group though.

The rest of the day was quiet and uneventful. It was a welcome respite after being chased by the feds. Except for the importance of the exodus, and the danger of being caught, they could almost imagine they were on a leisurely cross-country hike. They stopped in the evening to eat again but didn't waste any time and were back on the road soon after.

John noticed that the energy of the morning excitement had long since worn off. Everyone was slower getting up after each break and moving more stiffly, everyone except the kids. An hour after the dinner break John called a halt in a wooded area near a pond. He gathered everyone around before anyone could sit down or start to relax.

"We're close to Columbia and it's time to make a decision," John began. "We need to go west, around the city in the dark, to reach the bridge across the river. I'd rather not take the risk of stopping so close, or staying near the bridge, but it is a couple hours walk ahead of us to get across."

He looked around at everyone, letting them absorb the information. This was one of those times where he couldn't make the call on his own. He needed everyone on the same page.

"We have two choices and I'd like to hear what you all think. We can stop now and get a couple hours of rest before moving on and walk most of the day tomorrow, or we can keep going and stop across the river and sleep the rest of the night," John explained.

Looking around the group he could tell almost everyone was weighing the decision against the pain and exhaustion in their bodies and minds.

"I don't much like the idea of trying to get back up after lying on the ground for a couple of hours. I think I'd rather keep going," Hugh, one of older men said from the back.

Others were nodding or quietly adding their assent. John could only see a couple of people that looked like they would rather rest right then, but even they couldn't argue with the speaker's logic.

"I agree," John said. "It seems like I'm more tired and sore every day. I don't want to know what it feels like to try and get up after only a couple hours of sleep. We keep moving for now?"

He saw nearly everyone nod at his question. He wasted no time splitting everyone into even smaller groups and explaining the plan. They would wait five minutes after the group in front of them started before heading out. They would stay close to the highway until they reached the city, then turn west and follow the edge of town. Getting close to dark it would be easy to get lost in the fields around the town so they had to risk staying within sight of it. He remembered, from the map that the north end of town was mostly housing so much of their walk would be through fields, parks, and back yards. If anyone was stopped they would say their car broke down before curfew and they were on their way home. If they were captured their sacrifice and silence would mean the rest had more of a chance to get away. They all knew the risk when they left and they were prepared for the worst. Once they reached the west edge of town they would turn south to meet the highway and continue on to the bridge. Once across there was a wooded area about two hundred yards south of the highway. That's where they would stop and sleep the rest of the night. Everyone would move on at dawn without exception.

John's group led the way. They were down to Amanda, Todd, Jennifer, and two others. He didn't feel the need to look back or supervise the departure. He was confident everyone would stick to the plan so he set his eyes forward and picked up the pace. They walked for perhaps forty-five minutes when John stopped and looked around.

"What is it, John?" Amanda asked.

"Do you smell that?" John asked. When Amanda shook her head he went on. "Smoke, I think I smell smoke."

They kept walking for about fifteen minutes before everyone began to smell it. After a few more minutes they could see it as well. A couple streets in from the edge of town a house was burning. The orange glow flared in the sky like a miniature sunrise, and black smoke rolled through the neighborhood. John knew most cities had limited public services, especially at night. The local police and fire departments are always understaffed, and the night shift even more so. He only thought about it for a moment before he came to a decision.

"Guys," John indicated Todd and the other two. "I need you to help me. Amanda and Jennifer, you two stay here and wait for the next group. Tell them to move fast. It will take some time for the authorities to show up but they will and we want everyone far from here. If the last group goes by before we come back, go with them."

Amanda clearly disagreed with the plan. She knew what John intended, but she didn't argue. She also didn't intend to leave him this time but she would deal with that when the time came. John led the others toward the house. They moved through a couple of yards and crossed a street toward the next. The glow from the house fire grew brighter as they went and the heat started to intensify. When they reached the street the burning house was on, neighbors were outside, gawking in shock and horror. No one was doing a thing and there were no sirens or lights in the distance.

"What are you doing?" John yelled at the people nearest him. "Get your hoses, put water on that house."

People stared at him, clearly dumbfounded that some stranger was yelling at them while their neighbor's house burned. John heard a scream from one of the upper floors of the burning home.

"You three," John indicated Todd and the other two. "Get these people organized. We need water on that house. As many hoses as you can get. Use a couple to wet down the houses next to it."

Todd caught on right away and moved before John stopped talking. The other two were close behind. They pushed and shouted, startling people out of their stupor. John went to the nearest house and turned on the outside faucet. It wasn't attached to a hose and started pouring water onto the ground at his feet. He stripped off his jacket and shirt, getting both of them soaking wet. After wringing water out over his head and soaking the rest of him he put the jacket back on and tied the shirt around his face and neck. It only took a couple of moments, but to John it was too long. The screams for help were desperately tugging at him to hurry.

"John, what are you doing?" Todd asked when he saw his soaking friend heading for the inferno.

"Help isn't coming for a while. Someone has to go in for them."

He didn't stop so Todd walked with him. Todd and the others had organized the neighbors and everyone with a hose that could reach was working on getting them attached to faucets and pulled toward the burning house.

"Let me go," Todd said.

John looked into his eyes as they walked. Todd was serious. He'd gladly walk into that house if John let him. John just shook his head.

"No time," John said, indicating his wet clothes.

They had gotten close to the house and the heat made Todd stop. Even with the wet shirt the inferno took John's breath away. Most of the back side of the house and the roof was aflame and the air was scorching. The water covering John's clothes and hair made it bearable, but he knew it wouldn't last long.

"Amanda is going to kill you for this," Todd said. "And me for letting you do it."

"Tell her I love her," John shouted back over his shoulder.

John didn't hear if Todd said anything else. Climbing the steps of the porch the roar of the fire engulfed every other sound. He couldn't even hear the screams anymore and he prayed it was because the fire was too loud. He pulled his hand into his sleeve and tried the handle of the front door with the wet material protecting his hand. It steamed, but the door opened without burning his fingers. John stepped inside just as the first hose started pouring water onto the roof above.

Inside, the house was simple like thousands of others in the Midwest. He was in a large living room that would have been comfortable and homey, except for the flames crawling up the walls near the front door. The back of the room was engulfed in flames and they were starting toward the front of the house. He didn't see any stairs and had a door on his right and a large open doorway to a kitchen that seemed to be the source of the conflagration. He stepped through the door to the right rather than risking the wall of flames in the kitchen.

John found himself in a bedroom that was nearly untouched by the fire in the rest of the house. Smoke was pouring through and John crouched to avoid most of it. Like many of these older houses all of the rooms on the main floor were connected with no hallways, and he saw a door at the back of the room on the other side of the bed. Like the last room there was no one here so he went through the open door and into a large dining room.

The dining room was nearly as bad as the kitchen with flames dancing the walls and across the ceiling. The tendrils of destruction fascinated him for a moment, moving like living things along the old wood work in the room. On John's left were the stairs, climbing into a dark, smoky second floor. He could hear the screams above the flames and see what kept the residents trapped upstairs. The steps were clear but on the walls in the stairwell hungry little flames licked across the plaster. The fire moved like it had a mind of its own, working its way up the walls toward the second story. John pulled his steaming jacket up around his neck and rushed up the stairs before they became impassable.

At the top of the stairs was a loft, and what he thought were two doorways. The smoke was so thick coming up the stairs he wasn't sure, but he could clearly hear the screaming coming from the room on his right. He used his sleeve to protect his hand again and turned the knob on the door. The door was stuck on the towel the occupants pushed under it to keep out the smoke but he was able to force it open with his body. The bedroom beyond was miraculously free of fire, and had much less smoke in the air than the rest of the house. A woman and two children were huddled near an open window on the far side of the room, trying to get clean air. John remembered from being outside that window was too high off the ground to jump. It was at least a fifteen-foot drop straight down.

"Come on, we need to get you out of here," John shouted at them from the door.

The three turned, and John was relieved that the woman didn't hesitate. She picked up the smaller of the two children and pushed the other in his direction. He could tell she was terrified, but the fact that he came through the house must have reassured her they could make it back the same way. He pulled off his damp jacket and handed it to the woman.

"Here, cover the both of you with this."

He didn't wait to see if she did it, he untied the shirt that protected his face and draped it over the little girl's head before picking her up. He turned to the stairs and rushed down two at a time, praying the woman was following close behind. There was no time to be sure, so he did his best not to lose his way as he got the little girl out of her burning home. By some miracle the path he'd used to enter the house was still relatively clear, and he rushed out the front door moments after having picked up the child. He turned to look back and breathed a sigh of relief when he saw the woman and second child right behind him. The deep breath caused a coughing fit that wracked his body and felt like his lungs were being torn apart. He set the child down before he dropped her.

The scene outside was chaos as neighbors tried to get as much water as they could on the burning house and those next to it. Some moved forward to help the woman and her children, and others were helping find more hose, buckets, and anything else that would hold water. John had seen Todd holding Amanda, who had obviously come to see what was happening after directing the other groups on their way. When John collapsed in the yard Todd couldn't hold her back any longer.

John felt her arms wrap around him while he knelt in the wet grass. She held him until the coughing subsided and he was able to stand. The look on her face shifted from horror, to anger, to something John could only interpret as pride. She didn't say anything, and he didn't prompt her for words. She just looked at his face as if studying it for the first and last time, like she hadn't expected to see it again.

The moment was broken by the sound of sirens cutting through the night over the roar of the flames. John and the others didn't speak, they just turned to leave. The woman, whose house was slowly falling to a smoking ruin, rushed over before they crossed the street. She touched John's shoulder and he turned to find himself suddenly wrapped in a vice-like embrace.

"Thank you sir, thank you so much for saving my babies," the woman was sobbing.

John gently detached himself from her and looked down at the woman.

"Don't thank me, I just did what had to be done," John said.

The woman looked at him as if he were crazy for a moment, but just nodded, unsure how to respond to that. John gave her a sooty smile.

"If you want to thank someone, thank God, he's why we were passing by."

"You're an angel then?" The woman asked. "What's your name?"

"No angel, just John," he said, giving her hand a squeeze. He took Amanda's arm and together they turned and walked across the street and into the shadow between the other houses. They were on their way toward the bridge before the emergency vehicles arrived.

Chapter 35

The reeducation camps started out as acclimation centers for people who didn't fit into the new America. It was an easy way to get rid of political dissidents or enemies of the government. After all, America wasn't some third world dictatorship; they couldn't be dragged out of their homes in the night and killed. Eventually it was a place to send people who hadn't actually committed a crime. They just needed a reminder of how to be good citizens. I never knew anyone that came back from a camp. The way I understood it was if you went to a camp you were relocated after release. Of course that always led to rumors that no one was ever released.

-Excerpt from the Journal of John Evermann

Lieutenant Casey left the border post with a stuffed bear and the knowledge that several of the fugitives were well out of his reach. The children had been the most important ones to capture. They tended to be easier to educate when separated from their parents. Now they were over the border and he had no idea where the parents would be. He needed a plan and time to think.

He remembered signs for a town, Neosho, east of the border post. He turned his SUV onto the road leading the small town. With this new information he might be able to requisition a helicopter to help with the search. He doubted it, helicopters were expensive and very conspicuous, but he would try. His bosses would have to weigh the cost against the loss of a few citizens. They would also have to factor in how hard it would be to hide what was going on if it turned into a full-scale manhunt.

He pulled into town and easily found a motel with a diner. He hadn't slept the night before and no matter how good his plan he wouldn't get much done without a couple hours of rest. Like every establishment in the country Casey only had to show his citizen's debit card and he was given a meal and a room.

The meal wasn't anything special and Casey paid little attention to it. It was flavorless but nutritious, which was all that was required by the FDA. The diner was nearly empty, except for a coupe of elderly men who had the look of patrons that spent most of their day in the diner drinking the weak coffee. There was one bored looking waitress in a wrinkled uniform and the television was on the federal news station, which was regulation. Casey was glad to have some normalcy around him for a change. It helped him relax.

While he ate he called into the Peoria office on his cell phone. The reception was awful, as usual, but like Casey's dad always said, you get what you pay for. Technically these phones weren't paid for, but if they had been they'd be cheap. The desk sergeant picked up and Casey asked to be transferred to the duty officer.

"Lieutenant?" The voice on the other end sounded surprised.

"Simons," Casey recognized the voice of his subordinate. "I need a team to come down to post one-eleven and pick up our van."

"Yes sir, I'll send a team right away."

"How's the search for that missing girl?" Casey asked.

"They're still looking sir."

Casey cursed under his breath. That would make resources scarce for his case.

"I need you to call central, ask for Harbaugh. He owes me a favor," Casey said. "Tell him I'm asking for one helicopter to find these fugitives."

"I'll see what I can do sir," Simons said.

"Good, I'll call back after I get some sleep."

"Sir? What about the prisoner?" Simons asked.

Casey had almost put Benny out of his mind. Of course he had called everything in before heading down there so they were expecting a prisoner pickup as well as the vehicle retrieval. Casey just didn't see the point in putting Benny in prison or a camp. The bearded man had nothing to lose, nor did they have leverage they could hold over him.

He wouldn't change, or even become a productive member of society. He would just be a drain on the state. Casey couldn't see the benefit in incarcerating one man for the rest of his life when the goal was to reform them and get them back into society.

"There won't be a prisoner pickup," Casey said. They would want an explanation. "He wasn't who I was looking for."

Casey hated to lie, especially when it was about work, but he couldn't afford to be recalled to explain his decision. He would report the truth when he debriefed and face the consequences then.

"Understood," Simons said. "I'll try to get an answer for you today."

"Good, I'll call you later." Casey hung up the phone and finished his meal.

Casey knew his chances of getting real help were slim. His bosses wanted the fugitives stopped but not badly enough that they wanted to risk drawing attention to the situation. He knew they would rather see the people escape rather than a firestorm of public sympathy. At least if they left the country the media out of Texas could be controlled through the jamming stations.

"You look to be chewing on something pretty serious there son," one of the elderly men sat down across from him.

Casey looked up from his meal, knowing the man wasn't talking about the food.

"It's a private matter, citizen," Casey said.

"Bah, you can stuff all that comrade citizen talk. Name's Gordon," Gordon didn't hold out his hand, he just sat there looking at Casey.

Casey knew exactly what he was dealing with now. The man was a silent dissenter. They were people who didn't agree with the way of things. They just kept to themselves and weren't considered much of a threat. For the most part they were left alone unless they moved beyond the idle comment or two. Casey thought they were cowards. At least John and his people were doing something, as wrong as it was.

"Gordon, it's an official matter. I can't discuss it."

Casey put his head down and started eating again. He hoped Gordon would take the hint.

"If you want my advice son."

Casey sighed.

"Put your badge in the nearest dumpster and get yourself over to Texas. They need people like you there."

"Why do you say that Gordon?"

"Well, it's the weekend and here you are, obviously miles from home, and you're working a case. If I had to guess I'd say you're alone because everyone else put in their time for the week?" Gordon nodded, not really needing an answer.

Casey didn't like how easily a stranger could read him. That was his job after all. He thought about it and realized it probably wasn't that hard for someone who'd been around long enough. The plates on his SUV weren't local, and if that wasn't enough the vehicle was covered in bugs and dust from a long drive. His uniform was wrinkled and needed washed, and he must not look all that orderly himself. It was the weekend, when almost every command officer in the country would be at home, leaving the work to the off-shift officers.

"Way I see it," Gordon kept talking. "You are so focused on whatever it is you're looking for, that you can't bring yourself to stick to your contract. You're wasting your talent."

"I have a duty. I took an oath to hold to that," Casey said.

Gordon touched the side of his nose and smiled knowingly. He finished the dregs of the coffee in his little cup and stood up.

"Gordon, why aren't you headed there yourself?" Casey asked. The old man stopped and turned back.

"I'm too old and set in my ways to be any use over there," Gordon said. The way he spoke about it, it was like he was talking about some fabled city of gold, or the outdated idea of heaven.

"Was a time I thought about it, but I waited too long," Gordon nodded at Casey when he said that last part.

Gordon went back to his table with the other man and sat down. The waitress came by and refilled both men's coffee and they went back to their conversation as if the last few minutes never happened. Whether Casey knew it or not then, those few minutes would stay with him forever.

In that moment the conversation bothered Casey so much he couldn't concentrate on the problem of the fugitives. Even the tasteless meal, which was normally acceptable to Casey, seemed to turn his stomach. He decided it was exhaustion finally setting in and sleep moved to the top of his priority list.

The motel room was as sparse as the meal. The décor was identical to every other roadside establishment since about nineteen eighty, and smelled like it hadn't been aired out in as long. There was one double bed, a chair next to a small table, and a television on the dresser. The bathroom was no bigger than a closet but it had a shower so it would serve Casey's needs. He dropped his duffel, containing the much-needed change of clothes, into the chair and climbed into the cramped shower.

Finally clean, after the lukewarm shower, exhaustion truly set in. Casey dried off, flipped on the national news, and collapsed onto the bed. They were covering the missing girl and all the steps the federal police were taking to find her. Casey didn't make it through ten minutes of the story before he was asleep.

Hours later he woke with a start and it took him several seconds to break through the fog of sleep and remember where he was. It came back to him piece by piece and he sat up and looked at the television. It was later than he wanted to have slept.

Cursing his failure to set an alarm he grabbed his phone and called the Peoria office.

"Simons is out sir, but he left a message for you," the desk officer said after Casey asked for the junior officer.

"Give it to me," Casey said.

"It says the chopper is a no go and central would like a briefing on the prisoner at your earliest convenience," the desk officer read the message.

"Of course they do," Casey grumbled.

"Can I help you with anything else, sir?"

"No, thanks," Casey said and hung up the phone. He tossed it back on the night stand and rubbed at his face. He started to get up when the television switched over to local news. The lead story was an old house fire in Columbia, Missouri. He walked toward the bathroom but stopped. Columbia was in the fugitive's path and the timing was about right. He looked back at the television.

"The homeowner, Nancy Simmons, claims a stranger saved her family from the flames," the reporter was saying. The screen behind her showed a smoking hulk where a house had been. A fire truck and federal patrol car were on the street and neighbors stood around in robes and pajamas. A reporter on scene approached a woman sitting on the back of the fire truck receiving oxygen while two children clung to her.

"I swear, it was a miracle," the woman said when the microphone was put in front of her. She coughed and continued.

"He came out of nowhere, definitely not from around here. John's a hero," the woman finished.

"Where did this hero, John, go?" The local reporter asked.

"He just walked away with four others, right into the night," she said, pointing across the street.

Casey didn't hear the reporter's next question, or Nancy's answer. He rushed to get dressed and collect his things. He stuffed everything into his duffel and was racing down the motel stairs in a matter of moments. He had been in such a hurry he forgot to switch off the television or close the door behind him.

Chapter 36

Whether it was planned or not, the catastrophic breakdown of the welfare system became justification for many of the changes in the country. Between the two great wars Roosevelt started the welfare system that became so prominent in this country. The original plan was to assist widows, children, and the elderly who had lived longer than the normal life expectancy. Over the years, political promises, and crusader ideals, had expanded the system to include just about anyone who was 'down on their luck'. The trouble was, the more people on welfare, meant less people working, and the working people were the ones funding it. Eventually you reach a point where the balance tips and there aren't enough people working to pay for those who aren't.

That's what happened to us. The system fell right off the cliff. People demanded a solution, and rightly so. The government had promised to take care of them and suddenly it couldn't afford to. All of the other funds had been tapped out, all other programs borrowed from until there wasn't anything left. Just one of the symptoms of the perfect storm that led to what we see today.

-Excerpt from the Journal of John Evermann

The sun was starting to rise over the river the refugees had crossed the night before. The ripples in the water flashed silver as John watched the colors of the world change with the coming day. Everyone was asleep behind him, except for Todd who shared the last watch. The other man was stretching his legs, walking along the tree line but still within sight of his friend.

The night before, the refugees had all met just south of the highway on the west side of the bridge as instructed. They'd waited anxiously for the ones who stayed behind to fight the fire, relieved to see him and the others finally cross the bridge. John's head count, when he got there, confirmed everyone made it through. Despite their exhaustion John led them south for another hour to insure no one would stumble upon them by accident.

"Sun's been up awhile," Todd came back and sat down next to John and nodded toward the sleepers.

"Let them sleep a little longer, they've earned it," John coughed a little. His throat was still irritated from the smoke and his voice was raspy.

"How are you feeling?" Todd asked. Everyone was concerned about the smoke John had inhaled but Todd's worry carried a note of guilt.

"I'll be fine Todd," John patted his friend on the shoulder and smiled. "Remember, we have someone looking out for us."

"I don't think Amanda will ever forgive me for letting you go in there," Todd said.

"Todd, you couldn't have stopped me. She doesn't blame you."

It was true, despite Todd's doubt. Amanda had been upset about John's stunt but she didn't blame Todd. She reserved her anger for her husband. She was proud of him for rescuing the family from the burning house, but furious and terrified at the same time. John understood her conflicting emotions about it and sympathized.

By the time the sun was fully up everyone was awake and packing. They all ate and collected any stray garbage around the site as usual. Within two hours of sunrise the refugees were split into their groups and ready to move. With John's group in the lead they started walking south across old fields and woodland. More leaves had fallen with the previous night's wind and they crunched underfoot like piles of potato chips.

After a couple hours walk they reached an old road that traveled south. The pavement was broken and impassable for a car, but it could be walked on.

"What do you think?" Todd nodded toward the road.

"I don't think it's been used in years, and it would be faster than crossing these fields," John said.

John looked at the broken pavement, and weeds growing in the cracks. He decided it was worth the risk to save some time. He checked the map but the old highway wasn't on it. It was probably part of a network of old farm roads between the interstates. He guessed they could follow it south to the next major road and eventually the interstate they would use to guide them west.

"We should be able to follow this to the town of California," John said, tracing the route on the map with his finger. "We'll go around the town and stay on this until we're a couple hours south of it."

"It looks pretty small, it shouldn't be too much trouble," Todd said, looking at the map over John's shoulder.

The groups set off again on the old highway, moving steadily south. It was easier going than the open ground they were used to. As long as they watched for broken chunks of the road, and large cracks, they made good time. John was struck by how quiet it was along that stretch of road. Of course there were the sounds of wildlife, but they were used to hearing the sounds of the occasional car on a nearby road or farm and construction machinery in the distance. The only farms they passed were abandoned years before, and the further south they traveled the more decayed the road was.

They reached the outskirts of California, Missouri late in the afternoon. John opened the map, looking for an old farm road he had seen before.

"Here it is. We'll take this road around and meet up with the interstate," John was tracing the line on the map. "That will take us back to eighty-seven."

"John, wait," Todd was standing a few feet ahead, looking toward the town with his head tilted like he was concentrating on a sound he couldn't quite hear.

"What is it? What do you hear?" John asked, moving closer to his friend.

"That's just it, John. Nothing. I don't hear any cars, children playing, machinery, nothing," Todd said.

While it was true that fewer cars and fewer people meant towns were quieter it was still shocking to hear nothing but silence this close to a town the size of California. All the sounds of human habitation tend to blend into a miasma of unidentifiable noise unless one is close enough to a specific source to hear it. Even outside the town there should have been a steady drone of sounds punctuated by the occasional car horn, children at play, or lawn mower. Standing on the outskirts of California, Missouri, the sound of silence was deafening.

"Tell everyone to wait here, Todd and I are going to go take a look," John said to Amanda. He started to turn away.

"John," Amanda's voice was stern and he turned back. "Don't do anything reckless."

John smiled and stepped closer to kiss her on the forehead. "Don't worry dear. We're just going to take a look. I doubt there are any burning buildings to run into this time."

Amanda didn't smile at his joke but she nodded, giving his hand a squeeze. They both knew if doing the right thing required reckless action, John wouldn't think twice about doing it. It was part of the reason she loved him. It was also the reason she was always worried when he went off on his own. She just did what she always did, and prayed God kept him safe.

When John and Todd walked between the first couple of houses they noticed the overgrown yards and deteriorating buildings. That wasn't an uncommon sight in the smaller towns of the Midwest, as populations were moved and contracted toward the center of towns. Some yards had rusting cars, bicycles, and toys buried under the weight of nature taking back what was hers. They stuck to the streets, which were as cracked and broken as the highway had been, to avoid the dangers of the long grass. The refugees had been lucky so far, but they were always conscious of the danger of snake bites so far from help.

As they moved toward the center of town it became apparent why they had heard nothing from the highway. There was nothing to hear. Even in the center of town, where they expected to see the concentrated population of California, they found only a decaying shell. Broken glass littered the crumbling streets and sidewalks, mixed with bits of concrete, asphalt and brick from the streets and buildings. Grass grew in the street, across walkways, and anywhere else it could find a hold in the man-made landscape.

"Abandoned," Todd said simply, looking around at the empty buildings.

They had both heard of towns left to rot when they had nothing to offer. Their citizens moved to other towns and cities to be reassigned to work that would support society. Neither of them had seen it with their own eyes. John couldn't help but feel sadness creep over him at the sight. Empty and broken store fronts, where people had built their dreams, were staring out at the deserted street like the hollow sockets of a skull. Where a town at night just felt asleep, California felt dead.

"Let's head back," John said. "There's no need to go around."

Todd nodded and they turned around and headed back. John didn't like the feeling of the ghost town and he hoped to move everyone through it as quickly as possible. With the broken roads radiating out from the decaying town it reminded him of a cancer, a place of rot in the middle of America. How many such wounds marred the once great country, he thought. How many abandoned yards where children once played, or homes where families once lived? At what point did Americans go from a people who would defend their homes, neighbors, and towns with their very lives, to nothing but cattle to be moved whenever it suits the whim of the government? At least there was evidence that nature would eventually retake what was hers.

Chapter 37

I've never understood why people don't see the game that was being played out, and how they were used as pawns during the years leading up to the collapse. Some of it was subtle, easy to miss in all the noise. When politicians pitted people against each other it always amazed me how many played along. Why couldn't more people see through the lies and games? The biggest fight before the collapse was on abortion with both sides pitted against each other and politicians standing back and fueling the emotional fire. If you were pro-life then you wanted to take rights away from women, but then didn't that mean if you were pro-choice you wanted to take rights away from infants? Pro-lifers wanted to see less killing of the unborn, but some would gladly see abortion doctors lose their lives. A couple of people even made that a horrific reality. Pro-choicers wanted more rights for women, but given the choice would they have wanted their own mother to decide whether they got the chance to live or not? Was our blindness to this game a symptom of the ignorance that had us stand idly by while it all came crashing down?

-Excerpt from the Journal of John Evermann

Lieutenant Casey drove directly to the scene of the fire in Columbia. Fire crews were still cleaning up the mess, but there were no federal police on the scene when he pulled up. He stopped his SUV a few houses down and walked toward the burned-out hulk that had once been someone's house. He flashed his badge at the first firefighter to take notice of him.

"Any idea what caused the fire?" Casey asked.

"Not yet, sir," the firefighter said after looking at Casey's badge a moment.

"The news reported that the occupant said someone helped her out of the house. Where would I find her?" Casey asked.

"That's right, sir. Witnesses say a couple of strangers came out of nowhere and started helping. The strangers were gone before we pulled up. The citizen who lived here was taken to the hospital," the firefighter explained.

"Has anyone seen the strangers since last night?" Casey asked. "Or which way they went?"

"No to both, sir," the other reported. "Witnesses say after they got the woman and her kids out they just walked off that way."

He pointed north between the houses on that side of the street. Casey looked where the firefighter pointed. Of course in the dark no one would have seen them after a few dozen feet, and at the edge of town there weren't likely to be any other witnesses. John's group had probably been moving around to the western edge of town but Casey would have to guess whether they would keep going west or move south. He would need to check for prints but first he needed to talk to the woman.

The short drive to the hospital seemed to take forever. Casey hated every moment he spent in Columbia instead of on the road after John and the fugitives. He had to be sure though. He was unwilling to take the word of a media report and a second, or third hand witness. He was determined not to run off on anymore wild goose chases after rumors or shadows.

Casey easily found the woman and her children after talking to admitting. All three were being treated for minor injuries and smoke inhalation after their harrowing night. The hospital in Columbia was a stark contrast to the one Casey was used to seeing in Peoria. They didn't seem to have a problem with overcrowding but like Peoria they were light on staff. They just had fewer patients to worry about in the smaller city. The woman and her children were in the same room and she was sitting up, watching them sleep when Casey walked in.

"Mrs. Simmons?" Casey tapped lightly on the door frame.

The woman looked up. Her eyes were tired from an obviously long night, but she smiled anyway. Something was strange about that. People rarely smiled when a uniformed federal officer came to visit.

"I'm Nancy Simmons," she said.

"Is your husband here?" He asked, looking around the room and seeing no one else.

"He's on nights at the factory. He's sleeping over at his brother's so he can be back tonight," she said.

"Of course," Casey said. He started to speak again but closed his mouth when she continued.

"No days off when it comes to civic duty," she said it seriously but there was something in her tone that made Casey wonder. He decided to let it go.

"The man that helped your family last night, can you describe him?" Casey asked.

"Of course," Nancy said. She proceeded to describe the man that Casey knew as John Evermann.

"Did he say anything about where he was going or who was with him?" Casey asked.

"No, he helped us out of the house, said his name was John, and left with a couple of other men that were helping put water on the other houses."

"What about the others?" Casey asked.

"I didn't see them for more than a minute. Three men that all looked like they hadn't washed up in a few days."

"Thank you Mrs. Simmons, if I need anything else I'll be in touch," Casey said.

"Is it true? Is John leading people to Texas?" Her question stopped him on his way to the door. It seemed, despite the best efforts of the government media department, John's story was spreading.

"I wouldn't know anything about that ma'am," he said without turning around. He never could master looking someone in the eye and lying to them.

"Of course not," there was that tone again, like she had expected everything he was going to say and was just humoring him. He left the hospital room before she could ask any more questions he would have to answer with a lie.

When John got in the SUV the stuffed bear caught his eye. It had fallen on the floor and was sitting with its glossy plastic eyes staring at him. The unblinking gaze seemed accusatory, as if the inanimate object was judging him in some way. He knew the thought was completely insane but he couldn't shake it. He grabbed the bear and tossed it roughly into the back seat.

He turned back and looked at the part of the city he could see through the windshield from the parking lot of the hospital. Casey rarely looked at any of the cities and towns he passed through, always being so focused on the task at hand. The visit with Nancy Simmons had thrown his concentration off and he was having trouble focusing. He knew he should be working out the next step. He should be trying to reason out which way John went, and the best way to follow. All he could do tough, was stare at the people, and the town in front of him.

He was parked so that he looked right up a main street, with some federal businesses, but mostly abandoned ones on either side. The people that were out didn't walk so much as trudge, slowly making their way from one place to another. There was no purpose to their movement. It was as if where they came from mattered as little as where they were going. Almost like they accepted that life had nothing more to offer and they moved through it knowing that the only real change would be at the end.

He caught himself wondering if John had been like that. A year ago, if Casey sat watching a crowd of people in Stewart, would he have noticed John Evermann as someone with a purpose? Would he have been able to guess what John and his fugitives were about to do?

Casey finally pushed the thought away, forcing himself to turn his eyes to the dashboard, then the glove compartment. Opening the door to the compartment he pulled out one of the maps inside. He opened the map in front of him. Folding back the top half he laid it against the steering wheel.

He could only see two routes open to John and his group. At some point they would have to cross the Missouri river, and there were only two places to do that without going days out of their way. The southern route would take them through Jefferson City, which would be extremely risky. He wouldn't put it past John to take that risk. He was last seen on the north side of Columbia however, west of the main highway. So, it was more likely he went west. There was a bridge across the river a couple miles west of the city. From there the problem would be turning south. Few of the old farm roads were still in use this close to the Texas border, and the further west they went the worse the roads got. Most of those farm tracks weren't even on the map, but Casey knew there would be quite a few of them. Casey settled on crossing the closer bridge. He knew his challenge would be in guessing which road John would turn south on.

Casey pulled out of the parking lot and made the short drive through town to the highway that ran west to the river. He was occasionally distracted by the people he saw, and the new way they began to appear to him. He forced his mind to concentrate each time it wandered. He reminded himself that everyone had all that they required; all they needed was provided for them. There was no one suffering from hunger or homelessness, no one begging on the streets because they couldn't get work. Everyone was being taken care of.

It wasn't a long drive to the bridge and he soon pulled over near the first road south from the highway. It was an unused road, like most of the others he would find. He put the SUV in park and climbed out without turning off the engine. He looked for any sign that John and his people had turned this way. There was nothing, not a single piece of litter any different from what was normally found on the side of the road. Nothing at all to indicate this was the way they went. He went back to the SUV and pulled the map out, laying it across the hood. Of course the next road on the map that traveled south was some hours to the west. If he followed a generally straight line from where he was though, this old broken road should cross one major highway and meet up with another that headed further south and west. If he were John that would be the highway he'd follow to get to the old Interstate 49. The route would bypass all of the other major cities in Missouri, and despite 49 being a military route; it would still be the safest way for the fugitives to go.

Casey folded the map again and got back in the SUV. He decided to follow his gut and pull onto the closer farm road headed south. The pavement was broken in many spots but he hoped it remained passable for the vehicle. He dodged large chunks of torn-up pavement, and potholes large enough to lose a tire in. He drove for nearly an hour, slowing down for rough patches, but it was an unseen cavity under the pavement that stopped his rush south.

The road looked clear for a good distance so he had sped up. In the instant before it happened Casey considered how unwise it was to drive too fast. Some instinct told him to be more careful. Just as he started to slow down again the weight of the SUV collapsed the pavement over a spot where the ground underneath had been washed out. He hit the newfound pothole hard and fast. The impact was enough to cause him to lose control and swerve off the road, nearly rolling the vehicle on its side. The SUV fishtailed in the gravel along the side of the road and finally came to rest with the rear of the vehicle in the ditch. He had felt both passenger side tires hit the hole with a grinding crunch and feared the worst when he climbed out of the SUV.

He'd been right to worry. Both tires on the passenger side were shredded. The rubber was nearly gone completely on the front tire and the back was flat with several layers of the tread pulled back to expose the layers beneath. He only had one spare, but even if he had two he would have had no way to change them with the angle of the ground and how soft it was. His first instinct was to curse and complain about his poor luck, but he knew how futile it would be. He wasn't much of a complainer anyway but there was no one around to hear him shouting or to listen to him despair, and neither would get him closer to finding John. He got on the radio and called in the location of the vehicle so that it could be picked up. He had little hope for that, however. The desk officer in Peoria took his information and he could see in his mind the disinterested officer filing the paper at the bottom of a stack of things to get done. This far from any large city scavengers would pick it over for parts. By the time someone was able to arrange a truck to come get his SUV it would be stripped bare of anything useful.

Casey pulled open the back door and dragged his bag toward him. He stuffed the map of Missouri into a side pocket, and then he noticed the bear. The stuffed animal sat next to the duffel as if it was nothing more than a motionless passenger waiting for his next decision. He looked at the toy for a few moments and finally stuffed it inside the bag as well. He didn't understand why he picked it up. It just didn't seem right to leave it for the scavengers. At least the toy didn't weight much, he thought.

Pulling the bag from the SUV he turned toward the south and looked down the long road ahead. For a brief moment he considered turning around and telling his superiors the fugitives were too far gone. They expected him to find and stop a large group of people on his own, a task that was starting to seem more ludicrous every day. He was told help would be sent when they found the missing girl, but by then it could already be too late. He pushed the thought away, closed and locked the SUV, and started to walk south. He was too far from home to turn back now, and the only excuse his superiors were likely to accept would be losing the fugitives when they crossed the border. He didn't walk far before he had the bag over his shoulder and was jogging south to try and catch up to the slower group.

Chapter 38

I think the hardest thing for anyone to accept is; just because they like something, or think something is a good idea, doesn't mean everyone else should be forced to do it. That is why America was constructed as a republic and not a true democracy. It's often people who have a hard time with the first idea that say our founding documents are too restrictive, or that our government is designed poorly. They're the same people that use phrases like, 'for their own good,' or 'for the greater good.' It's because they have an idea that they think is better than all the others and are determined to force it on everyone else, whether anyone else likes it or not.

-Excerpt from the journal of John Evermann

The refugees had passed through the abandoned town of California without incident. The silence was palpable as they walked through the corpse of the Midwestern town. The empty houses and store fronts they passed were depressing and everyone felt the weight of it. The rest of the day's travel had been uneventful and they stopped for the night a couple hours north of a town marked on the map as Eldon. John figured their best route would take them around the east side of the Lake of the Ozarks, then south west toward Joplin. As best he could tell from the map, this would avoid any more river crossings or large towns.

John took the last watch before morning, and was listening to the sounds of insects and animals when he heard a sound that was out of place. He'd grown accustomed to the subtle music of nature, especially at night. He knew the difference between a person and an animal walking nearby. Someone was walking through the dried leaves that littered the ground all around the wooded area the refugees were sleeping in. They were trying not to make much noise, taking slow steps with long pauses, and sometimes finding spots clear of fallen leaves. Despite their caution the interloper still made enough noise to catch John's attention. The air was cold, and fall was fully upon them, and it was one of the reasons John picked this spot. He didn't expect to be followed. With all the fallen leaves on the ground though, it would be impossible for anyone to sneak up on their camp. None of his people had left their blankets recently so he knew a stranger was nearby.

John moved close to Todd, who was sleeping a few feet away, and quietly woke him. He gestured for Todd to listen. He started to ask what was going on, but John waved him to silence. Todd heard the sounds of the intruder right away and nodded. John motioned for Todd to circle around the stranger on the west side, and watch. He indicated he would go directly toward the sound. John drew the pistol he rarely touched out of his waistband and pulled back the slide slowly to chamber a round as silently as he could. Flipping off the safety he stood and they both quietly moved toward the sound along their own routes.

It didn't take John long to get close enough to see the person through the trees. From the size of him, and the way he walked, John could tell it was a man. He was wearing dark clothing and was carrying a large bag at his side. The stranger was looking at the ground, trying to watch where he stepped, so he didn't see John in his path with the pistol leveled in his direction.

"I can't let you go any farther, stranger," John said evenly.

The man dropped his bag and reached toward his coat, but stopped when John spoke again.

"I wouldn't do that. I don't have a lot of practice but this close I doubt I'll miss," John said firmly. He didn't like the idea that he might have to back up that threat, but when it came to protecting his own he was prepared.

The stranger slowly lowered his hands and moved them away from his body where John could see them. Then he raised his head to look at John.

"Lieutenant Casey?" John was surprised and confused, but had sense enough not to lower the pistol. He hoped never to see the federal agent again and certainly didn't expect to see him walking on his own in the middle of nowhere.

"Hello, John," Casey said. "I've been looking for you."

Even facing down a gun the federal officer was calm. It worried John but he relaxed a little when Todd approached from the side.

"He's alone," Todd assured his friend. John nodded in relief.

"Toss your gun on the ground toward Todd, carefully," John ordered.

Casey did so, slowly pulling the pistol from the holster under his jacked and tossing it to the ground at Todd's feet. Todd picked up the weapon and held it, pointed at the ground.

"What are you doing out here on your own?" John asked, hoping to get a sense of the other man, and his intentions.

"I've come to take you in John," Casey said. The confidence with which he said those words unnerved John.

"I mean, where's your backup? Why are you on foot, by yourself?" John asked. They both knew John held the advantage, so he didn't see a point in arguing Casey's first statement.

"I had to abandon my truck a few miles back. An accident took out both tires," Casey said.

John wanted to turn Casey around and send him on his way, but the officer had followed them this far, alone, and without his vehicle. There was no guarantee he wouldn't continue to follow them. He might find a way to cause harm to the group farther along their route. He couldn't take the chance that Casey would get help and come after them, or simply follow them and try to hurt them a little at a time. John didn't know why Casey was alone but it was too much of a risk to think he would stay that way.

"Check him," John said to Todd.

While Todd patted down Casey's coat and checked his pockets John considered his options.

"You'll have to come with us, we can't take any chances leaving you behind," John said. He then motioned Todd to the bag after the other indicated the officer was unarmed.

"You're the one holding the gun," Casey said. He held John's gaze while Todd searched the duffel.

Todd pulled out the bear, a change of clothes, and other personal items. Satisfied there were no weapons in the bag he put everything back, zipped it up and stepped away. He didn't even realize the bear belonged to one of the children of their group.

"All right, let's go," John said, gesturing with the pistol for Casey to walk in front of him. Todd led the way and the officer picked up his bag and followed. John went last, keeping his eyes on the officer's back.

The encounter with Lieutenant Casey had taken long enough that the sun was beginning to lighten the horizon, and people were stirring when they got back to the camp. People watched in curious alarm as John marched the federal officer into their midst at gunpoint. For his part Casey took in the scene as understanding slowly dawned on him. He saw only adults and older children, no toddlers or babies. The children that were with the group didn't match up with his memory of the case files. He couldn't remember all of the faces, but the ones he could recall were not present. It confirmed everything he had suspected after finding the bear in the back of the van.

"That was very clever, John. Using Benny and our van to get the kids out of the country," Casey said, stopping to turn back to John.

"What do you know about that? Have you seen Benny?" John couldn't help his curiosity. He kept his distance though, fearing Casey might be trying to get him to lower his guard.

"He was caught at the border. I'm sure he was covering so the others could get across," Casey said calmly.

"Did you send him to one of your camps?" John asked. They all knew the consequences for getting caught doing what they were doing, but part of him hoped that it still wouldn't happen.

"No, we let him go. He is far beyond any hope of rehabilitation," Casey didn't see any point in lying to John. Behind him subdued but hopeful cheers rang out as people spread the news they overheard.

"Why?" John asked.

"Call it fiscal responsibility. He wasn't ever going to change so the cost to try wasn't justified," Casey shrugged.

Even though John's friend was saved a life sentence in a miserable camp, it was still chilling to hear Casey talk about him like he was no more than an entry in a ledger. It reminded John that, to the people in charge, that's all they were. They were faceless, nameless numbers to be managed. They weren't much more than livestock. They could be shuffled around, moved from home to home, city to city, to better serve their place in the new American society.

"So, what now John?" Casey asked, pulling the other man out of his dark thoughts. The officer's eyes dipped to the gun still pointed at his chest, then back to John's face.

"I can't take any chances," John put the pistol on safety and tucked it into his waistband again. "You'll have to come with us, at least as far as the border crossing."

Casey couldn't hide his surprise. He honestly didn't think they would kill him, but some small part of him thought they might. He never even entertained the possibility they would take him along. His plan had been simple, get close, find out how many there were, and how well armed, and try to find help between them and Texas. He didn't count on being caught, but it was something he could have worked with. Now his entire plan was turned on its head. He was alone, without supplies, or a weapon, and stood little chance of escape with so many of them to keep watch. He knew he was running out of time and would have to watch for any opportunity that might present itself.

"Whatever you say, John. You're in charge," Casey said calmly. He knew that keeping himself calm, and especially the fugitives calm, would be key to turning things around.

Chapter 39

Can one fairly cast blame on another person who has been taught that what they believe is right. Can we blame them if they're led astray by people they trust? All through history there are examples of awful things done by people because someone they believed in told them it was right. Of course it's easy to sit back and say they should have known better. We didn't live their lives, nor do we know why they put their faith in something we find wrong. That's why we are charged not to judge. The challenge is overcoming the hate or anger long enough to see that.

-Excerpt from the Journal of John Evermann

The refugees traveled south in their usual staggered groups. John kept Casey with his group so he could personally keep an eye on him. John also kept his weapon ready. The day was chilly, heralding the approach of winter. There had been frost on the ground that morning, which disappeared with the sun. The changing temperatures added a little urgency to their weary trek. John didn't expect a drastic shift in the weather, but the Midwest was well known for surprises on that front.

The plan was to travel south, and around the west side of the Lake of the Ozarks area. The map showed quite a few small towns and housing areas, as well as bridges crossing the small inlets and rivers that fed the lake. John remembered, from the news over the years, that most of these towns had been abandoned. With no practical use to the country, resort towns were shut down. Areas with no agricultural or industrial value were also closed up and their citizens relocated to places they could work for the common good. He was praying he was remembering the reports correctly, as well as hoping the bridges were still in good enough shape for them to cross. The area could take days to go around if a bridge was out.

They walked in silence for most of the morning, passing through the small town of Eldon two hours after starting out. Eldon was abandoned as well and the mood of each group that passed through was subdued by the sadness of it. They walked by empty buildings, broken windows, and decaying remains of cars where once had been a vital town. As with each community they passed like that it appeared as if everyone had simply vanished and everything was left as it was at that moment. The refugees did take a little time to look for food but none was found in the buildings along their route. None of them wanted to waste the time to spread out from the main road. Everything of use had been taken years before.

As usual John's group was last through the town. While the others made one more sweep for food in a corner convenience store, John and Casey were standing outside what had once been a used book store.

"Such a waste," John said.

"I was thinking the same thing. Why would anyone have opened a store like this?" Casey asked, misunderstanding John's meaning.

John turned to him, anger and surprise showing clear on his face.

"What?" Casey asked, genuinely oblivious to what could have raised the other's ire.

"This was someone's dream Casey, their life. They were forced to abandon it," John said, his anger causing him to speak louder than normal.

"To sell old books and profit from his neighbors?" Casey asked skeptically. "Sounds like a selfish dream to me."

"People used to like to buy books to read. To collect them or pass them on," John said. He wasn't surprised by Casey's comment, it was a common mindset, but it still frustrated him to hear it face to face.

"I remember too John, but that's what libraries are for. No one needs to own books or half the other garbage people used to buy," Casey answered expectantly.

"Right, so because some faceless politician in Washington decided what we need and don't need, we lost the right to choose?" John's voice rose, echoing down the empty streets of Eldon. Amanda stepped out of the convenience store across the street to see what was wrong.

"What right do you have?" John continued. "What right does anyone have to say what I need or don't need?"

"Steps have to be taken to maintain the welfare of the whole, John," Casey said calmly, again sounding like a government pamphlet.

"Don't you once want to do something for the welfare of yourself? Haven't you ever wanted to go somewhere just to see it, or choose a different path just to experience it?" John asked, desperate to see something in Casey other than a parrot of government propaganda.

Casey, hands in his pockets, just looked at John for a few moments. The passion in John's words was unmistakable, and Casey couldn't deny how alluring such freedom sounded. It was clear that John believed, with every fiber of his being, that what he said was concrete truth to him. Casey realized the car was in his hand, its smooth, cold metal sliding against his skin sparked memories of childhood dreams of racing cars. He jerked his hand from his pocket.

"Freedom without consideration for others is irresponsible," Casey recited.

"My freedom does consider everyone Casey," John said. "Your liberty is as sacred to me as mine is."

"But," Casey stopped him with a hand up, "It doesn't benefit me or anyone else. If your liberty isn't properly directed it's just you doing whatever you want."

For John, in those moments, the irony of it all was almost laughable. In fact, he would have laughed if he hadn't been so upset. America had long ago given up almost every vestige of religion, with most people publicly claiming atheism or agnosticism. Believers had been forced to keep their religion to themselves, but right here before him was a shining example of the new religion that had filled the void. He wasn't surprised that Casey was so dedicated to his cause, repeating the words almost like a recitation of scripture. He was, however, disappointed. Casey was so dedicated to his job and logical in his pursuit of it. John hoped that in Casey he might also find someone with a mind open enough to accept something other than the status quo. John just shook his head in speechless defeat and turned to continue down the street as the others exited the store. He knew Casey would follow, so he didn't bother to wait.

Casey looked again at the storefront, with its broken windows, faded sign, and shelves of books that had been exposed to the weather. Further to the back he could see books on shelves that had been protected from the wind, rain, and sun. They were lined up in order, most likely organized so that shoppers could easily find what they needed. Despite the order to it there was also a maze-like layout to the shelves, almost begging anyone who entered to wander rather than be able to walk a straight line to a desired section. Casey could imagine walking through the store. The act of navigating the maze would reveal more discoveries than one would find in a well-organized library.

Despite the smell of mildewed and decaying books near the windows, he could also smell the dusty and aged paper in the back. It was a smell he'd noticed in the rarely visited sections of the library in Peoria, where the older books were kept. It was something he always remembered. It brought to mind wandering the stacks of the library when he was younger, looking at the old hardback encyclopedias that nobody seemed to check out. The weight of the toy car in his pocket pulled at his mind and he turned away from the store in frustration. These rambling thoughts of childhood dreams and memories were distracting him from his mission. He saw the was group near the end of the block already and jogged to catch up with them.

When Casey reached them Amanda and John were talking quietly. It appeared as if she were trying to calm him while he explained why he was so frustrated. To Casey the scene was just another thing he didn't understand about people. He'd never had a lasting or meaningful attachment to anyone, especially a woman. He understood the concept, but he had never experienced it. Despite his own failings he could clearly see that he was witnessing two people that cared for each other, and understood each other enough to lean on one another in times of stress. The strength of that sort of relationship was undeniable. Even without having experienced it himself he was starting to understand how strong the bond was among the fugitives. He was starting to see why they eluded him for so long. He still didn't get that it was their devotion to individualism that drove them to care for each other so strongly. To him it was just another example of the entire group's need for each of them to put the welfare of the whole above the individual. While the ends are the same, the means were vastly different.

John seemed to calm down after speaking to Amanda for a few minutes, and the group continued on in silence. John avoided talking to Casey, which was fine with the lieutenant. It gave him an opportunity to study the people he had been trailing for days. He was impressed with how quickly the group of civilians had adopted sensible tactics about moving through open country. Separating into smaller groups, noise discipline, and using hand signals were things he expected from a military unit or law enforcement. None of the files he had on the fugitives indicated that kind of experience in their past. He hadn't been able to get a complete file on the recluse, Bernard, and suspected the bearded man might have been the source of the knowledge.

Casey saw more evidence of why the fugitives had been difficult to pin down when they stopped to eat. There had been a predetermined time for the first group to find a place to stop where they could sit in relative concealment. They didn't talk much, keeping their voices low when they did. No group waited for any other, they sat down together, ate, picked up any trash, and left. This kept the whole group moving, and maintained their intervals on the trip. The officer was again impressed by their efficiency. If one group did talk to another it was to share food or news. In all, the experience was another conundrum for the federal officer. He'd always been taught that people who held to the old philosophy of individualism had no concern for other people or the world around them. In spite of that these people were showing great care for each other. Even outside family units they made sure everyone was well, had food and water. They also showed concern for the environment by packing up their trash. Casey knew the motivation for that was to make it difficult to track them, but they could have accomplished that by burying the garbage. He was finding John's people were very different from what was been taught to expect.

While he watched the others Amanda gathered a little food from everyone in the group and brought it to Casey, along with a cup of water. It wasn't much, part of a protein ration, some crackers, and a few pieces of dried apples, but Casey was still surprised by their generosity. They obviously didn't have much and he was an extra mouth to feed.

"Thank you," Casey said, accepting the food and water. Amanda sat down next to him, clearly taking her turn to keep an eye on him. He didn't see a weapon on her, but he expected she had one close at hand.

"Welcome," she responded, looking out over the small group.

"Why did everyone give up food for me?" Casey asked between bites.

"Letting you go hungry would be unnecessarily cruel," Amanda replied without looking at him. "It's the right thing to do to help other people when they need it."

"So why are you running then? That's all your country asks of you is to help everyone," Casey said.

"There's a big difference between helping someone by choice and being forced to do it for them," Amanda said, looking at him now. "Rest assured Lieutenant, if you had means to get food you would be expected to contribute just like everyone else."

"How is that any different though? You're all expected to contribute to the whole, for the welfare of everyone," Casey smiled, thinking he had found a weakness in their ideology.

"Choice," she said simply. "They all chose to be here, chose to do this, and can leave whenever they want. Your way supports those who can't help themselves, but also those who won't. Your way makes everyone a slave to his neighbor, we would rather be brothers."

"I don't see the difference," Casey said. He'd finished his lunch and held the wrapper in his hand.

Amanda stood and took the garbage from him along with his empty cup. She looked at him for a long moment, the same look in her eyes John had in front of the bookstore.

"That's exactly why John was so upset earlier," Amanda said, starting to turn away.

"Why does he care if I understand? Why do you?" Casey asked before she could walk away.

She stopped and looked back.

"We believe everyone has the right to choose, even you."

She left him with a lot to think about, but still, few answers that made sense to him. His views were all he'd ever known. Parents and teachers had believed it all as strongly as he did, and it had become an ingrained part of him. Everything that John's people believed, and did, went against what he had always known to be true. Whether he understood it or not, he couldn't ignore the fact that the fugitives believed it so strongly that they would throw away their lives in America and try to get to Texas. To him, that made them dangerous.

Chapter 40

When Texas broke away from the rest of the country there was a catastrophic change in America's military. Not since the civil war had soldiers been ordered to fight other Americans. The modern military was more like a brotherhood than before, but to many, orders were orders. Even so, military personnel in Texas and the other seceding states felt obligated to friends and family on one side of the border or the other. There was also the matter of personal political views, and in how each soldier viewed their oath. Everyone in the military, before the removal of the founding documents, had taken an oath to defend the constitution and country from all enemies, foreign and domestic. For quite a few the removal of the constitution was a domestic threat but so shocking and unexpected that no one knew how to react. When they were ordered to turn their weapons on other Americans, on American soil, it was the final straw. Mass defections, insubordination, and outright mutiny followed. When the dust settled the military was so depleted it was nearly powerless.

-Excerpt from the journal of John Evermann

After John's group finished eating they took one last look around the area to make sure they hadn't left anything behind. Satisfied the area was clear, John led them south after the other groups. The day was still clear, and bright, with the slightest hint of the coming winter in the chill breeze blowing across the lake to the west.

They would spend a good portion of the afternoon walking around the eastern side of the lake. There were several bridges crossing inlets and waterways along the highway they followed, and to John's relief the first one was in tact, and safe enough to cross. John continued to pray their luck would hold out until they crossed the last bridge on their map.

They made good time around the lake, and stopped once more to eat a couple miles north of the small town of Camdenton. John expected it to be abandoned like the others but he didn't want to take the chance. The bridge was close enough to the town that anyone living there might see them if they crossed during the day. He sent Todd ahead to stop the first group early so they could plan out a night time crossing of the bridge.

Casey noted that the evening meal was more of a familial gathering than lunch had been. People talked a little more freely and didn't eat as fast. They still kept vigilant watch, spoke in low voices, and minded their garbage. However, they permitted themselves to relax just a little and give the impression of an old-fashioned family gathering and dinner. Casey sat alone, watching the group as he ate. After a time, John came to sit by him.

"What do you know about the area ahead?" John asked without preamble.

"This isn't my district John, all I know is what I saw on my drive to the border," Casey said, not looking at the man beside him.

"Why are you so worried then?" John asked. He had noticed an uneasiness come over Casey since they started rounding the lake area.

Casey was always impressed with John's ability to read his own people, seeing their needs and fears before they expressed them. The lieutenant didn't expect John to be able to read him so well. Casey was worried about being near the lake. He hoped he was hiding his concern, but apparently not well enough.

"There are reports that this is where some of the extreme militants and military traitors came to hide out during the war," Casey answered, seeing no point in lying to the other.

"Traitors?" John couldn't keep the sarcasm from his voice. "You mean the men and women that wouldn't shoot at their neighbors?"

"Yes, John. The soldiers that refused to follow orders and ran from their duty."

John just shook his head. It was always a wonder to him that two people could look upon the same event and see it from such polar opposition.

"You think the rumors are true?" John asked.

Casey shrugged and finished the last of his food.

"If they are, it could be dangerous for all of us."

"We haven't seen anyone yet," John said.

Hearing Casey's suspicions worried John as well. He knew the officer wasn't prone to exaggeration. Lieutenant Casey was a man of facts and rules. If he gave enough credit to these rumors to mention them, then there was likely some truth to it.

"Maybe there's nothing to the rumors," Casey shrugged, seeming to dismiss it.

"Or they have been following us to see how many we are and what we're doing here," John said. Either of those could be true, but John wasn't willing to take the chance and bank on the rumors being just that. Casey nodded as if confirming John's thoughts.

"Not a chance I'd be willing to take," Casey said firmly.

John sat in silence for a time, looking out over the group. They had one last bridge to cross. If there was someone with dark intentions following them, the bridge is where they would carry out whatever plan they formed. He knew about the militias and deserters that hid out in remote parts of the country, some with ideas of taking back America, and others just wanting to be left alone. They might have left the refugees alone, if it weren't for the Federal officer's presence. That simple detail would cast a large shadow of doubt over the refugee's intentions in the area. To the militia it changed a group of average citizens into a threat.

"Thank you for the warning," John said, starting to get up.

"Why are you thanking me?" Casey asked.

"You didn't have to say anything. You could have just let us walk through here blind and then taken advantage of whatever happened," John said.

"We're all in the same boat on this one John. If there is militia here they won't be kind to you if they see me," Casey had been thinking along the same line as John. "That is, if they haven't seen me already."

The implications of that weighed heavily on John as he went to gather the people leading the individual groups of refugees. Any contact with militia could be tricky depending on their political leanings and past. If they were just deserters, they would most likely have ignored the refugees or asked for food or supplies. If they were independents, looking to continue the war, they could see anyone else as a threat. With Casey in their group the refugees would surely be seen as cooperating with the feds. Possibly spies trying to find and report on those same militias. John briefly considered having the officer change out of his uniform, but every instinct told him it was too late.

John gathered the men and women that led each group in their formation, and took them a few yards away from the rest. Everyone found a place to sit, making a circle so they could see each other. John gave them all time to settle in before he started.

"You probably already know we stopped early so that we can cross the next bridge tonight," John started, including everyone by looking at them in turn.

"It's too close to Camdenton to go around, and people could still be living there," he continued.

All of those around the circle nodded in understanding. They were all used to the need for caution and adapting their routine on the fly.

"I want everyone to be aware that the feds have reports of armed militia in the area," John said. The reaction was instantaneous as people looked at each other in alarm. A murmur of concerned comments and questions began to build among the group but John raised his hand to forestall them.

"We haven't seen anyone yet so I don't want any of you to panic. I just want everyone prepared for the possibility of running into hostile strangers," John said.

Everyone sat as calmly as they could in light of that information, and listened as John continued.

"Stay together in your groups and stay calm. Everyone is looking to you for stability and guidance," John said. He gave them time to absorb that before continuing.

"If you see anyone, don't hesitate, just run. We don't want to take the risk of finding out if they're friendly or not. We'll all meet at the old golf course here," John pulled the folded map from his back pocket. Opening it he put his finger on a spot on the map that was marked as a golf course a few hundred yards north of the highway and west of Camdenton.

"Just like before, don't go there if you're being followed. We'll stay the night there and leave in the morning. If you get lost, or don't make it in time, you know the route," He looked at each in turn and they all nodded their understanding.

"Do you expect that federal officer to make trouble or draw attention to us?" Calvin Jacobs asked. The large, dark-skinned leader of the first group had a deep voice that reminded John of the radio announcers they would hear over the federal broadcasts.

"No, he'd be worse off than we would if the militia caught him," John said. "Besides, he's the one that warned me about them."

"Why is he even here, John?" Cathy Smith asked. She was a younger woman in charge of one of the middle groups.

"If we let him leave he could come back with help. We have to keep an eye on him until we're close enough to Texas that it won't matter," John said.

"Is that the only reason?" Calvin asked. John had known Calvin for years and he had never met a more intuitive person.

"No," John said. "Everyone deserves a choice Calvin. Maybe the Lieutenant will see the wrong in all of this."

None of them looked convinced but they understood. Calvin nodded as if confirming what he already knew. He was first to stand.

"I think we all know what to do then," Calvin's voice boomed.

The rest stood and started to return to their groups. Calvin stopped near John and put a large hand on the other's shoulder.

"You know it's a slim hope that man will change," Calvin said. It wasn't a question, so much as confirmation of what they both knew.

"I know, but even a slim chance is worth it," John said.

Calvin smiled and cuffed John's shoulder firmly. They parted without another word, heading back to the others.

The refugees waited until the sun was about an hour from the horizon before starting out again. They remained in their individual groups and intervals, and it would be well past dark before the last group entered Camdenton. Their planned route would take them around the south edge of the town to avoid the concentration of buildings that were more likely to have people living in them. John's group brought up the rear of their formation.

The outskirts of the town were made up of houses, spaced far apart and set along curving dirt roads. They passed a couple of schools on the south end of town, their large windows broken out and yards overgrown. There were bleachers and playground equipment, basketball courts with cracked asphalt, and even a football field that nature was taking back with a passion. It was only recognizable by the metal uprights at each end of the field.

The couple of rows of houses they had to pass through had nearly been reclaimed by the woodland that surrounded the town. The roads and homes had originally been built close to the forest and without anyone to keep nature at bay, the trees, vines, and brush had spread right up to and even through the homes. It was as if the forest and buildings were becoming one entity, forming a new and almost alien landscape.

As they walked through, John realized that this town would be the perfect place to hide a large group of people. If his group had wanted to remain in America, this would be the place to stay. They had the lake to fish from and plenty of woods to hunt in. The trees provided shelter and camouflage from the air. As long as people stayed away from the highway through town no one would suspect people were hiding nearby. The thought had him on edge the entire time. He felt the reassuring weight of the pistol in his waistband, with the cold metal pressing against the small of his back. He never liked violence, but the idea that he had the means to defend himself, and his people, made him feel a little better.

A loud crack echoed through the wood to the group's right. John knew it was close and the stick small, but it sounded as sudden and sharp as a gunshot. Everyone hesitated for just a moment before John's urgent whisper.

"Go!" The word was like a starter's pistol. The group sprang away like startled deer.

A real gunshot rang out in the trees behind them and John heard the hiss and snap as a round passed him and struck a nearby tree.

"Spread out!" John shouted, no longer worried about being quiet.

His group scattered into the trees, but still making their way toward the bridge. John kept close to Casey as the two lost sight of everyone else.

John ducked around a tree but was unable to avoid the low branch on the other side. Another shot rang out as the limb made contact with his face and he went down. For a brief moment John thought he had been shot, until his mind caught back up with reality and he remembered the tree limb. Pain lanced through his head and neck, but he tried to ignore it and scramble to his feet.

"On your feet, John," Casey said as he took hold of the straps of John's pack and pulled him up.

John held onto Casey's shoulders a moment as the pain subsided to a dull throb. Blood was running freely from his nose and he could feel a stinging split in his lip.

"We need to move, John. Are you ready?" Casey looked into John's eyes to make sure the other was coherent.

John nodded, and winced as the pain shifted. They both started to run again, spurred on by the sounds of someone running through dry leaves behind them. They heard a shout ahead to their right, followed by a gunshot but there was no sound of a bullet passing close. John was sure now that there were others after them and they were shooting at the fleeing members of his group. He prayed as he ran, hoping no one was shot.

John's previously injured ankle and throbbing head were slowing him down, and both men knew their pursuer was going to catch up soon.

"You keep going, I'll take care of the guy behind us," Casey said. He looked at John and waited as if looking for permission.

John looked over, his doubt about letting Casey out of his sight clear on his face.

"Don't worry John, I won't be asking them for help. I want to be across that bridge and away from here as much as you do," Casey said and veered off to the right.

"Don't kill him," John said, hoping it was loud enough for only Casey to hear. Casey gave no indication that he heard John as he disappeared into the trees.

John ran as fast as his pain-wracked body would carry him. He heard another shout ahead, followed by the sound of a large branch breaking and another gunshot. Soon after, he heard the sounds of a scuffle behind him in the trees.

John didn't slow down or turn around to look but he found himself hoping that Casey would be all right. He didn't want anyone getting hurt, but the stranger was just that, a faceless stranger in the dark and Casey was someone he had come to know. Clearly the he and the agent were not friends, but a connection had been built during their adversarial cat and mouse chase across the Midwest. He found himself not only praying for his wife and friends, but for the federal officer and the strangers in the woods. He hoped everyone would come out of the encounter alive.

"That's quite far enough," a voice shouted ahead of John.

John stumbled to a stop, facing an older man in an old military uniform. The man had a hunting rifle leveled at John's chest and his finger was barely brushing the trigger.

"We don't want any trouble, we just want to get across the bridge and out of your area," John said, raising his hands to the side and breathing heavily.

"We saw that fed with you. You helping them?" The man punctuated the question by raising the rifle so that John was looking right at the tip of the barrel.

"No, we're just passing through on our way to Texas."

John saw movement in the trees behind the man, but was careful to keep his eyes on the rifle. Someone was coming up behind the stranger, but he couldn't tell if it was friend or foe.

"Can't take that risk pal," the stranger said. "Where's your friend?"

"Here," Casey said, stepping around a tree behind the stranger. John saw a rifle Casey had picked up from one of the others. The man turned toward the officer and as soon as his rifle was pointed away from John, Casey brought the butt of the rifle down on the stranger's head. The stranger hit the ground before he even completed the turn.

John went through a moment of relief, then one of panic when Casey raised the rifle to point at him. The officer must have taken the weapon from the one that had been behind them. His mind was a confused morass of emotions and it took him a minute to focus and realize Casey was talking.

"I may not be able to stop the others but you, you're the one they consider the ringleader," Casey was saying.

"What?" The situation was so surreal it was hard for John to think.

"I'm taking you back, John. Turning you in might salvage this entire fiasco," Casey said, indicating with a shake of the rifle that John should turn around.

Everything became clear, as if lightning flashed in the pitch black of the last few minutes in John's memory. He had gone from worry and fear, to panic, and then certainty that he would probably die at the hands of an unnamed rebel. Relief was then replaced by disappointment when his savior so suddenly became his enemy again.

"Casey, don't do this. They'll come looking for me," John shifted his weight, his mind searching for the familiar feel of the pistol tucked in at the small of his back. He couldn't feel it and wondered if it had fallen out during the chase.

"That's not the plan John. Everyone is to make for the old golf course. No stopping and no turning back. They'll leave in the morning and we'll be long gone," Casey said.

John had known desperation before. He had struggled with the knowledge that, at any moment in this journey, he might have to risk his life. He knew he was facing another one of those moments and slowly started to reach behind his back, praying the pistol had just shifted but was still close at hand.

"Don't bother looking for your weapon, John," Casey patted his holster, which had been empty since his capture and how held the pistol John had been carrying. The officer had taken it sometime during the run through the woods when John was distracted.

John's desperation turned into defeat. Casey was right about the plan. No one would come looking for him. They all knew their part and each person had to stick to the plan to make sure all the others made it to safety. He nodded once and turned to walk the way Casey indicated. A soft voice stopped him.

"You aren't taking him anywhere," it was Amanda, speaking behind Casey somewhere in the dark. There was a tone to her voice, dangerous and sure, that John had heard few times in his life.

Something in her voice kept Casey from turning around, and his instincts proved correct. John turned to see her walking slowly toward the officer, another captured rifle pressed against her shoulder and pointed at Casey's head. Todd was coming from another direction, his pistol also pointed at the officer.

"I don't want to shoot you but I will," Amanda said.

"I believe you," Casey said, lowering the rifle and holding it out, by the barrel, to Todd's reaching hand. John's friend also took the pistol out Casey's holster.

"Now, you move," Amanda said with finality.

Chapter 41

The road that got us here was paved with good intentions, as the saying goes. Every plan, law, or initiative started out as a way to help people, protect people, or increase opportunity. Somewhere along the way those good intentions were taken advantage of by the corrupt opportunists that found ways to game the system for their own political gain. The corruption changed our mindset. A system designed to help those who could not help themselves became a system that helped those who would not. One of the clearest symptoms of the fall was the rise in unemployment due to a failing economy. Some people found it was more profitable to not work and as unemployment continued to rise government felt compelled to continue helping with more benefits. It became a vicious cycle that, for many, justified the sweeping changes to come.

-Excerpt from the Journal of John Evermann

"We can't take him with us after what he did!" Amanda's voice was quiet but the strength of it was as potent as a shout.

The group leaders were gathered on the overgrown fairway of the dark golf course. The refugees had made it there safely and three people, with the captured rifles, watched the east to make sure they weren't followed. Todd was watching Casey, who had his hands tied behind his back and was being kept apart from everyone else.

"We can't leave him here either, the militia are sure to come looking," John said.

"Is that so bad, John?" Kyle asked. He and his husband were the last to join John's group before they left Stewart, and he tended to be a bit more cold-hearted when it came to dealing with people outside the group.

"He did try to hurt us, and his people did kill Steve," Kyle finished.

John didn't need a reminder of how the federal officers had hurt them.

"Leaving a man to die is no better than killing him yourself," John said.

"Then we should let him go and take our chances," Amanda said. She was still furious about finding a gun pointed at John's face only hours after her friends had sacrificed some of their rations to feed the officer.

"We can't take the chance he'll be able to get help at the border," John explained.

It had been a long night and John didn't foresee any sleep in his immediate future. He was exhausted, and worried about being followed, but he knew he couldn't push the group any farther without rest. He was growing frustrated with the situation, but took a deep breath and reminded himself of a saying his grandfather was fond of. God never gives you more than he knows you can handle. He took a deep breath to clear his head and calm down.

"He's going with us at least until we're too close to the border for him to warn anyone," John said with finality.

He could see the decision wasn't popular but everyone accepted it. The rest moved off to join their groups and get what little rest they could. Amanda stayed behind while John watched them leave. She still looked angry but he could tell it wasn't directed at him.

"I still think it's too dangerous to keep him around," Amanda said.

John nodded, staring off after the others.

"I won't leave him to die or take the risk of letting him go yet," John said.

"We don't know the militia will kill him," Amanda said, but her voice betrayed her own uncertainty on that.

"I'm not willing to bet his life on it."

"You're too decent for your own good sometimes, John,"

She gave him a hug and kissed him before returning to their camp to sleep. Despite the danger, and her previous anger, she was proud of him. She rolled up into her sleeping bag. Knowing John had more to do and wasn't likely to get any sleep himself she didn't wait for him to follow.

John found Casey sitting against a tree in the dark. His hands were tied behind his back and Todd was standing nearby holding a pistol. Todd's eyes were flinty and they never left the federal officer. Casey watched John approach, his face betraying no emotion.

"So, what's the verdict John?" Casey asked when John was close enough he didn't have to shout. "You leaving me here for the militia or finishing me off yourself?"

It bothered John that Casey thought those were the only two options open to him.

"Neither," John said. "I can't let you go either, you're coming with us."

Both Casey and Todd were shocked speechless by that statement. Todd looked like he wanted to argue, but couldn't find the words, and seeing the look on his friend's face he decided that was probably best. John was in no mood to argue about it any further.

Casey had fully expected to die soon, either at the hands of the fugitives or the militia. He knew that would be the risk when he pulled the rifle on John in the woods. He hadn't even expected to make it out of that situation alive the moment he heard Amanda's voice in the darkness behind him. Being kept with the group wasn't even a consideration while he waited to hear his fate.

"I can't imagine that was a popular decision," Casey said. He had seen Todd's reaction and knew the others had to feel the same. What had that decision cost John, Casey wondered.

"The right choice isn't always the easy one," John said.

John sat down across from Casey with his back against a tree, leaning his head against the hard trunk and holding his pistol firmly in his hand.

"Get some sleep, both of you. Early start in the morning," John said without looking up.

The conversation was over and neither Todd, nor Casey minded. It had been a long night for everyone. Todd returned to his sleeping bag that was laid out near Jennifer's, and Casey rested back against his own tree. They were both asleep in moments and John was left alone in the dark with nothing but the wind and night sounds to drown out his worry.

* * *

The next four days were relatively uneventful for the refugees, and went a long way to raising their spirits. They weren't being chased by federal agents. The towns they did pass were mostly empty, and morale rose as the once harrowing flight from Illinois turned into a peaceful excursion in the country. John was the only one that wasn't able to relax. He was worried the change wasn't so much a respite from the storm as the calm before the worst of it.

John used the time to plan, moving along their line of travel, from group to group. He reminded each group leader about the rest of the route, going over the map that he carried, and making sure each knew the destination in Oklahoma. If anyone was separated from the group

John wanted to be sure they knew where to go, and how to find everyone else. He also prepared everyone for the last obstacle between them and the border, Fort Joplin.

Everyone in America knew about Fort Joplin and the role it played in the civil war. It's location near the border, large airport, and connection to several major highways made it the perfect spot for the American war command. Fort was a loose word, as the city was not surrounded by a wall, or even a fence, except around the airport and important military buildings on the north side of town. So many troops, tanks, helicopters and other assets were located at Joplin, and the surrounding towns, they had become the largest military installation in America. John knew they had no choice but to go around, but how far around was the question. He would need to be close enough to see it to know how far away they needed to be to avoid patrols, searchlights, and fly-overs.

Near the end of the fourth day after escaping the Ozarks area the group was camped on the north side of a small rise about a mile away from Fort Joplin. They were surrounded by trees with a canopy thick enough to shield them from the air. Just in case no fires were lit and everyone was instructed to move around as little as possible. The refugees all sat in small groups, eating and talking quietly, but mostly waiting in nervous apprehension for what lay ahead.

John, Todd, and Amanda were crouched low on the rise overlooking Joplin. Even with the war at a virtual stalemate, Joplin was an active installation. Military vehicles moved in every direction on unknown errands. Important buildings, or what John guessed were important, were lit up with massive banks of lights. Formations of soldiers could be seen moving in different areas, and the airport was lit up and busy with activity. There was one dark spot in the landscape between the two towns that made up the Fort, but other than that there were lights everywhere, as if the place never slept.

"Why did we come this way again?" Todd asked the rhetorical question everyone was thinking.

"Too far out of our way to go around on a different highway and everyone is already exhausted," John answered anyway.

They had considered the possibility shortly after leaving the Ozark area, but they decided it was too much of a risk to hope one of the smaller farm roads was still there. The closer they got to the border the more the military had altered the landscape from what the map showed. The refugees being unfamiliar with the area, and having limited cross country navigation skills between them, the odds of getting lost were too high.

"There's our shot," John said, pointing to the band of darkness between the towns.

Fort Joplin was made up of the city of Joplin on the west and Carthage in the east. They were separated by about five miles of old housing divisions, grassland, and trees. The two towns were connected by a major highway that had regular traffic, even at night, which meant military traffic since curfew kept civilians inside at that time. As far as John could tell the old homes were unoccupied since no lights had been visible in the windows, even close to sundown when they settled down to watch.

"There's a lot of traffic on that highway," Amanda said, watching the crawling, twin lights in the distance.

"There," Todd said, pointing. "That looks like an overpass. We might be able to slip through in small groups without being seen."

Todd was indicating a spot in the highway that was well lit and seemed to rise up over the flat land. From that distance it was hard to tell but it did look like the highway spanned a depression of some sort.

"We'll have to get closer to know for sure, but it's worth the risk. I don't want to be caught anywhere near here when the sun comes up," John explained.

"We'll need to move quickly," Amanda said. Once again, she was glad they had sent the children ahead in the van, despite the pain of being separated from them.

"Do you suppose it's always this active?" Todd asked.

"I don't know but let's pray if something is going on it has nothing to do with us," John replied.

John's leg was better, though he still had a bit of a limp when they jogged back to the waiting refugees. John explained the plan to the nervous people back at the camp. The idea of crossing such wide-open terrain close to the two towns didn't help their anxiety but everyone was definitely glad to be on the move.

With fear fueling them, the refugees moved as fast as the darkness would allow. Everyone sensed the danger even before they reached the same overlook where the others had scouted the area. There was a tension in the air everyone could feel, like right before a storm. When the first of the group did reach the overlook, the sight below stopped them in their tracks.

The fort below was even more active than when John left it. When the lead group stopped he and Todd moved up to see what was wrong, and the change worried him. Before, Fort Joplin just seemed to be busy but upon their return the entire place was on full alert. Search lights were scanning the sky and ground around the city, more vehicles were moving on the roads, and the whole installation was lit bright as day.

"You don't think they knew we were coming, do you?" Todd asked, unable to take his eyes off the spectacle below.

"I can't imagine how," John said. His voice didn't sound too sure.

"The highway seems busier," Todd pointed out apprehensively. It did appear that more vehicles were moving away from the city.

"Right, we need to move now. We have a long way to go and I don't like the looks of all this," John said.

Todd nodded and started ushering the first of the refugees down the hill. The light from the moon and the fort cast a dim glow across the landscape that made travel safer, so everyone moved a little faster when they started down toward the highway. After the last person was over the top of the rise Amanda stopped and tilted her head to the side.

"What's that?" She asked.

"What?" John stopped and looked at her curiously.

"I don't know, it's like a sound I can't quite hear but I can feel it," she put a hand to her chest. "Here."

John listened for a moment, and then he heard and felt it too. The realization of what was coming hit them both at the same time, but it was John that vocalized it.

"Helicopters," the urgency in that one word was enough to start them down the hill at a run.

John didn't know the purpose of the helicopters but from the sound there were a lot of them. He feared that this was the end of the line for him and the others. He could see the others running ahead. Todd with Casey, friends and neighbors, and people he had met on the journey. He had led them all to this place, this time, and all the forces against them were converging. All they could do was run for their lives but he feared it wouldn't be enough.

A flash of light banished the night from the direction of the airport. Seconds after the flash the sound and shockwave hit the refugees, knocking many to the ground or to their knees. Some screamed and all turned their eyes to columns of flame birthing from the airfield.

"What is happening?" Amanda shouted over the roar of the explosions.

"I don't know, just run," John shouted. He was staring in horror at the scene opening up over the fort. The helicopters they had heard were coming in from the west, over Fort Joplin, and the streaks of tracer fire highlighted each of the aircraft as they rained hell the ground beneath. John snapped out of it with the realization that the helicopters were not there for him and his people.

"Just run," he shouted again.

Chapter 42

An old adage that we lost sight of was, if you let government give you rights, you are also subject to having government take them way. We forgot that government is meant to protect those rights we, by nature's laws, already have. When Washington offered to give us things we should have been earning ourselves, all under the guise of more rights, we accepted with closed eyes and open arms. Then when those 'rights' became too expensive we started to lose them again. So many were surprised.

Our basic rights are considered inalienable because no one need give them to us, and while a person or government may try to take them away they are ours to protect. These basic rights need no other person to supply them. No one must become a slave to us to maintain them, nor do we need to be slaves to another. We carry them with us everywhere and they are free, but may cost everything. We forgot that for a time, but I promise to remember it forever.

-Excerpt from the Journal of John Evermann

Years later John would have trouble recalling the Battle of Joplin. The events all blended together into a frightful flight under flashes of light and rumbles of explosions. When time dulled the memories, he would be reminded of that night in every thunderstorm, or loud noise and flash of light. He would always remember the fear and doubt about whether he had done right. He would remember the anxiety about whether they would survive his decisions. His only consolation that night was that his children, and the children of his friends, were safe and would grow up in a better place.

The refugees raced across the field toward the highway. Distant sounds of gunfire and explosions caused people to flinch away and cry out, even though the battle was taking place more than a mile away. John shouted for everyone to keep running and helped those who stumbled or fell behind. At some point Casey's bindings were removed, probably so he could maintain his balance, but John didn't care anymore. He'd rather the officer escape than hurt himself.

"What's happening, John?" Amanda shouted.

"I don't know but this distraction is a miracle," he said as he helped someone who stumbled over a tree limb. He didn't let on that he was afraid the miracle was actually a disaster. The others needed hope against their fear. He couldn't afford to show his own.

Their flight to the highway overpass seemed to take forever, but it was faster than it would have been without the danger of the nearby battle. All the while the fighting was confined to the larger city of Joplin.

They were close enough to hear and feel the explosions and see the flashes of lights, but too far to make out details. The highway traffic seemed to swell as civilian vehicles fled the city and military trucks headed in. When the refugees reached the overpass, they heard a loud rumbling from the east, in the direction of the smaller town. The rumble had a metallic clanking accompaniment that set John's teeth on edge. John wondered what new horror was descending upon them.

People were waiting near the overpass when John made it to the shadow of the concrete bridge. They were unsure what to do after the plan changed. John could hear the whooping sound of helicopters coming close.

"Move, just move. The plan's shot we need to get out of here," all their planning had gone up in smoke in the chaos of the battle. John could only pray now. He prayed everyone would get to the other side alive, and whole.

People rushed en masse under the concrete roadway, moving around the supports to get clear of the overpass. Trucks roared on the pavement overhead and the rumbling, clanking sound in the east grew louder. When John stepped out from under the bridge himself he thought he could hear the helicopters getting closer as well, and then he was sure of it when he saw the lights. The aircraft were scanning the ground as they approached the highway. The sense that something awful was about to happen crashed over John like a tidal wave. His fear and anxiety peaking.

"Todd, we need to get everyone as far from here as possible," John shouted to his friend.

"Move now, let's get across this field," he said to those closer to him.

People ran for the trees that bordered the old field about a hundred yards to the south of the highway. The ground was uneven and dangerous, but when someone fell their neighbor helped them up and they kept running. John was last, making sure no one fell behind. He looked up at the sound he'd been unable to identify and saw the metal bulk of tanks rolling across the overpass above.

As they neared the trees the sounds of approaching helicopters became much louder. The aircraft roared overhead and flew toward the road. The trees nearly bent double at the downdraft and many of the refugees were forced to their knees or knocked off their feet. The vehicles were so low it was like standing in a hurricane. The refugees watched in horror as the night was lit up by sudden bursts of light and streaks of tracers when the tanks on the highway opened fire on the helicopters.

The pilots above returned fire with rockets launched from pods on mounted on the sides and a large gun extending from the nose of the aircraft. John didn't know much about weapons, and nothing about helicopters, but the display was impressive and horrifying. Burning streaks of light and streamers of smoke lit the night all around the terrified civilians. The resulting explosions sent the refugees running into the trees to get away from the scene. John stayed long enough to see a rocket, fired from somewhere along the line of tanks, hit one of the aircraft and send it spinning to the ground. The metal monster hit the dirt, its blades churning earth like a terrible plowing machine as the vehicle tore itself apart in the crash. He didn't wait to see anymore.

Acrid smoke joined the sounds of battle and the refugees pushed through the trees and ran across the next field. John rushed ahead and started directing people to head south and west so they could make their way around the fort about a mile beyond.

"Who's attacking Joplin?" Todd asked when John got close.

"I don't know, maybe rebels," John said.

"It's forces out of Texas," Casey said nearby, breathing heavily from the run and bleeding from a cut on his forehead. John was surprised that the officer was still with them.

"How can you be sure?" John asked. "There hasn't been fighting for years."

"The flags," Casey said, working to catch his breath as they ran. "Texas flags on the choppers."

John nodded. He'd missed seeing any emblems on the aircraft.

"I also heard a report," Casey began again. "A report at the border post that there was a build-up."

"Why now?" Todd asked, dodging a tree limb that was in his path.

"Can only guess, but a hit this big is probably a message," Casey said, now holding a hand to his side. "We've been probing the border near Colorado. This is meant to make us stop."

Their running conversation was interrupted by a group of old humvees driving through the field across the refugee's path. The vehicles were speeding from the east, bouncing and careening across the uneven terrain toward Fort Joplin. John guessed they were reinforcements from Carthage.

One of the gunners riding with his head and arms outside the top of a humvee must have noticed the large group of people in the field and mistaken them for invaders. He tugged back on a lever on the weapon in front of him and swiveled the gun toward the John's group. The flash and thump of the machine gun made John jump and the refugees scatter. Todd pulled Jennifer out of the way as the weapon raised tiny geysers of dirt while the solder brought the weapon to bear. Tracers raced through the group like rocket propelled fireflies. Miraculously no one was hit.

While John watched the raw violence of the scene the murderous fireflies started arcing up into the sky and were joined by others. The convoy had stopped and the gunners were firing at something above the refugees. It was then that John realized he was hearing, and feeling, the helicopters again. The aircraft were coming back for the humvees and John's people were caught in the middle.

"Everyone down, now," John shouted and waved his arms.

People dropped to the ground and pulled their neighbors down with them. The helicopters screamed overhead and people screamed below, covering their heads as if fleshy shields would protect them from anything the two armies rained down. John pulled Amanda down and covered her with his own body, but couldn't help watching the battle unfold around him. Machine gun fire from the convoy lit up the sky, burning arcs of light toward the helicopters. The aircraft received the hits and some even seemed to be damaged by the curtain of devastation they were flying into. All of them fired their main guns at the ground vehicles, apparently out of rockets after their battle with the tanks earlier.

The fight was over in moments and John's eyes saw nothing but spots and flashes after. The helicopters flew away, leaving behind a line of burning wrecks and stunned civilians in the churned and scarred field. John saw one of the pilots look down at the huddled civilians when the helicopters passed close to the ground. He wasn't sure if that was a good or a bad thing.

With the destruction of the convoy and the disappearance of the helicopters everyone started to get to their feet and run for the trees again. They skirted the burning hulks of the humvees and avoided looking at the bodies of the former occupants. When someone did look they shuddered at the sight of bodies burned and decimated by fire and bullets.

The sounds of battle were again a distant thunder for the refugees. They ran, stumbled, and fell their way through open fields and clusters of trees for more than a mile, always moving steadily south and west. John, Todd, Amanda, and the other leaders just kept everyone moving despite pain, exhaustion, and fear. It seemed that everyone was hurt in some way. Cuts from flying bits of metal, scraped knees from falls, and twisted ankles from the rough terrain were all too common. John saw them all and thanked God everyone made it in one piece and was able to keep moving.

When the battle seemed like ancient memory behind them the group started to slow and collect themselves. People sat down right where they stopped, or bent near double, coughing and trying to catch their breath. Most of the refugees had lost their bags but they still had all of the firearms they had picked up along the way. John was relieved to see Casey was still with them.

"Is everyone still mobile?" John asked Todd. John and Amanda were sitting on the ground, back to back, supporting each other while they caught their breath.

"I think so, just tired," Todd nodded.

"We need to keep moving, but I think we can take it slower," John said.

"Just a few minutes longer," Amanda gasped between deep breaths.

"Shhh," Todd held up a hand and the two fell silent but didn't hear what had caught his attention.

"I heard something," Todd whispered to their questioning looks. Others were starting to notice and all fell silent.

After a moment John heard it too. There was a rustling sound in the trees south of them as if someone were trying to walk quietly through dry leaves. John waved everyone to stay quiet and drop down.

Everyone did, lying as flat in the grass as they could. While they watched a large group of armed soldiers walked out of the trees, and scanned the clearing ahead of them. They were all armed with military rifles and wore heavy body armor over camouflage uniforms. They weren't a group of back-woods militia, but professional soldiers. For a brief moment John's instinct was to defend himself and the others but he quickly stifled that thought. They stood no chance if it came to a fight.

"Don't shoot, we're just civilians," John said loudly before the soldiers could stumble upon them. He slowly rose to his knees and raised his arms so they could see his hands.

The reaction of the soldiers was instantaneous. They all stopped and raised their rifles to their shoulders. Three focused on John but others started scanning the area with goggles that were attached to their helmets. Something to see in the dark John figured. John stayed on his knees and didn't move.

"There are others with me," John said. "We have weapons but we're no threat."

John couldn't see any insignia so he knew either way this was the end of the line. The soldiers were either American reinforcements, and their bid for freedom was over, or they were Texas soldiers who might help them if he played his cards right.

"Identify yourself," a commanding voice shouted from among the soldiers.

"John Evermann, from Illinois," he said, squinting into a flashlight someone had turned on his face.

"What in God's name are ya'll doing out here, John from Illinois?" The commanding voice asked.

This was the moment that would decide it all and John knew it. If the soldiers were Americans he could lie and hope they just sent the refugees home. If they were Texans he could tell the truth and hope they believed him and helped his people. He'd quickly made up his mind to tell the truth when the decision was made for him.

"Sir, that's him," a voice behind the lights said. "The John Evermann, from the radio."

"Explain, Sergeant," the commanding voice was quieter, as if he turned to talk to another.

John couldn't hear the conversation between the two so he waited patiently in the grass. Two soldiers, at their commander's request, did start letting people sit up but asked that they lay their firearms in front of them. They were moving among the refugees, checking for weapons and helping people up. They even checked wounds to make sure none were life-threatening. One of them stopped a few feet behind John when he realized he didn't know where Casey was.

"You can sit up sir. Do you have any weapons on you?" The soldier said to whoever was lying in the grass behind John.

"I'm not armed," John heard Casey say, followed by a rustling as the agent sat up.

"Whoa there," the soldier said, and John heard a rattling sound as something shifted against the soldier's harness. John imagined he was shouldering his rifle.

"We have a fed over here," the soldier called out.

The entire scene turned nightmarish as soldiers stepped forward with their weapons raised again. People were shouting things like spy and traitor, and John's people were cowering in the grass under the intimidating effect. He was thankful none of his people went for their weapons.

"Wait," John shouted. "He's with us, he helped us."

Everyone was shouting at once so John wasn't sure if anyone heard him. He didn't want to move, to provoke the soldiers, but he couldn't sit by and let something happen to Casey either. A sharp whistle cut above the shouting before John made up his mind on what to do.

"Hold on now, stand down," the commander shouted above the noise.

Discipline and training took over and the order was followed. Soldiers lowered their weapons to a ready, but less threatening position, and the source of the voice stepped into the light followed by another. John could now see clearly and recognized the Texan flag on the officer's shoulder, as well as the man beside him. Their uniforms were identical to those American soldiers wore, but bore different insignia. The two men approached John.

"So, you are the man everyone's been talking about," the shorter of the two said. John recognized his voice as the one calling the shots. The officer offered his hand and helped John to his feet while he shook it.

"I don't know about that sir, I'm just John and these are my friends and family," John said, again embarrassed that someone outside their group, especially someone in another country knew who he was.

"And this officer?" The officer nodded behind John. "He's your friend?"

"Not exactly, sir," John said. "He's been trying to stop us but we had to bring him along after we caught him. Too risky to let him go until we reached Texas."

"I heard about your trip," the officer nodded. "What should we do about your friend now though?"

"I offered him a choice to come with us and I think he should still have that chance, sir," John said. "Everyone has a right to choose. Let him come with us, or go home, whichever he chooses."

The two men looked at each other, each measuring the other. John saw a slight smile turn up the corner of the officer's mouth but as soon as it was there it was gone again. The serious soldier was back in place, and back in command.

"This is your unit, John," the soldier waved his hand at the civilians. "Your call."

"Sir?" The man beside the officer looked concerned.

"There's no danger to us, Sergeant. By the time the fed gets anywhere we'll be long gone," the officer said.

John nodded and turned to Casey. Casey hadn't moved, still kneeling in the grass with his hands laced behind his head.

"Lieutenant, I asked you once if you wanted to come with us. That opportunity is still open," John said. He wasn't of a mind to try convincing Casey, and he knew it wouldn't help if the many had made up his mind already.

"I can't John, that's not my world. I can't change to fit it and it won't change to fit me," Casey said.

John nodded, expecting that answer. He started to turn back to the officer but Casey stopped him.

"Wait, John I have something you might want to take with you," Casey reached for his bag and the soldier closest raised his rifle.

"Whoa there, what're you reaching for?"

Casey stopped midway to his bag.

"Stand down, Corporal," the Texan officer commanded.

The soldier lowered his weapon a bit and Casey slowly opened his bag and showed the soldier what was inside. The corporal looked slightly embarrassed when Casey retrieved a stuffed bear from the bag.

"I found this in the van at the border. Someone might be missing him," the federal agent stood and handed the toy to John.

John took the bear slowly. He was surprised Casey had kept it, and wanted it returned. He looked down at the glass eyes of the toy, staring up at him. It seemed like the horror of the flight past Fort Joplin melted away as his children came to mind. He was thankful that they were safe, and that he might see them soon.

"Good luck, John."

John looked up through moistened eyes and took Casey's hand in a firm grip, shaking it in goodbye. Not another word passed between the two, and Casey just nodded to the corporal before turning and walking north toward Fort Joplin. Everyone watched him go, but no one moved until he was into the dark trees behind them.

"Sergeant, we're going to need a lift out of here," the officer said. The man beside him stepped aside and started speaking into the radio on his shoulder. The officer turned back to John.

"I admire ya'lls determination to get to Texas, John. Doing this all on your own and all that is a big deal, but I hope you don't mind if we give you a lift the rest of the way," the officer said with a smile.

John looked around, his own relief plain on his face. There were smiles and nods from everyone, sighs of relief and even subdued cheers. John let out a breath, one he felt like he'd been holding since walking out of his house in Illinois and turned back to the officer.

"We'd appreciate that, Sir," John said, holding out his hand.

Debriefing

Texas isn't a perfect utopia. Be careful of anyone peddling that word. You can be sure their version is not the same as yours and they only care about one of them. We have our share of issues, disagreements, and stress but at least it's for the right reasons. People understand that it's good and healthy, and above all we're free. We all know what it looks like when people try to solve disagreements by removing freedom or bullying others into like-mindedness. Will we remember in two hundred years? I don't know, it might all happen again but we've got another chance to do it right. Someone once said that America was the last bastion of freedom, but whoever said that was wrong. The human heart is the last fortress of liberty and the last hope for freedom. As long as a human heart beats it will beat to be free. Some people will ignore it, and some are afraid to listen, but as long as enough people are around there will be some who will do anything to have it.

-Excerpt from the journal of John Evermann

Lieutenant Casey sat in a straight-backed metal chair across the plain metal desk from his supervisor. He waited patiently, staring at nothing, while his boss read Casey's report on the last few days. He didn't look around, or fidget. There wasn't anything to look at anyway. The same gray walls were bare except for a picture of the President. The desk was free of anything except the necessary tools for the officer's job. There was nothing else in the small office because nothing else was needed.

"So, this fugitive Bernard," the other officer said after setting the pages down. "You let him go because you don't think he could be reeducated?"

"That's correct sir. It would have been a waste of resources."

"Are you trying to take an analyst's job away, Lieutenant?" The other officer asked?

"No sir, I..."

"Your job isn't to think, Lieutenant," Casey's supervisor cut him off. "The analysts think and it's our job to uphold the letter of the law."

"Yes sir."

"Why did you fail to capture the fugitives before your men's contract time was up?"

"I had some of them sir, but they are resourceful people," Casey said.

"Resourceful? They were just common workers. How resourceful could they be?"

"The perspective is different in the field sir, and they had help," Casey said, slowly letting his anger slip as he realized the failure of his mission was going to fall squarely on his shoulders. The barb hit its target and Casey's supervisor sat back stiffly and his eyes narrowed.

"Lieutenant Casey," the officer said in clipped tones. "Since you have shown obvious inadequacies in the field of command you will be reassigned as a junior field agent."

Casey nodded.

"Further, your record will permanently show that you failed to follow orders, complete your mission, and were in violation of your contract time. A poor example for your subordinates."

Casey didn't react. With that stain on his record he would never be more than a field agent again. The ignorance of the charges was almost laughable. He wondered if he would have felt the same had he not met John and his people. Before, duty had been everything, but now to be charged with failing in his mission and also reprimanded for working past his contract to try was beyond reason. He resisted the urge to laugh out loud.

"Officer Casey, you're dismissed," his supervisor said in exasperation. Casey looked up at him.

"The girl, sir?"

"What girl?" Casey's supervisor snapped.

"The politician's daughter, the missing person's report that pulled most of my men away. Was she found?" Casey asked.

"Oh," his supervisor dismissed that with a wave of his hand. "She was found the morning after the Fort Joplin incident. She was unharmed and said her abductor didn't abuse her or demand anything."

"Strange. Did they capture him?"

"No sign of him, she wandered into a station house in Hope, Maryland, the morning after the battle."

"Thank you, sir," Casey stood up and left the office.

* * *

The office of the chief of immigrant affairs was not what John expected, or rather not what he was used to. The immigration official sat behind a large wooden desk that was a mosaic of organized chaos. Light tan walls were hung with pictures of family members, friends, and coworkers. The flag of the Republic of Texas stood in its stand in the corner. There were books on a shelf across the room from John, who sat in one of the two comfortable chairs opposite the official. Rather than a reflection of society, as John was used to, the room was a reflection of the man that worked in it.

"We have a bus ready to take you folks wherever you want to start over," the official was folding some papers and sliding them into a small passport book.

Everyone had made it, and been reunited at a military base near the border. Sarah's group had been picked up shortly after breaching the fence and after telling their story she, and the children, had been moved to the facility to wait for the rest. Even Benny had made it, crossing the border further down the line two nights after his release. The toy bear had been returned to his excited friend.

"Thank you, sir. We appreciate it," John said. He was still overwhelmed with being in Texas, even after a week in the processing station near the Oklahoma-Missouri border.

"Call me Eric, John," the official said. "Now, there's enough money in here to get you started."

John hadn't expected a handout and started to protest.

"Whoa, John it's a loan. It's not free money so don't worry," apparently Eric had been following John's journey enough to get a sense of the man.

"Your passport is done, and your temporary citizenship papers are in here," Eric continued. "When you decide on a place to settle stop in at the local immigration office, they'll help you make the transition."

John took the packet and looked through it while Eric watched. The papers reminded him of all the regulation in his old life, the forms, identification, and numbers that told him where he fit in to best help society. He kept telling himself they were needed to make sure he could find his own place wherever he wanted.

"Can I ask, why did ya'll leave Illinois? Why did you risk everything to come here?" Eric asked. It appeared to John as if the other had been waiting to ask that the entire time.

John took a moment to think, knowing Eric wasn't asking just to hear a generic answer about freedom or patriotism.

"The kids mostly," John began. "I was tired of waiting in the same lines, for the same work and the same food. Sending my kids to the same school, so they can do the same work for the same rations, all so everyone can be the same. I couldn't stand to look at everyone standing in the same line anymore, but most of all I didn't want my kids to grow up thinking that was normal. Everyone back there is either dead without knowing it, or struggling for breath and I want my kids to have room to breathe."

The answer seemed to satisfy Eric's curiosity and he smiled, sitting back.

"What do you plan to do now, John?" Eric asked.

"Whatever I want."

Made in the USA
Lexington, KY
22 December 2018